Electrifying
IN A KILT

Other Books by Anna Durand

Electrifying

IN A KILT

Hot Scots, Book Sixteen

ANNA DURAND

JACOBSVILLE BOOKS · MARIETTA, OHIO

ELECTRIFYING IN A KILT

Copyright © 2024 by Lisa A. Shiel
All rights reserved.

ISBN: 978-1-958144-62-6 (paperback)
ISBN: 978-1-958144-63-3 (ebook)
ISBN: 978-1-958144-64-0 (retail audiobook)
ISBN: 978-1-958144-65-7 (library audiobook)

Manufactured in the United States.

Jacobsville Books
www.JacobsvilleBooks.com

Names: Durand, Anna, author.
Title: Electrifying in a kilt / Anna Durand.
Description: Marietta, OH : Jacobsville Books, 2024. | Series: Hot Scots, bk. 16.
Identifiers: ISBN 978-1-958144-62-6 (paperback) | ISBN 978-1-958144-63-3 (ebook) | ISBN 978-1-958144-64-0 (retail audiobook) | ISBN: 978-1-958144-65-7 (library audiobook)
Subjects: LCSH: Highlands (Scotland)--Fiction. | Man-woman relationships--Fiction. | Scots--Fiction. | British--Fiction. | Romance fiction. | BISAC: FICTION / Romance / Contemporary. | FICTION / Romance / Romantic Comedy. | FICTION / Romance / Later in Life. | GSAFD: Love stories.
Classification: LCC PS3604.U724 V35 2024 (print) | LCC PS3604.U724 (ebook) | DDC 813/.6--dc23.

Prologue

Iona
Six Months Ago

Couples float across the floor in the great hall, enjoying a chance to flaunt their dancing talent or just shuffle along, not caring if they aren't light-footed. Valentine's Day has never been my favorite holiday, and I always do my best to avoid this time of year. Some might say I avoid it like the proverbial plague. Watching everyone else couple up and get lovey-dovey makes me feel…unwanted. I know that's ridiculous. Plenty of people love me—my family and friends, naturally. I've never made any enemies, as far as I know. A journalist will inevitably annoy some people, but I've always treated the subjects of my stories with respect.

Aye, everyone likes me.

But tonight, I wish I could just hide in a closet or become invisible. Why? Because I've been roped into attending the Valentine's Day bash organized by my brother Thane and his new sweetheart, Rebecca Taylor. I'm thrilled for Thane. He's waited a very long time to find the right woman, and Rebecca has quickly become one of my best friends.

How long will Thane and Rebecca wait before they try to set me up with someone? I expect that to happen at any moment. I wrap my arms around myself, lean against the wall, and listen to the music. My vision retreats into my mind. I hear the songs, but I don't pay attention to anything else as the minutes tick by.

Evan MacTaggart approaches me. "Iona, would you care to dance?"

I hunch my shoulders and shake my head. "Thank you, Evan, that's very sweet. But I'd rather be an observer. It's my journalist nature to watch and not participate."

Evan seems vaguely disappointed, but he walks away and finds his wife, Keely, among the crowd. They begin to dance and laugh.

Maybe I should try harder to enjoy this event. But I cannae muster any enthusiasm for…anything.

The hairs at my nape lift. A journalist needs finely honed intuition, and mine just spiked. Oh, aye, someone is coming toward me. It's Thane, and I have a strong suspicion about his intentions.

Who will he set me up with tonight? I see Sorley MacKechnie among the crowd, hovering at the periphery. His partner, Fergus MacRae, is here too. Thane strode past the two constables and took the time to chat with them briefly. Fergus grinned at whatever my brother said. Did Thane suggest Fergus should coax me onto the dance floor? It wouldn't surprise me at all.

I'll make a polite excuse for why I don't want to dance.

Thane stalks around the periphery of the great hall until he reaches me. "Iona, why aren't you dancing? You love a good ceilidh."

I try to remain placid, but my whole face begins to tighten. "Dinnae feel like dancing, Thane. I'm the only one here who doesn't have a significant other."

"Eric Taylor is single too."

"Aye, but he's almost twenty years younger than I am." Does Thane honestly believe I want to dance with a much younger man? His girlfriend's son? *Bod an Donais.*

My brother leans against the wall beside me. "What's really bothering you about this ceilidh?"

I look at Thane and bluster out a sigh. "It's a ball, Thane, not a ceilidh."

"Well, it all sounds like the same thing to me." He tips his head down to stare into my eyes as if he believes that will make me do what he wants. "You haven't answered my question. What's really fashing you?"

"I'm old, that's what fashes me. I'm well into my forties, and no man wants to date me because I have two children. The fact that they're adopted only turns men off even more." Why on earth did I spout all that rubbish? I rub my neck and gaze out at the dance floor. "Besides, I'm a nosy journalist. Men like that even less. I might as well hang a shingle on my front door that says 'old maid lives here, run away now.' "

"Ramsay isn't married anymore. Dinnae see him standing in a corner having a self-pity party." Thane commandeers my hand and hauls me away from the wall. "Come with me, Iona."

He maintains his iron grip on my hand while he stalks onto the dance floor.

I dig my heels in, refusing to budge. "Leave me alone, Thane."

"Cannae do that." He tosses me over his shoulder. "If you won't cooperate, I'll make the decision for you."

Thane marches across the floor, forcing other people to scatter to get out of the way, and halts in front of one man. Then he sets me down. "Iona needs a dance partner. Eric, would you care to escort my sister round the floor?"

What did I say to Thane a moment ago? I don't want to dance with a man who's half my age. Did my brother listen? Of course not. I have half a mind to flee as fast as I can. Dating is not on my agenda, and neither is dancing with Eric Taylor. He's a sweet laddie, but not my type.

Eric flicks his gaze between my brother and me, then he offers his hand. "Come on, let's have some fun. I bet you're a great dancer. I noticed you're very graceful when you're walking around."

Thane smirks as if he's dead certain Eric is the one for me.

But it isn't Eric's fault that my brother has become the nosiest, most interfering person in the whole of Scotland.

While Thane walks away, I accept Eric's hand. He leads me out into the middle of the dance floor and adopts a decent approximation of a ballroom posture. And we begin to shuffle across the floor.

Eric smiles. "You look really pretty tonight, Iona."

"Um, thank you." I catch a glimpse of my brother Ramsay dancing with Jamie Douglas, wife of Gavin Douglas. And for reasons I can't explain, I do the most ridiculous thing. I start a conversation with a virtual toddler. "Eric, tell me about your job. It's geology, right?"

"Yeah, I'm a geologist."

"What aspects of geology do you specialize in?"

The way he lights up at the chance to talk about his job tells me a great deal about him. Eric still gets excited about his career, unlike me. I'm ashamed to admit I've lost most of my vigor—career-wise and emotionally. Still, I listen while Eric expounds on his geology career.

"Field mapping is my favorite thing, although most geologists I know think that's not a sexy discipline." Eric deftly guides us around another couple who seem oblivious of where they're going. "I work for an independent company that does all sorts of stuff—geotechnical mapping, logging, hydrogeology, geoscience, engineering geology, and lots more."

The laddie tells me more about those disciplines, but I lose focus the longer he talks. It's all too technical for me. Even when the song stops, and another one begins, Eric goes on blethering. His excitement about his career drives him to take us around the floor faster and faster until I begin to feel dizzy. But I don't want to offend him.

"Eric, I'm hungry. Let's go to the buffet."

"Oh, jeez, I'm sorry. You must be bored to tears by all that geology stuff. I rambled on and on."

"Dinnae fash. But I do want some food."

"Sure, let's head over to the buffet." He reaches toward my hand, then seems to think twice about that. "Come on. There's nobody at the food tables right now."

Our trip to the buffet satisfies my grumbling tummy, but Eric makes me laugh with silly jokes. Then I try to gently get rid of Eric by taking my plate and saying goodbye to him. The laddie still won't give up, though. When I find an open seat at a table and sit down, Eric appears and takes the seat beside mine. He talks more about his job, and I do my best to seem attentive and interested, strictly to be polite.

But I'm getting tired, and I want to go home.

Even when Thane puts on a dance routine, hoisting Rebecca above his head, all I can think about is the nice, soft pillow on my bed. I do cheer when Thane proposes to his lass, and she says yes. I'm genuinely thrilled for them.

Mhac na galla, I'm about to faint, I'm so jeeked.

I kiss Eric's cheek and rise from my chair. My face feels warm because I'm jeeked. Sleep sounds like heaven, if I can ever escape this laddie. "Goodnight, Eric. Thank you for keeping me company."

"Let me walk with you down to the vestibule."

I'm too exhausted to argue. "Aye, fine."

Our journey from the great hall to the vestibule takes time, mostly because I'm wearing high heels. The spiral staircase has many steps. By the time we reach the vestibule, I have to put my foot down.

"Time to say good night, Eric. No ifs, ands, or buts. Enjoy the rest of the party."

He touches my hand. "We could go outside and look at the stars. It's really romantic."

"No, I just want to go home."

Eric touches my hand again. "Please."

"You're sweet, but I—"

He lifts my hand to kiss it. "You're the hottest, smartest woman I've ever met. Don't leave yet. Go outside with me."

"All right. We can look at the stars for a moment, that's all."

The laddie grasps my elbow, leading me outside and onto the gravel drive. But when he tries to guide me toward the garden, I've broken my last straw.

"We can see the stars from the driveway, Eric."

"May I kiss you, Iona?"

"Eric…"

"Just one kiss, please."

If it will get rid of him, I suppose one kiss can't hurt. "Yes, fine."

The look of sheer joy on his face makes my stomach churn. When Eric touches his lips to mine, I feel nothing romantic toward him. The moment he pulls away, I can't disguise my discomfort.

"Let's try that again, Iona, please. I'll do better this time."

"The problem isn't you. It's me. I'm simply not attracted to you, and nothing will change how I feel. I'm sorry, Eric."

And then I walk away.

But my troubles have just begun.

Chapter One

Iona

When a woman in her forties lets a man in his twenties kiss her, nothing can or should come of it. But that one brief moment of madness has become the bane of my existence. Eric Taylor is a sweet laddie, but I am not attracted to him. That kiss proved it. With other men I've dated, one touch of our lips led to something more—but not with Eric. I told him so. I've continued to tell him every time he shows up at my work or at my cottage. Eric is relentless, in a strangely sweet way.

But no, I do not want to date or sleep with him.

Our one brief kiss has become a distant memory—for me. Eric has other ideas. Or he did. The laddie hasn't pestered me in at least five days. That's a miracle.

Despite my unwanted suitor, I woke up this morning feeling bloody good. The sun is shining, a somewhat rare occurrence in the Scottish Highlands. So, I wander out into the garden and settle down on an Adirondack chair to enjoy the lovely weather.

Ahhh, this is heaven.

My mobile chimes. I instinctively reach for it and swipe to turn the screen on. The first thing I see is a notification from…Eric Taylor. I groan as I open the text message. Though I do not want to talk to him right now, I suffer from an overabundance of politeness when it comes to such matters. Naturally, I can't stop myself from reading Eric's missive.

May I see you today? Miss you so much.

Och, when will that boy give up? I don't miss him, and no, I do not want to see him today. This is getting ridiculous. His mother, Rebecca, is marrying my brother Thane in seven weeks. I haven't told Rebecca about her son's behavior because, honestly, I haven't told anyone. It's embarrassing, and I won't risk upsetting Rebecca or Thane by sharing my problems with them. They have enough stress, what with all the wedding preparations. Rebecca doesn't need to hear about her son's antics and the fact that Eric has become a stalker—a sweet, well-intentioned one.

Not responding to his message seems like the best option.

But my mobile chimes again. *Please, Iona, I need to talk to you.*

I throw my head back and growl, unleashing a slew of Gaelic obscenities. Then I slump in my chair and try to pretend I'm not deeply annoyed. I count the seconds until I realize more than a minute has passed with no text messages. At last, I can allow myself to relax a wee bit. After five minutes tick by with no texts, I begin to genuinely unwind, shutting my eyes, letting the soft sizzle of the wind rustling through the trees ease the tension inside me.

Until this moment, I never realized how lovely and necessary silence can be. The sound of a vehicle approaching barely registers in my mind, until the tires crunch on the gravel in my driveway. If that's Eric...I'll flee into the pasture behind Raghnall MacCrum's homestead. Surely, Eric won't trudge through cow patties to harass me.

Someone pounds on my front door, battering it so ferociously that the sound echoes through the entire house and out into the garden. *Mhac na galla.* Eric is driving me insane. It's time to give him the verbal lashing he's earned.

But I'll do it politely.

I jump out of my chair and fling the back door open, making it bounce back, and stomp through the house all the way to the front door. There, I pause for just long enough that I can catch my breath. Then I finally fling the front door open.

And I gawp at the stranger who's glowering at me. "Who the bloody hell are you?"

He slants toward me a wee bit. Spittle sprays from his lips as he snarls, "I'm the man who's going to destroy your life, and you are the slag who seduced my son."

"What are you talking about? I have no idea who you are, but I'm dead certain you have no right to shout at me." His accent proves he's British, but I still can't fathom why a stranger is shouting at me.

The man slaps his palms down on either side of the door frame. "Do you deny that you're Iona Buchanan?"

"Why should I deny or confirm anything for you? I have half a mind to ring the Loch Fairbairn Police Station."

"Go on, then. I can wait." One corner of his mouth kicks upward the slightest bit. "I would love to watch the coppers handcuffing you."

Oh, I've had enough of this *bod ceann*. "I'm ringing the police right now. Best scurry away or else the constables will come—and they're my friends."

I slam the door in his face. Well, I try to do that. But he shoves his hand in the way, stopping me from locking him out.

"Do you mean to continue lying to me?" the *bod ceann* says. "Toby Knight is my son."

"Never heard of the laddie." Maybe that isn't entirely true. Eric's best mate is called Toby, but I can't say for certain he's the one this *bod ceann* is shouting at me about. Toby is a rather common name, especially among British erses. "Last chance, Mr. Knight. I'll ring the police in five seconds. Four, three, two—"

Mr. Knight takes one step backward and adopts an arrogant stance. He spreads his feet a wee bit more and crosses his arms over his chest. The *bod ceann* lifts his chin too.

What a pigheaded lout.

"Have it your way," I tell him. "Time to bring in the authorities."

I make somewhat of a show of raising my mobile and punching in the digits. Then I turn on the speaker so this ersehole can listen to the phone ringing at the other end. We both hear it when someone picks up the call.

"Loch Fairbairn Police Station. How may I assist you?"

"Hello, Fergus. This is Iona Buchanan." I can't resist smirking at Mr. Knight, who now sighs and rolls his eyes. "I have an intruder who's trying to get into my house."

"We'll be there in five minutes, Iona."

"Thank you, Fergus." I disconnect the call and slap my mobile down on the table beside the door. I lift my chin. "Still want to stay here?"

"Yes."

"Fine." I cross my arms over my chest, just like he did. "We can wait right here."

I count the minutes, one second at a time, while the bod ceann grows more and more impatient. He begins to tap his fingers on his elbows, which are still bent thanks to his arms being strapped across his chest. He must have sizable muscles. The suit he wears is stretched taut over his biceps.

Four minutes and ten seconds to go.

My mobile rings, and I see my oldest brother's name on the screen. He sent me a text message, which must mean Thane has heard about this altercation. News travels fast in Loch Fairbairn.

I lift the screen, tilting it toward the *bod ceann*. "If one of my brothers knows about this, that means they both do. Thane and Ramsay are tough men. They'll make mince meat out of you."

Mr. Knight huffs. "I've been struck by lightning. Your brothers don't frighten me."

He must be lying. Struck by lightning? He's only saying that to prove how tough he is. Almost no one actually gets hit by lightning.

Another text message chimes on my mobile. This time it's Ramsay. I glance at the two texts. Aye, my brothers are barreling toward my cottage right now.

Two minutes and forty-nine seconds to go.

"Would you like a glass of water while we wait, Mr. Knight?"

"No," he snarls.

I shrug. "Have it your way."

Seconds later, I hear a siren wailing in the distance, clearly heading this way.

And still, the *bod ceann* does not move.

The police car pulls into the driveway, blocking Mr. Knight's vehicle. Two constables climb out—Fergus and his partner, Sorley. The laddies march straight up to my unwanted guest and take up positions at either side of him.

"So, you've been harassing this woman," says Fergus. "That sort of thing is illegal, you know."

The British *bod ceann* rolls his eyes.

Sorley shakes his head. "Better tell us why you're harassing Ms. Buchanan. Otherwise, we'll have to throw you in the boot of our car."

Mr. Knight snorts. "You can't arrest me for standing on the porch."

"Aye, we can," Fergus declares. "Iona, do you swear this man was harassing you?"

I nod. "Absolutely."

Another car comes racing up the road, tires squealing as it halts at the curb. Thane and Ramsay leap out and stomp up to the porch.

Ramsay thrusts a finger toward Mr. Knight. "Is this the bastard who assaulted our sister?"

"There was no assault," I tell my brother. "He was being extremely obnoxious and making false accusations against me."

"What accusations?" Thane demands.

I stab a finger at the British *bod ceann*. "He accused me of seducing his son."

Thane squints at the Brit. "Who are you? And who is your son?"

"I am Rafe Knight, and my son is Toby Knight."

"As if that explains everything."

Rafe lifts his chin even higher. "He's best mates with Eric Taylor. The boys have been in Scotland on an extended holiday. That's how Toby met this woman."

He made the word woman sound like a heinous insult. Why on earth does Rafe Knight despise me? I met him less than ten minutes ago.

"Och, men," I grouse. "You're all behaving like rabid lions. I don't know Toby. I only know Eric because his mother is marrying Thane."

And the laddie is stalking me, sort of. Can I rationalize having Rafe thrown in jail when I've allowed Eric to pester me? I'm so confused.

"You need to arrest him," Ramsay announces. "We'll figure out what's going on here down at the station. Thane and I can keep Rafe Knight company in his cell."

"Aye, we can." Thane cracks his knuckles. "With pleasure."

I throw my hands up. "Och, will you lot stop behaving like lunatics? This has gotten wildly out of hand."

Fergus looks at me. "Are you saying you don't want Mr. Knight to be detained for questioning?"

"Well…I don't know."

"Then we have to take him in. Better safe than sorry." Fergus pulls out his handcuffs and secures them around Rafe's wrists. "Time to go, sir."

Rafe glowers at no one in particular. "I'll sue the lot of you."

"You'll have the right to a solicitor if we decide to book you for harassment."

"What about his car?" I ask.

"Dinnae fash, Iona. We'll deal with that once we've sorted out whether to arrest him."

Surprisingly, the Brit allows the constables to lead him away without any fuss at all. They help him into the backseat, then climb into their seats and drive away.

I turn to my brothers. "You didn't need to come running. The constables could've handled the situation."

Thane grasps my shoulders. "You're our sister. Of course we'll always come when you need help."

"Aye," Ramsay concurs. "At least Maeve and Rowan weren't here."

I sigh. "My children are strong lasses who can take care of themselves in any situation."

Ramsay winks. "Just like their mother."

"Their strength isn't my doing. I can't pass along my genes to my adopted daughters."

"No. But you have raised them to be just as strong as you."

Every muscle in my body slackens now that the uproar is over with. "I need a wee lie-down."

Thane squeezes my shoulder gently. "Are you sure you want to be alone? Rebecca and I would be happy to have you join us for lunch at our house."

"I appreciate the offer. But I'd rather be alone."

My brothers both kiss my forehead, then they get into Thane's pickup truck and drive away.

Though I shuffle into the bedroom and flop onto the bed, I can't manage to sleep. My thoughts keep returning to Rafe Knight and what the constables might do with him. Does he deserve to be arrested? Maybe his anger stems from pain. What sort, I can't say.

Mhac na galla. Now I'm empathizing with a British erse who shouted at me. I sigh. Not only do I allow a young laddie to essentially stalk me, but now I'm giving serious consideration to the idea of telling the constables not to charge Rafe.

Aye, I'm a hopeless case.

Chapter Two

Rafe

I gaze at the bars of my tiny cell and contemplate my situation. Have I done something wrong? Should I apologize to that woman? The longer I sit here, drumming my fingers on my knees, the less charitable I feel. Maybe I had begun to wonder if my assumptions had been invalid. The study of human nature has never been my forte. People, particularly women, have often confounded me. Even science can leave me baffled. No matter how deeply I study all the journals and papers written about my chosen field, I know I will never fully understand it. No one will. Nature is a fickle mistress.

Perhaps I do deserve to be incarcerated. That's what most everyone who knows me might say.

I lean back on my narrow cot and hook one knee over my opposite leg as I stare up at the ceiling. I have a window, but it's so bloody tiny that I suspect it was designed for squirrels or perhaps cats. No full-grown man could possibly escape through that small rectangle even if such a gent could break the glass. The bars make that almost impossible. I might have halfheartedly studied the nooks and crannies of my cell while waiting for someone to tell me what they mean to do with me.

Yes, I can admit that I've been an arse of the first order. But Iona Buchanan needs to explain her behavior. I will gladly rot in a Scottish jail cell for as long as it takes to get the truth out of her. Of course, if I'm in jail I can't get the truth out of anyone.

My plan has a number of flaws.

I decide to lie down on my cot and attempt to squeeze my entire body onto the narrow space I've been given. Only an elf could sleep on this flimsy so-called bed. I shift about several times, but I still can't get comfortable. I imagine only a drunken sailor could manage to sleep under these conditions. Finally, I settle down and lock my hands under my head as a sort of pillow.

Ah, yes, this is the life.

What did you expect, you sodding arse? Harassment is a crime in Scotland—I assume. So, I can't explain what I expected would happen when I pounded my fist on Iona Buchanan's front door.

"Wake up, Mr. Knight. You have a visitor."

The voice of the constable—Fergus, I believe is his name—rouses me from my musings. I yawn and stretch. Only then do I turn my attention to the two people standing just beyond the bars of my cell.

And I spring up into a sitting position, dropping my feet onto the floor.

Iona Buchanan gazes at me dispassionately.

The constable touches Iona's arm. "Will ye be all right alone with him? I could cuff him to be sure."

"No, that's unnecessary. But thank you, Fergus."

The constable shuffles out of the cell block, which consists of one other cell just as minuscule as mine. Fergus has left, and the door clicks shut behind him.

Iona Buchanan steps forward, almost touching the bars.

And I suddenly notice her clothing. She's wearing a different outfit than the last time I saw her. The ensemble consists of a frilly, pale-blue dress that conforms to her bust and has thin, frilly straps too. The hemline stops above her knees. *Bloody hell.* She has the most perfect knees I've ever seen. I'd love to kiss them.

No, I don't want that. This woman is my enemy.

I clear my throat. "What do you want? Unless you're going to assure me you'll never shag my son again—"

"Haud yer wheesht."

"And that means what? Sounds like gibberish."

"I said shut your mouth, Mr. Knight."

My brows lift. "My surname doesn't sound anything like any of those words you spoke. And I demand you—"

"Shut up, Mr. Knight." Iona puckers her lips. "I have never shagged any laddies who are half my age. Whatever your son told you, it was pure rubbish."

"My son doesn't lie to me."

Iona rolls her eyes. "Oh, aye, no child ever lies to their parents. What does your wife think of you running off to the Highlands to harass me?"

My jaw tenses, and my nostrils flare. This always happens when someone brings up the topic of my ex-wife. "My family is none of your concern."

"If you want to be left alone, I recommend you stop banging on strange women's doors."

Before I can spew more vitriol at her, a constable opens the door just far enough to reveal his face. Fergus looks at Iona. "Does he want a solicitor?"

"You should be asking me that question," I snarl. "I am the prisoner, after all."

"Aye. So, do ye want a solicitor, Mr. Knight?"

Iona turns round to face Fergus.

And I get a bloody fantastic view of her back. That dress has no back at all, only a slender strap of blue fabric tied three-fourths of the way down her spine. And what a lovely spine she has.

"Why don't we let Mr. Knight think about that," Iona says. "He might be released without needing legal assistance."

I stalk over to the bars and grasp them in both hands. "I have my own solicitor. Don't need a ruddy Scottish lawyer who probably makes his arguments in Gaelic."

The bloody woman sighs as if I'm the one being ridiculous. "You can go now, Fergus."

As soon as the constable departs, Iona whirls around to scowl at me. She sets her hands on her hips. "You are the most obnoxious man I have ever met, and I've met a fair lot of your kind."

"What group are you claiming I belong to?"

"The erseholes of the world."

I laugh with no small measure of derision. "You've met every bastard on the face of the planet? My, my, you do get around, don't you?"

She inches closer to the bars. "Maybe I should find your son and have a poke with him, strictly so I can watch your head explode."

When did I move closer? My body is crushed to the bars. When I speak, I can manage only a hushed yet rough tone. "I'd wager you aren't married, Ms. Buchanan. What man could possibly put up with your holier-than-thou attitude."

"Don't blame religion for your atrocious behavior."

I push my face between the bars, and my gaze flicks down to her cleavage. *Blimey.* The slopes of those breasts are driving me mad. That's only because I haven't been with a woman in such a long time. My growing lust has nothing to do with Iona Buchanan.

She glances down at my groin and licks her lips. Then she swerves her attention back to my face. "Maybe I should tell Fergus that you need to be locked up overnight."

I thrust a hand between the bars to grasp her chin. That results in our lips grazing each other.

The beautiful but evil woman stares directly into my eyes.

Fuck. I'm getting harder by the second. That might explain what I do next.

I crush my mouth to hers. For a few seconds, she remains perfectly still with her eyes wide open. I'm staring into her eyes too. Our irises are the same shade of deep blue. Her tits brush against my chest. Then our eyes shut at the same instant, and she moans just as I flick my tongue between her lips.

Iona Buchanan relaxes her jaw, inviting me to devour her mouth.

When she hooks two fingers inside my waistband and tugs me closer, I ravage her mouth like I've just come home from a ten-year tour on an interstellar spaceship where the entire crew was male. She gives as good as she gets, lashing her tongue around mine while my cock grows harder every second.

Just when I'm ready to do my damnedest to fuck her through the cell bars, Iona jerks away from me. She stumbles backward several paces. For a moment, she simply stands there gawping at me.

Then she stalks up to me and smacks my face.

"Bloody hell," I snap. "That hurt."

"You deserve the pain." She flounces over to the door but pauses with one hand on the knob. "You are the most vile, despicable, arrogant, odious cretin I've ever met. You will never see me again, Mr. Knight."

Iona flings the door open and races out of the jail. Just as the door begins to swing shut, I hear her shout, "Set him free, Fergus. Send him back to England in a cargo crate, if possible."

That bloody woman. A crate? If she wanted to set me free, she wouldn't have suggested such an idea. Then again, she might not have meant it.

Why am I giving her the benefit of the doubt?

My favorite copper pushes the door open, holding it there with one foot wedged against it. "Ready to go home, Mr. Knight?"

"I'm ready to leave this lovely little cell, if that's what you mean."

"Aye, that's what I meant." Fergus holds a set of keys in his hand, and now he twirls them repeatedly—probably in an attempt to unsettle me. It does not work. "All right, you're free to go."

"Not until you unlock the cell door."

Fergus ambles up to the bars and smirks. "Oh, aye, I almost forgot to do that, eh?"

"At least you've remembered now." I can't help the disgust in my voice. Perhaps I deserve this treatment, but I have good cause for the way I've behaved.

The constable unlocks my cell and swings the door open. He leads me out of the jail area, down the hallway I'd been perp-walked down earlier, and finally takes me out into the main room where desks and all sorts of equipment fill the space.

My new best mate guides me over to the main doors, pushing one open. "There you are, Mr, Knight. If you're on holiday here in Scotland, try not to annoy any more women. We take harassment seriously."

"And 'annoying' females is considered to be harassment, is it? I gather persecuted men don't get the same treatment."

Fergus gives me a long-suffering look. "Best get that chip off your shoulder, or you'll get yourself into more trouble. I'd rather not have to slap cuffs around your wrists again."

I understand his meaning. The Loch Fairbairn Police Station will drag me in again if I annoy Iona Buchanan.

Why on earth did I kiss her? She's a harpy. But her lips were soft and warm, and she tasted like strawberries. I hadn't kissed a woman in a very long time—until today. I despise Iona Buchanan, but I wouldn't mind shagging her once or twice.

If I can tape her mouth shut during sex.

Fergus hands me a set of car keys. *My* keys. "Thane and Ramsay brought your vehicle to the station for you. Wasn't that neighborly of them?"

"My gratitude is voluminous." If they didn't put a bag of rotting rubbish in my car, I'll be shocked. But I behave like an adult and shake the constable's hand. "I appreciate your kindness under these bizarre circumstances, Constable…What is your surname? Sorry, I'm being rude again."

"Not at all. MacRae is my name, and my partner is Sorley MacKechnie."

"I hope you won't take this the wrong way, but I pray I never see either of you again. I'd say 'unless it's outside of work,' but I doubt you'd want to see me at all."

Fergus MacRae slaps my arm. "Dinnae fash. We don't hold grudges. Do we, Sorley?"

"No, never," Constable MacKechnie says from across the room. "We're neutral on flaming erseholes, but completely biased when it comes to Iona Buchanan. She's done more for this village than most anyone else has done in ages."

"In what way?"

"Ye haven't earned the right to know."

I want to ask what he means by that statement, but I decide my curiosity is liable to get me into more trouble. Instead, I shake Fergus's hand and wave goodbye to Sorley. But as I'm walking out the door, I stop and turn back. "By the way, could you point me to a hotel or bed-and-breakfast? I'm too knackered to drive anywhere."

Fergus snatches a piece of paper off a bulletin board and hands it to me. "This is the only place in the village. It's good, though. Dinnae worry about that."

I accept the flyer. "Thank you. I'll be on my way now."

"Ah, one moment," Sorley calls out. He snatches up a sheet of paper and rushes over to me, offering another flyer. "The hotel doesn't provide meals. You'll need to visit the café for that.»

"You've both been exceedingly kind. Thank you."

My charitable attitude lasts only until I climb into my car, which I drove here all the way from England. As soon as I've climbed in and shut the door, I notice a folded sheet of paper lying on top of the dashboard. What, is this a parking ticket? That would figure.

I unfold the sheet—and groan. It says, "Upset our sister again, and we'll do more than give you a wee gift. We will well and truly batter you." It's signed with the names Ramsay and Thane.

What did they mean about a "wee gift"?

The meaning becomes clear once I've driven down the road for a few blocks. Then the stench reaches my nostrils. I slam on the brakes and twist round to search for the reason why the car smells like rotting rubbish. That's because it *is* rotting rubbish. Thane and Ramsay Buchanan left me a small bag full of it.

Even that won't stop me from getting to the truth about Iona and my son.

Chapter Three

Iona

Going back to the scene of the crime hasn't made me feel relaxed or relieved or whatever I'm supposed to feel after today's events. When I walk through the door and turn around to shut it, I experience a flashback of Rafe Knight glowering at me, accusing me of seducing his son. Toby Knight is a stranger to me. I've never met the laddie, and I never heard of him either until today.

Why did Rafe kiss me? More importantly, why did I reciprocate?

Something is horribly wrong with me. That's the only explanation. I've been celibate for so long that I'm desperate for a good shag. *Mhac na galla*. Even I'm not that desperate. The moment I first saw Rafe Knight, I'd felt something stirring within me. Oh, what rubbish. He is attractive and has a good body. His lips felt slightly chapped when we kissed, yet somehow, that turned me on even more.

I don't know what's wrong with me. I cannae be attracted to that *bod ceann*. Thinking the Gaelic phrase for dickhead makes me picture what his cock might look like and how it might feel inside me.

"Och, woman, you've gone insane." Talking to myself is a bad sign, that's for dead sure. But I can't stop myself. "You need to get out of this house for a few days, don't you? Just in case Rafe Knight decides to assault your home again."

I've gone off my rocker. And it's all the fault of that man.

Where can I go to hide from him?

A hotel seems like the best choice. I race into my bedroom, gathering everything I might need for a wee holiday, though I'm not sure fleeing my own home counts as a holiday. Hiding out in the village's only hotel doesn't seem like absconding either. Dinnae care about definitions right now. I want to escape from the scene of the crime.

I carry my overnight bag out to the car and head straight for the Loch Fairbairn Arms. The car park isn't packed, with only a few vehicles here and there. This is a sleepy village most of the time. Occasional events draw in tourists, but this time of year is always a wee bit slow. At least I don't have trouble finding a space for my car.

When I stride into the lobby, Mrs. Agnew greets me with a smile. "Iona, dearie, what are you doing here? I hope you aren't writing an exposé of the hotel."

"Nothing like that. I, um, just need a place to stay for a few days." What sort of lie should I tell to explain my need for a room? Not sure why I feel the need to lie, but I do. "A pipe burst in my house."

Mrs. Agnew winks. "Is that what the young people are calling it these days?"

"What?"

"You know." She winks again, this time wagging her brows too. "If you need an anonymous place for a shag…"

"No, that's not at all why I'm here." When did the words burst pipe become synonymous with sex? Mrs. Agnew is in her late sixties. Maybe her generation has a strange fixation with sexual metaphors that involve plumbing. "Honestly, I just need a room for a few days. Because of the pipes."

"Did you ring for a plumber, dearie?"

If I say yes, she'll realize I've lied. Mrs. Agnew knows everything that goes on in this village. My best strategy is to avoid my moronic lie. "Could I just get a room, please? I'm exhausted."

"Of course." She signs me in, then hands me a room key, the electronic sort. I miss real keys. "If I see Mr. Knight, I'll let you know."

The sly tone of that statement irritates me, but I won't snap at Mrs. Agnew. She's a wonderful woman who happens to have a penchant for teasing everyone she knows.

I find my room easily. Mrs. Agnew gave me one that's on the second floor and has a beautiful view of the village and the mountain that lies on the north side, Beann Dealgach. The hotel had been renovated several years ago, so now every room has a spectacular view of either the mountain or the foothills. I've never stayed here before. Maybe I can write a review while I'm here and publish it in *The Lock Fairbairn Daily News*.

Just as I'm almost done unpacking, my mobile rings. I grab it and announce myself with my standard greeting without thinking. "This is Iona Buchanan of *The Loch Fairbairn Daily News*. How may I help you?"

"Oh, Mam, I wish you wouldn't say that when you know it's me."

"Rowan? I'm sorry, love, it's habit. Did you need something?"

"Aye. To know where you are. Maeve and I stopped by the house, but you weren't there." Rowan lowers her voice to a whisper. "Is it true? Did a British man assault you?"

"No, love, it wasn't like that. He was angry, but I'd rather not discuss the incident. I've taken a room at the hotel for a few days to relax, that's all."

"Is he hot?"

Before I can respond, a shuffling sound interrupts and another voice comes on the line. "Mam, tell us the truth. Are you having an affair with a British man?"

"No, Maeve, I am not. That man should be on his way home by now, anyway."

"Oh, no, he hasn't left. We bumped into Uncle Ramsay after we left your place, and he told us that British *cacan* decided to hang around for a while." Meave switches to a whisper now. "Why would he do that unless you two mean to have a poke or two?"

"Or three," Rowan interjects. "Mam, you need to get some action."

I groan. "Are you two done? Because all you need to know is that I wanted to stay at the hotel for a while and I am not having a poke with anyone. Understand?"

Both lasses mumble their agreement, though they sound disappointed.

"Good. Now, go about your own business and leave me be."

"All right. Love you, Mam."

"Aye, love you too, Mam," Maeve adds.

Finally, my children disconnect the call. Where they got the idea that I'm shagging Rafe Knight, I can't fathom. Well, we did kiss. But Fergus and Sorley wouldn't gossip about that. I hope.

Then my mobile rings again. I almost don't answer but then decide I'll feel guilty if I don't. "Hello, Thane. I've already heard from Rowan and Maeve, so you might as well get your two cents in."

"I cannae believe that man chased you out of your home. If you don't file a complaint, I will."

"What are you talking about? No one chased me away. I wanted a wee holiday with room service and a gorgeous view of Beann Dealgach, that's all."

He says nothing for a moment. "Dinnae believe you, Iona. Ramsay doesn't either."

I throw my head back and moan. "You two are driving me off my head. You're almost worse than Rafe Knight. Can't you both just let me enjoy a wee holiday on my own?"

"Aye, all right. We'll back off, but only for a few days."

"I signed in for three days. That's all. Now, I want to get back to relaxing. Goodbye, Thane."

For the next half hour, I try to think of what I want to do on my wee holiday in the town where I live and work. Does that still qualify as a holiday? I'm not even leaving the village limits. Maybe I should at least go for a walk. To all the places I've already been to over my entire lifetime so far. I won't actually be getting away from it all if I stroll down the streets and meet my friends and relatives along the way.

I reckon I might as well take a walk, anyway. At least I'll get some exercise to clear my head of thoughts about that vile, odious man. I'm wearing the same dress as when I visited Rafe at the police station. It isn't exactly walking attire. But I don't feel like changing, so I'll stick to the area around the hotel. I do have a straw hat, so I'm not completely unprepared for the outdoors.

Just as I shut the door to my room, I hear a door across the hall click shut too.

I turn around and gasp. "You! How dare you stalk me."

"Stalk?" Rafe says with a slight chuckle. "You flatter yourself."

"Being followed by a toerag like you is not flattering. Obviously, you were stalking me, waiting outside until I checked in."

He takes two steps toward me. "I've been here for two and a half hours. When did you check in?"

"Well, ah…"

Rafe smirks. "Later than that, eh? I'd wager you just arrived."

"My arrival time has nothing to do with you. Now who's flattering yourself?"

He stomps up to me and leans in close enough that I can smell his aftershave. It's a woodsy aroma that has an odd effect on me. That sort of cologne has always made me randy, but not to this degree. My nipples have tightened.

Rafe leans in even closer, our faces millimeters apart. "That was no casual kiss earlier. You kissed me passionately, Iona."

"You started it."

"But you didn't tell me to stop, and you participated actively." He glances down at the neckline of my dress, where my stiff nipples are impossible to overlook. He keeps his head down as he lifts his gaze to mine. "You want me."

"I'd rather have a poke with a sumo wrestler who has bad body odor."

"No, love, you want me. Can't hide your lust."

I bar my arms over my chest. "Leave me alone, or I'll have you dragged off to jail again."

"On what charge? Turning you on?" He chuckles with a sort of deep sensuality that arouses my body, the parts I'd rather stayed asleep. "Admit it, Iona. You want to know what fucking me would be like."

"Please. I hate you."

He sets one hand on the door beside me, and his lips graze my cheek. "I can't stand you either. But sometimes hate makes for the hottest sex."

Maybe it has been a long, long time since I had a poke with anyone. Rafe might be a raging ersehole, but he is attractive and sexy with a body I'm sure could take me to the heights of ecstasy.

No, no, no, I won't debase myself that way.

But couldn't I try it just once…

Rafe curls those luscious lips into an expression of pure lust. His voice grows deeper too as he lowers his head to within millimeters of my mouth. "You're like me, aren't you? Sexually frustrated, not looking for a relationship, just needing one bloody fantastic shag."

"I think I could put up with you for a quickie. If I don't look at you and just use your body."

He freezes and stares into my eyes with a starkness that almost makes me want to apologize—for what I dinnae know. After a moment, his expression hardens, and he pushes away from the wall, taking two steps backward.

Then he pivots on his heels and walks away swiftly.

I gape at the back of him. The *bod ceann* wanted a quick shag, yet he just stalked off without even kissing me. Not that I wanted him to do that. Ugh, of course I did. I cannae believe I almost let that despicable man seduce me. That must have been some sort of trick to humiliate me.

But Rafe didn't insult me, not to my face. Instead, he purred the most sensual words I've ever heard and got me so wet that I can't walk around in public anytime soon. So, I rush back into my room. And yet I can't stop thinking about Rafe and how much I wanted him to fuck me. I'm off my head in the worst way. I have only one option to get that man out of my system.

I shut the curtains and rub myself off.

And *mhac na galla*, thinking about that odious man makes me come harder than I ever have before.

Chapter Four

Rafe

I can't look at that woman anymore, but I can't stop thinking about her either. Iona Buchanan is a succubus, luring men into her traps only so she can devour them. What she said…No, I refuse to think about that. It might trigger memories I prefer never to relive. But my mind insists on forcing me to hear those words again. *I think I could put up with you for a quickie. If I don't look at you and just use your body.* After that statement, I no longer have doubts about ruining Iona's life, and I'm now certain that she has been shagging my son.

Why, then, did she want me released from jail?

Suddenly, I realize I have no bloody idea where I am. I recall stalking out of the hotel and crossing the car park. After that, everything became a blur. I'm walking down the pavement, trying not to trip off the edge and onto the street. Why I feel off balance is no mystery. It's the fault of that woman.

The beautiful, sensual Scottish lass.

No, that's not what I meant. I was referring to the psychopathic succubus known as Iona Buchanan.

You aren't worth bothering with anymore, Rafe. You don't exist in my world.

I stop dead and bump into some bloke or other. The memory of those words always derails me. I shouldn't let any woman have that much power over me, yet I seem incapable of letting go of the memories. Iona Buchanan didn't speak those words. Another woman uttered them.

"You're blocking the foot traffic."

For a moment, those words can't penetrate my brain. I stare at the man who spoke them, but I can't recall who he is or why he's glaring at me. The pavement is wide enough for three people to walk side by side, yet this bloke seems to think I've committed a crime by standing still.

And then I realize why. This man is Thane Buchanan.

"The pavement is yours," I say as I attempt to push past him.

But Thane moves in front of me. "You and I need to have a wee chat."

"No, thank you. I've had my fill of 'wee' chats today."

"Then let's have a large one." Thane grips my shoulder. "You have two choices. Walk into the café on your own power, or else I'll drag you in there by the scruff of your neck."

"Hmm, let me think about it." I squint my eyes briefly. "No, I'm going to pass on that offer."

When I try to move past him, he squeezes my shoulder hard and snaps a pair of handcuffs around one of my wrists. I felt him doing that. Then he snaps the other cuff in place. But when I glance down, I get a strange surprise. The cuffs have fluffy pink padding. What the bloody hell is this man doing?

"Let go of me, you Scottish Neanderthal."

"There never were Neanderthals in the British Isles." Thane grasps the chain that holds the cuffs together and starts dragging me toward the café he'd mentioned a moment ago.

Since I seem to have no choice—unless I want to tackle Thane—I give in and follow him into the café. We sit down at an outdoor table.

My captor picks up a menu and starts browsing.

What the fuck? I've never visited Scotland before, but if the Scots I've met today are any indication, I doubt I'll ever return. Assuming I can escape. They might have me thrown in jail again if I refuse to comply. With what, I haven't a clue.

A waitress approaches us. Her gaze shifts to my pink handcuffs, but only for a brief moment. Then she smiles at Thane. "Good morning, Mr. Buchanan. What can I get for you and your friend?"

I snort and shake my head.

"We'll both have haggis, neeps, and tatties," Thane announces. "And a bottle of Thane Black Label too. Thank you, Bonnie."

This arse has a beverage named after him? I suppose he owns the entire village too. That would be just my luck.

Our waitress toddles off to work on our order. Not that I intend to eat or drink anything. This man will probably sprinkle cyanide into my food and drink. Maybe I have caused a great deal of trouble since I arrived in this village earlier today, but I don't give a toss about what a bunch of barmy Scots think of me. Saving my son from a succubus is all that matters to me.

Moments after Thane placed our order, it arrives at our table, before we've even had time to glower at each other. Once the waitress leaves, I can't hold back my curiosity. Instinctively, I try to fold my arms over my chest. But I can't do it. The fucking cuffs prevent it.

Instead, I lean back in my chair and squint at Thane. "Are you paying for the meal? Or am I required to cough up the money myself?"

"Dinnae fash. I'm paying." He opens the bottle of whisky and pours a dram into two glasses, then hands one to me. "You'll feel better after a taste of my Black Label."

"Not a fan of whisky. I prefer vodka."

"You won't leave this café unless you try my single-malt Scotch."

"Getting me drunk won't help you get rid of me." But I give in and pick up a shot glass, knocking back the contents in one swig. "Satisfied?"

Thane clucks his tongue. "That's no way to enjoy a high-quality single malt. Try it again, more slowly this time."

He pours me another dram.

I stifle a growl and take a sip.

"Let it roll over your tongue and down your throat," Thane tells me. "Take it slow, don't rush. The flavors will awaken your senses little by little."

I smack my glass down. "Enough. I tasted your sodding whisky. Now I want to go back to my hotel—alone. I don't need an escort."

Thane clucks his tongue again. "You're the impatient sort. Does that bleed over into your sex life? Must not be much of a lover."

"If you don't release me from my shackles, I'll flip this table over and strangle you with the handcuffs."

The bizarre Scot studies me for a moment while smiling slightly. "I was going to order you to stay away from my sister, but I've changed my mind. Iona can take care of herself. If you should hurt her in any way, Ramsay and I will hunt you down like the rabid dog you pretend to be."

"Who says I'm pretending?"

"My gut says so." Thane releases my cuffs and slaps a handful of Scottish notes on the table, then he rises. "The whisky is yours to keep. And I do recommend eating something before you get drunk. Enjoy the haggis."

Thane Buchanan saunters out of the café, disappearing down the street.

I stare at the food on the table, my brows wrinkled, and try to deduce what in the world just happened. Thane bought me enough food for two people, gifted me with whisky, and then walked away.

Well, I am hungry. Haggis can't be as revolting as it looks. Might as well give it a go.

I scoop up a spoonful of haggis and cautiously consume it. The Scottish pudding isn't as revolting as I'd assumed it would be. This won't become my favorite dish, but at least I'm in no danger of vomiting. Tatties and neeps aren't vile either, but then, they're simply potatoes and turnips. As much as I loathe admitting it, Thane's whisky is the highlight of my meal. It's the best single malt I've ever tasted.

No, I won't share that revelation with Thane or Iona or any other Scots.

When Bonnie comes to clear off my table, I hand her several bills that amount to a twenty-pound tip. Her eyes widen when she sees that, but she doesn't question the amount.

I walk out of the café carrying the bottle of Thane Black Label. I briefly wonder where his distillery is and if guests are allowed to tour the facility. Then I realize the last thing I want to do is meet the Buchanan brothers again. They don't frighten me. I've simply had enough negative excitement for one day.

Going back to the hotel seems unwise. Iona might still be there, and I don't care to risk speaking to her. All I want is to find my son. But I keep forgetting to ask these barmy Scots where he and his best mate are staying. They're here on a six-week holiday, that's all I know.

I won't ask his mother. That would result in the equivalent of setting off a neutron bomb.

To waste time, I amble down the pavement heading toward nowhere in particular. I turn two corners, paying no attention to where I'm headed. After about fifteen minutes, I halt in front of a strange establishment. The name of it seems to be in Gaelic, and I have no idea what the words mean. But I do recognize the sort of merchandise being peddled inside the shop. It's New Age bollocks.

Since I'm rather lost, I simply stand here like a vagrant. Might as well try to ring Toby for the eighteenth time, strictly so I won't look like I'm loitering. But Toby's mobile rings and rings and rings, finally switching to voice mail. I leave yet another message.

"Please call me back, Toby. I need to speak to you. I'm in Scotland, and I just want to see you and know you're all right. Cheers."

I sounded pathetic, didn't I? Begging my son to return my call.

The door to the shop swings open, and a group of cheerful women exit. They smile and give me appreciative looks. At least I haven't lost my appeal for all women, only the Scottish ones who are sleeping with my son. I trudge into the shop strictly out of curiosity. Don't know what to do with myself now. I've been dragged off the jail, threatened by Scottish louts, and given a free meal for reasons I cannot comprehend. Of course I'm bloody confused.

As I wander about the shop, not really paying attention to the wares being hawked, I notice a woman behind the sales counter is watching me. She doesn't seem interested in me as a man. I think the woman is simply wondering why a single bloke would visit a place like this. The only other patrons have just left. I must seem like the largest sore thumb in Scotland.

"May I help you find something?" the woman calls out to me.

Now that she's spoken to me, I can't reasonably ignore her. All I can do is trudge over to the counter. "I wasn't actually looking for anything. Sorry. I think I'm a bit lost. Never visited this village before."

"Well, then, let me be the first to welcome you." She thrusts a hand out across the counter. "I'm Kirsty Turner, and this is my shop."

I shake her hand. "Thank you for not clubbing me to death. I'm Rafe Knight."

"Oh, aye, you're the British man who harassed Iona and got locked up at the police station. I gather you aren't interested in my metaphysical wares."

"No. Sorry. And yes, I am that arse." I rub my forehead. "Actually, I'm trying to find my son. Toby is on a six-week holiday in the Highlands with his best mate, taking a break from his job as a computer programmer."

She tips her head to the side. "Are you Toby Knight's father? He's best friends with Eric Taylor, an American laddie. Eric's mother is marrying Thane Buchanan."

"Thane? I met him earlier. He threatened me with haggis and whisky."

Kirsty laughs. "Aye, that sounds like Thane. But why don't you ring Toby?"

"I tried. Had to leave a voice mail."

"What about texting him? Younger people prefer that."

Texting? I've never mastered that. My fingers are too big, and I can't understand how anyone manages to type anything on their mobile phones. But I suppose I'll give it a go. "Gah! The bloody autocorrect thinks it knows what I want to say better than I do."

Kirsty smiles, holding out her hand. "Would you like me to type it for you? Just dictate your message to me."

"That's very kind. Thank you." I pause to collect my thoughts, then start dictating. "Toby, it's your father. I'm worried about you. Please get in touch right away."

Kirsty hands my mobile back to me. "There you are."

"I'm grateful for your help. But I think I'll walk while I wait to hear from Toby."

While I shuffle out of the shop, one thought plagues me. Why doesn't my son want to speak to me?

Chapter Five

Eric

"Wake up, mate, it's time to harass Iona Buchanan again." My roommate gives me a strong shake—not once, but three times. "Come on, Eric. You're the one making me lie to my father, so the least you could do is order and pay for our meals. I'm starving."

"Cook something," I mumble, still half asleep.

"It's afternoon, Eric." Toby slugs my arm. "Next time I'll punch you in the face, you arse."

"Go on, punch me in the ass."

My roommate blows out an annoyed breath. "I said I'd punch you in the face. Want your mum to wonder why you're black and blue? I'll tell her."

I sigh and still can't rouse myself.

Toby kicks me in the ass. "If you don't get up, I'm going to tell your mother that you've been stalking Iona. She'll tell Thane, who will tell every other Scot in the Highlands. You'll be roasted on a spit by this evening."

"Roasted hot dogs do sound good."

Toby makes a frustrated noise. "I give up. You can starve and get burnt on a cross like a ruddy witch."

Finally, I yawn and roll over onto my back. Then I yawn again and rub my belly. "Where's the food?"

Toby hurls my sleeping bag at me.

"Okay, okay, I'm sorry." I push up into a sitting position and glance around. "Where are my shoes?"

"No idea. I'm not the keeper of your wardrobe."

"Oh, there they are." I pull my sneakers on and tie them while I speak. "You know, it was your idea to rough it in the Highlands. 'It'll be so amazing,' you said. 'We'll have a blast in the great outdoors,' you said that too."

"Is it my fault Scotland is the world capital for midges? At least the insect repellent works."

"Yeah, that's awesome." I study our tent, which is kind of small for two full-grown men. "I need to find Iona."

Toby groans and flops back down on his sleeping bag in a dramatic gesture that's completely unnecessary. Then he winces. "Ow, that bloody hurt."

"Could've told you it would. The ground is hard."

"This is all your fault. We had to drive to Scotland so you could woo your dream girl, who's twice your age and not interested."

I sit cross-legged as I conjure Iona's face in my mind. She's so beautiful, so kind, so wonderful. But my mom would never understand. I'm twenty-five years old, but she acts like I'm still a kid.

Toby's phone chimes. He glances at the screen, then aims a lopsided frown at me. "It's my dad. He wants to know where I am."

"So tell him. What's he gonna do? You're in Scotland, he's in England."

My best friend sighs and types a response. After a brief delay, his phone chimes again. "Blimey. It's doomsday."

"What are you talking about?"

"My father is here in Scotland, in the Highlands."

I shrug. "Let's have lunch with him. Then maybe he'll quit pestering you."

Toby moans again, this time adding a bit more drama to his performance. "Bloody hell. You don't know my father. He'll demand to know the precise location where I'm staying. Dad isn't a moron. I'm sure he's figured out something is going on." Toby shuts his eyes and shakes his head. "He'll find out that I've been covering for you."

"So, pretend you didn't get his text."

"He's far too clever to fall for that trick. Besides, it's juvenile."

I know Toby's right, but I can't risk my mom finding out that it's me, not Toby, who's trying to win Iona's heart. Sure, Iona keeps telling me she doesn't feel that way about me, but if I could just get her alone for a few minutes…She'll probably still think I'm a psycho. Why do I keep pestering her? I don't know. I've gone temporarily insane, I guess. No, that's not it. I have real feelings for her, and we did kiss at the Valentine's Day shindig.

Maybe my dogged determination to win her over has something to do with the fact my longtime girlfriend dumped me.

No, I genuinely have deep feelings for Iona.

Toby pulls his shoes on, eying me with a half frown. "You're my best mate, Eric. We're like brothers. But this thing with Iona has gotten out of control. There's definitely something else going on with you, though I don't believe it's only because Alice threw you over. That certainly didn't help. You'd been with her for five years. Please tell me what's got you wound up so tight these days."

Alice didn't just dump me. I'd bought a ring and asked her to marry me.

She had slapped me in the face and flounced away in a huff.

Guess what? Three weeks later I heard she got hitched to some rugby player. Yeah, my life sucks the big one.

But that's not why I'm chasing Iona. I honestly love her.

I stand up and stretch, groaning. "What should we do today?"

"Avoid my father at all costs, for one." Toby gets up too and plants his hands on his hips. "You know, when we were out and about in the village yesterday, I saw a house that had a sign on it."

"Uh-huh. A sign for what?"

"A psychologist who specializes in therapy for couples, families, individuals, and slightly barmy geologists."

I roll my eyes. "Therapy? Come on. Mom wanted me and Courtney to get therapy after Dad ran out on us, but we only went once. It was dumb."

"Your sister isn't deranged. You are." Toby throws his hands up. "I'm saying this as your best mate because I care about you."

I stuff my wallet into my hip pocket, then grab my baseball cap and sunglasses. "Let's go into the village to get some grub."

"And then you'll harass that poor woman."

"No, of course not. But I need to apologize for the, uh, texts I sent her this morning." I scratch the back of my neck. "And the other days too."

"As long as that's all you do. I'll go with you for moral support."

Toby really is the best friend any guy could have. He's put up with my recent behavior when any sane person would have called the cops.

We both grab our phones, then head out. None of our clothes would be worth stealing, so we haven't worried about that. Scotland seems like way too nice a place to have a serious crime problem.

Just as we reach the village limits, someone shouts at us.

"Toby! Get your arse over here! Immediately!"

Oh, I recognize that British voice. And I also recognize the tall guy who's running across the street toward us.

Toby's eyes bulge. His jaw drops. His face goes a little paler too. "Fuck."

I doubt Rafe Knight could hear that since Toby whispered the solitary word.

Mr. Knight halts directly in front of us, and he doesn't seem happy. No, his expression kind of reminds me of the way I'd expect a rampaging bull would look. "Toby, why have you been avoiding me? I want to know what the bloody hell you think you're playing at. Iona Buchanan is twice your age. The only reason I'm not locking you in the boot of my car is because that woman seduced you."

"No, she didn't. Iona is a nice person," I blurt out. Did I think that through before I spoke? Of course not. That's kind of my MO.

"A nice person?" Mr. Knight huffs. "She seduces boys half her age and has innocent men imprisoned."

Imprisoned? What the hell is he talking about? Iona absolutely wouldn't do that without serious provocation.

Toby's brows knit together. "I don't understand. Who was locked up?"

Mr. Knight compresses his lips and flares his nostrils. Maybe he is a rampaging bull after all. "Iona Buchanan had me detained at the Loch Fairbairn Police Station."

"Whuh—But why?"

"Because I confronted the slag about her inappropriate relationship with you. Perhaps your mother wouldn't give a toss about that, but I do."

Oh, I wish he hadn't brought up Toby's mom. It's one of his triggers. The ex Mrs. Knight is one nasty piece of work, but that's not Toby's fault. Neither is Mr. Knight's anger. That's my doing, and I suddenly feel like a heel. "Uh, Mr. Knight, about Iona—"

"I don't want to hear another word about the slag. Toby, you are coming home with me right now."

My best friend adopts a demeanor not unlike his father's thunderous expression. "I am not a child, which means you can't order me around. I'm staying."

He locks his arms over his chest to hammer that point home.

Oh, shit. Mr. Knight is mad at Toby and Iona, but it's all because of me.

I clear my throat. "Listen, I need to explain something to you, Mr. Knight. The one who's been chasing after Iona is actually—"

"Me," Toby interrupts. "I'm sleeping with a woman twice my age, and there isn't a bloody thing you can do about it. Maybe you shouldn't have broken up our family without a second thought. Maybe then I wouldn't have turned out to be a selfish prick, just like you."

Oh, yeah, my best friend just went scorched earth on his dad.

Chapter Six

Iona

Ahh, I feel so much more relaxed this afternoon. My encounters with Rafe have faded from my memory, and I enjoyed a lovely meal at the café, alone. Maybe I would've liked to have a companion. A friend, not a lover. Just someone to talk to so I wouldn't look like a pathetic woman in her forties who cannae get a date.

Rafe Knight probably found his son by now. I pity that laddie, having a raging erse for a father.

I took a long walk through the village too, so I needed a shower once I got back to my room at the Loch Fairbairn Arms. Oh, the steamy water felt wonderful and relaxed all the kinks caused by stress. Caused by that bloody man. He had been doing rather well with trying to seduce me—until he suddenly scowled and stormed away.

Maybe he has a split personality.

After my shower, I pulled on a plush terry-cloth dressing gown. It's much softer than what I can buy in a shop. I love the feel of it against my skin.

Just as I've sat down on the bed to watch television, someone pounds on my door. I shuffle over there and swing the door open.

Rafe stares at me. He has one hand on the door frame and looks like a maniac—the lustful sort. His hair is mussed, he's breathing hard, and four of the buttons on his shirt are undone. His skin glistens with a light sheen of sweat.

And in one hand, he holds a box of condoms.

Suddenly, I have trouble catching my breath. "Rafe? What do you want now?"

He grasps the belt on my dressing gown and tugs me closer. The sweaty scent of him has a strangely arousing effect on me. "You."

"Dinnae understand."

"You asked what I want." He tears my belt away. "You, that's what I want. My cock buried inside you, no talking, just a hard, hot fuck."

"Ahmno interested in being your revenge poke."

His gaze shifts downward to my mound. He already tore open my dressing gown, so he has a clear view of my entire naked body. "Are you going to deny you want me inside you?"

Aye, absolutely. That's what I should say. But there's something about this unkempt ersehole that turns me on more than I'd like to admit. I've lost my mind and all my self-control. Why else would I debase myself the way I'm about to do?

I grasp the waistband of his trousers and drag him across the threshold. "Keep your obnoxious mouth shut unless you're saying something filthy. Understood?"

"Yes." He kicks the door shut and picks me up only to fling me onto the bed. "Get rid of that dressing gown unless you want me to rip it to shreds."

I cannae move. Rafe unleashed is something I never expected to see. My body grows wetter and achier every second while I watch him disposing of his clothes. He rips his jacket off, flinging it halfway across the room where it lands on the dresser. Then he stumbles around trying to rid himself of his shoes and socks. Even his clumsiness makes me want him like mad.

The despicable man had better give me the hottest sex in history.

Rafe drops his trousers, kicking them away, revealing a surprising fact.

The man has no underwear on. That gives me a clear view of his big, hard cock. The tip is red and glistening. I'd already figured out Rafe has a muscular build, but now I can rove my gaze over every inch of his body and all those beautifully defined muscles.

Oh, aye, I need him inside me. So, I shimmy out of my dressing gown, tossing it onto the floor.

He rips open the box of condoms and flings it onto the nightstand, sending the packets flying every which way. Then he climbs onto the bed, crawling toward me on all fours. Once his face is hovering above mine, he rocks back and forth so slowly that I feel every millimeter of his cock brushing against my belly. My pulse beats hard enough to make me feel a wee bit lightheaded. But when he shoves a hand between my thighs, roughly cupping my mound, I release a desperate cry. Dinnae care if I'm behaving like a pathetic, sex-starved eejit.

Well, I am one of those.

Rafe hoists my knees onto his shoulders and dives his head between my thighs. He latches on to my clit, suckling it fiercely, grunting like a ravenous beast. My nub pulsates, and so does my sex. I clutch his head while he devours me with his tongue, his lips, and his teeth, and my state of arousal intensifies to a level I've never experienced before in all my life. It's intoxicating. The second he thrusts his longest finger inside me, I jerk. My head thrashes and my whole body folds in on itself as I cry out. The orgasm struck so suddenly I had no time to consider what I'm doing with this man. Never before has my heart thrashed so wildly that it seems to want to explode, but it does now.

I clench my fingers in the pillow and unleash a wild, ululating cry.

Rafe rises to his knees. His cheeks have turned pink, sweat drizzles down his chest, and he snatches up a condom, ripping the packet open with his teeth and spitting it out. Despite his almost crazed state, he manages to carefully roll the condom on. Then he grasps my wrists, pressing them to the mattress at either side of my head.

"Keep your hands here," he commands. "Understand?"

"Aye." I love the harshness of his voice and his bossy command. "Whatever you say. Just fuck me already."

He hoists my legs again, urging me to lock my ankles behind his neck. And at long last, he plunges his cock inside me as deeply as possible, holding that position while his expression grows tight.

My back arches. My fingernails make a scraping sound against the pillowcase.

Rafe sets his hands at either side of my hips and begins a brutal pace of pumping in and out, in and out, going faster with every thrust. My cream runs down my inner thighs. Noises erupt from my lips, desperate sounds that can't possibly come from me. No man has ever taken me with so much determination and force, as if he means to brand me with his cock. I can't swear I'd mind if he did do that.

The bed begins to creak and scrape across the floor. My cries escalate into high-pitched shouts. The nightstand wobbles and thumps into the wall again and again.

Rafe shoves an arm under my lower back, hoists me into a semi-sitting position on his lap, and clutches me to his body while he goes on fucking me like a maniac. I throw my head back, thrashing it side to side, lost to the incredible sensations he's giving me. When he begins thrusting upward, I bounce on his cock.

"Yes, oh God, yes, don't stop, you sodding ersehole!"

"I hate you, but I'll fuck you into submission however long it takes."

"*Mhac na galla*, I despise you but—Oh, God, yes, yes, yes! Don't you dare stop!"

"Ahhh!" He slams me down on the bed. "You love my cock. Say it, Iona."

"I love your cock, you bloody bastard."

"You're an evil succubus, but I'll make you come anyway."

Rafe shoves my legs apart and slaps his hands down on either side of my head. I can just barely see him in my peripheral vision. The tension on his face matches my own. The need to come has turned into a demonic force inside me, and inside him too, I'm dead sure.

He pumps into me like a demon, and the furniture begins to shake and scrape and shiver once again. I push up onto my elbows, tipping my head back, so aroused that it's almost painful. Rafe's grunts escalate into throaty shouts while I let out more high-pitched cries and my sex tightens in anticipation of a climax that I know will blow us both apart. My nipples have grown so sensitized that the slightest breeze intensifies my need.

This time, my orgasm gives me no warning. I scream as my inner muscles contract around his cock so many times that I lose count.

Rafe punches into me twice more, roaring like a beast, his release so powerful that I can feel it inside me. Then he freezes briefly, releases a deep groan, and collapses onto the mattress beside me.

"Bloody fucking hell, woman. You are a wild banshee."

"You are a raging bull with a cock to match."

He moves only his eyes to glance at me sideways. "I still despise you."

"I hate you too."

We both spoke in a softer tone of voice that seems to belie our statements. Cannae believe I had a poke with Rafe Knight, the beast who pounded on my door this morning, making false accusations. I've lost my mind. Nothing else explains it.

But I cannot ever do that again. If anyone found out...

Rafe's lips form a charmingly lopsided smile. "That was the best shag since the beginning of time."

"Aye, it was." I fan my face with my hand. "Whew. You have a shocking amount of stamina for a man your age." I look at him. "How old are you, by the way?"

"Fifty-one. What about you?"

"Forty-six."

He smirks. "I suppose that makes me a dirty old man debasing a younger woman."

"You aren't that much older." I roll onto my side, facing him. "Want to give it another go?"

Rafe grins, and it's the most enticing expression I've ever seen. "Yes, I want that. But afterwards..."

"We still despise each other."

"Exactly." He pulls me on top of him. "You can do the honors this time. But I will need a little while to recover first."

Someone knocks on the door. "Um, Iona dear, is everything all right in there?"

That's Mrs. Agnew.

Rafe and I exchange guilty looks, then I call out, "Everything is fine."

"Dinnae know what all the racket was. Sounded like an earthquake, but I didn't feel anything. And the screams—"

"It was the television. I'm fine, I promise."

"All right, if you say so. I need to get back to the front desk."

Rafe looks at me.

I look at him.

And we both burst out laughing.

Once we stop doing that, Rafe lifts his head as if he's searching for something. "Do you have any food? I'm famished."

"I have some potato crisps and chocolate."

"Perfect. Where are they?"

"Over there, on the wee table. I have some water bottles too."

He leaps off the bed, and I sit up to get a perfect view of his backside. That taut erse. Those powerful thighs. The elegant planes of his back. He is a beautiful man. I might want to date him if it weren't for his despicable nature.

Rafe brings our snack to the bed, climbing in beside me.

We both lean against the wall while we gorge ourselves on junk food. Rafe holds a strawberry truffle to my lips and holds it there until I give in and let him slide it onto my tongue. Once I'm done, he offers me another candy. But I take it from him, waiting until he parts his lips for me, then I set the truffle on his tongue. He devours it slowly, keeping his gaze on me the entire time. Then he feeds me another candy, this time butter caramel.

Once I've consumed it, my journalist curiosity rears up. I need to ask him a question. "Why did you come to my room determined to have a poke? You looked like you'd been in a right rammy just before you pounded on my door."

"I pounded *you* even harder."

"You know what I meant."

He shoves a peanut-butter chocolate into his mouth and uses chewing as an excuse to avoid my question. Even once he's done eating, he stays quiet.

"Rafe, I want to know why you were in such a wild, disheveled state."

All the humor and playfulness has evacuated his expression. "It's none of your concern. Fucking you doesn't obligate me to share anything about my life with you."

"Except when you're shouting at me about your son."

"I shouted because you've been shagging him." The anger he'd shown me earlier seems to be returning. "You don't need to know anything else."

"Considering your behavior today, I have every right to know."

He flies off the bed, knocking the chocolate box onto the floor, and snatches up his clothing. While he gets dressed, he refuses to look at me. But he does not refuse to speak. "I came here to find out what my son finds so intoxicating about a Scottish woman who's twice his age. When did you last shag him? Early this morning? During the lunch hour? You'll probably seduce him again once I've left the premises."

Bod an Donais. Why did I ever let this man touch me?

Chapter Seven

Rafe

Iona stares at me as if I'm a deranged lunatic who escaped from an asylum a few hours ago. Maybe I have done an excellent impression of a raging bastard who's off his rocker. Iona wants explanations, and all I've given her is vitriol and madness. I feel as if I've gone mad, that's for sure. Steady, calm, reliable—those used to be the words most often ascribed to me.

"Get out of my room," Iona declares. "Never come within five miles of me ever again. If you do, I'll file a harassment report at the police station."

I ignore her statement because I have no valid response to give. She's correct. She should file that report and have me thrown in jail again. I use hunting for my shoes as an excuse not to look at Iona. Once I've found them, I have no reason to stay in this room.

Without saying a word, I walk out and shut the door behind me. My feet seem determined to drag across the floor as I head for my room directly opposite Iona's. Yes, I should go into my room. But that's the last thing I want right now. My behavior of late has shocked me more than anyone else. My wife rejected me. My son rejected me. Even the woman I shagged a few minutes ago rejected me.

I don't feel like a man anymore. I've become the beast from that fairytale, punishing a kind woman for my own problems. I doubt Iona will volunteer to rehabilitate me.

As I shuffle out of the hotel, I pull out my mobile and search the built-in maps to search for someplace I can go to cool down and figure out what I hope to accomplish here in Scotland. I should leave Iona alone. Yes, that's bloody obvious. But my son…Toby is all I have, and even he despises me.

Toby, you are coming home with me right now. Oh, yes, wasn't that the clever thing to say to my adult son. Toby has always been trustworthy. I know that. But when I found him earlier, I'd treated him like a child. Naturally, he lashed out at me. I deserved it.

I'm sleeping with a woman twice my age, and there isn't a bloody thing you can do about it. Maybe you shouldn't have broken up our family without a second thought. Maybe then I wouldn't have turned out to be a selfish prick, just like you.

Of course he's angry about that, even years later. I let him believe I'd initiated the divorce. He loves his mum, and I couldn't let him find out what she'd done.

After a long stroll down the streets of Loch Fairbairn, I drop my arse onto a bench that sits at the edge of a small playground. It's full of various things children like, such as a jungle gym. But I don't see any children playing. Maybe they're in school. I haven't a clue what day it is. Monday? Saturday? Who knows. All I can say for certain is that I need to give Toby time to calm down before I try to explain.

I bow my head, gazing down at my hands.

"Ah, there you are. It's been quite a search to find you."

That Scottish voice does not sound familiar. When I glance up at the man who spoke, I don't recognize him either.

The stranger sits down beside me, offering his hand which I do not accept. "I'm Jack MacTaggart. And you are Rafe Knight, the evildoer who upset Iona Buchanan."

"Aren't you so bloody clever? I'm probably the only British male in this town." No, I won't dispute his description of me as an evildoer.

"Not quite. Alex Thorne and his wife Catriona live just outside the village limits."

"I don't know who those people are."

"You'll find out eventually." Jack thrusts his hand at me again. "Let's be friends, eh? The alternative isn't as pleasant."

I'm too exhausted to argue with this bloke about anything, even a handshake. So, I grasp his hand. "Can't say it's a pleasure to meet you. A vague threat isn't friendly. How did you know where to find me? Even I haven't got a bloody clue where I am."

"You're on the high street, one block away from Kirsty Turner's metaphysical shop. I understand you visited the shop earlier."

"By mistake. But where the bloody hell am I?"

My new mate chuckles. "On the high street."

"Oh, yes, that clears up my confusion, doesn't it? A man who has never set foot in Scotland before today should instantly understand the street layouts."

Jack MacTaggart sighs as if I'm an errant child and he's the tolerant kindergarten teacher. "You're holding a great deal inside yourself, aren't you? I can help if you'll cooperate. I'd like to get to work on your inner-directed anger as soon as possible."

I swivel my head toward Jack MacTaggart, suddenly certain that I do not want to go anywhere with him. I've sussed out his agenda. "You're a psychologist or a therapist or something of that nature."

He grins and punches my arm. "Good job, Rafe. I could tell you were intelligent when I first saw you. I'm a psychotherapist, as you correctly surmised. Now, let's turn that intelligence on you."

"You want to analyze me here on a park bench."

"No. I recommend we go to my home. That's where I see my clients."

"Lovely. Do I get a free meal too? Perhaps your wife and children will watch while I bare my soul."

Jack stands up. "Come with me and you'll find out. A wee bit of therapy can't hurt."

I huff. "Can't hurt? That's a shedload of bollocks."

"Sounds like you've had experience with therapy, and it didn't work out for you."

I huff again.

"Give me a chance," Jack says. "If you hate it after five minutes, I won't bother you again—and the session will be free of charge. Does that sound reasonable?"

"I suppose so." I crane my neck but can't see anything beyond the corner across from us. "How far must we walk? I'm knackered."

"No walking required. We'll go in my car." He waves toward a vehicle I hadn't noticed before. A bush had partially obscured it until I bent forward. "Might as well give in, Rafe. If you don't, Thane and Ramsay are on standby to dump you into the nearest rubbish bin headfirst."

I groan and heave my body off the bench. With all the resignation of a condemned man, I tell Jack, "Let's go."

The drive to Jack's home takes only a few minutes, and his car is quite comfortable. I couldn't help noticing a child's toy stuffed into a corner of the backseat. Jack must have a wife and child, perhaps more than one child. Only one wife, though, I assume. These days, you never can tell.

Jack's home is a lovely cottage on the outskirts of the village. He has neighbors close by, but not so close that it would be annoying. I doubt the therapist would care if his neighbors pester him. It's his job to care about everyone. Not that I'm an expert on psychotherapy. Far from it.

The moment we walk into the house, I know I've misjudged Jack. The first thing he does is kiss his wife, who sits on the sofa with a toddler who resembles his father and his mother. The beautiful blonde smiles at me, her green eyes sparkling.

Jack ruffles the toddler's hair. "This is our son, Michael. We like to call him Micky. And the bonnie lass beside him is my wife, Autumn. Say hello to Rafe Knight, *mo chridhe*."

"Welcome to our home Mr. Knight." Autumn says with a smile. "Whatever help you need, I'm sure Jack will get you fixed up lickety-split."

I suddenly feel itchy, but I resist the urge to scratch my entire body. "Ah, thank you, Mrs. MacTaggart. I gather you're American."

"Yep. But please call me Autumn. We aren't formal in this house."

"That's kind of you, Autumn. Please call me Rafe." Has she not heard about my rampage through the village? If she's been home with her child all morning, she might not have known about that. But Jack knows all about it.

Autumn smiles. "Good luck, Rafe. I'm sure you boys have a lot to talk about."

Jack grips my shoulder. "Time to therapize you, laddie."

"I don't think 'therapize' is a word."

"Not technically. My wife invented it." He nods toward a hallway. "My office is down there."

Since I agreed to this rubbish, I have no choice but to follow Jack down a short hallway to a closed door. He opens it, waving for me to enter the room, and follows me so he can shut the door—for privacy, I assume. Well, at least I'll have a measure of confidentiality. His office is not what I expected. Don't therapists always want their clients to lie down or at least sit down on a couch? Since I don't have much experience with therapists, I shouldn't have assumed Jack's methods would be identical to those of every other psychologist.

He has a desk, and there is a chair across from it. But I don't see a couch. Two high-back, upholstered chairs are positioned on either side of a window seat. At Jack's suggestion, I approach the window seat and settle onto the nearby chair. Actually, this is a rather pleasant place to sit and have my head examined by a professional. The view is lovely too.

Strangely, I feel more relaxed in this room than I did when I was at home in my house.

Jack takes a seat on the chair across from me. Then he sets one ankle on the opposite knee. "Let's get started. How do you feel?"

"Ah, so you're the cliché-loving sort of therapist." I drum my fingers on my chair›s arms. "How do I feel? Like smashing my fist through a concrete wall, that's how."

If Jack is shocked, he hides it well. "Why are you so angry, Rafe?"

"Because I am."

"That's not a useful response. How can I therapize you if you won't cooperate?"

I sense a note of sarcasm in his voice.

Jack waves toward the window. "Try gazing out at the bonnie blue sky, then slowly allow the memories to unfold in your mind."

"Are you trying to hypnotize me?"

His lips curl into a mischievous smile. "Aye. Is it working?"

I've met a number of Scots in my life, though always in England or America or some other country. The Scots I've met in this village are by far the strangest on the planet. If Jack's tactic is to drive me insane, his plan is a roaring success. But I refuse to give him the satisfaction of knowing that.

So, I relax into my chair and casually glance out the window. "It is a lovely day. I understand sunny weather isn't the most common sort in Scotland."

"Inane conversation won't make me forget why you're here."

"Because you dragged me to your home, that's why. Showing me your child won't turn me into a sentimental sod. And your hypnotism routine won't work either."

Jack taps his chin with one finger. "Hmm, you are a difficult one. But if I could reform Alex Thorne, I can do the same for you—with or without your cooperation."

I grunt.

And he smiles. "I think you're ready. Now, tell me why you're so angry?"

"Because Iona Buchanan is shagging my son."

"Why does that upset you so much? Toby is an adult, after all. Perhaps he has genuine feelings for Iona."

I grunt again. "She seduced him. That's the only explanation for why he took up with a Scottish woman and never even told me about it."

"How did you find out?"

"Well, ah, you see I…installed tracking software on his mobile phone."

Jack's brows shoot up.

"Yes, I know, it was a terrible thing to do. To be fair, though, I installed that with his permission on the day he went away to university. I sort of forgot to remove it later."

"I see. And you used that software to track him down." Jack tips his head to the side, and his eyes narrow ever so slightly. "Did you read his text messages? I doubt you could've learned about his supposed love affair with Iona any other way."

"Yes, that's how I did it. Toby began texting her regularly whilst he was still in England. Then he and his best mate, Eric Taylor, drove to Scotland without telling me."

Jack studies me for a moment, and my skin begins to itch again. "How does Toby's mother feel about the situation?"

"She doesn't know. My ex-wife rarely sees our son."

The man determined to therapize me sits up straighter and smiles at me as if he's uncovered a vital clue. "Now we're getting somewhere. Tell me about your marriage, Rafe."

Bloody hell.

Chapter Eight

Iona

I unlock the front door and drag my feet across the threshold, kicking the door shut behind me. I've come home. That fact should make me feel better, but instead, it engenders a sense of disappointment. I love my little cottage on the outskirts of Loch Fairbairn. I love the few neighbors I have too. Why, then, do I feel dejected? It's rubbish.

And it cannot possibly have anything to do with Rafe Knight.

That man...He might be incredible in bed, but he's a flaming ersehole the rest of the time. The vitriol he spews at everyone, including me, does not endear him to me or anyone. Once I'd checked out of the hotel, I drove home while still fuming about that odious man.

No more. I will not allow Rafe to ruin my day.

I drop my purse on the table beside the door, then shuffle over to the sofa. Once I flop down on the cushions, I realize I haven't even removed my shoes. I'm sitting here fully clothed, still wearing my dress and my sandals. But I'm too exhausted to get up and change into something casual. So, I let my head fall back against the sofa and prop my sandaled feet on the coffee table.

Memories filter into my mind. Rafe naked. His thick dokey waving about. The erotically determined look on his face.

"*Mhac na galla*," I curse at the ceiling. "Ye cannae even banish that *bod ceann* from your own thoughts. You're off your head, woman. Snap out of it."

I had planned to take a day off anyway, so at least I'm not shirking my work responsibilities. Despite the fact it's Wednesday, not Saturday, I might as well forget about my job for a while. Tomorrow, I'll get back to work on the raft of scintillating exposés I've accumulated for the next edition of the *Loch Fairbairn Daily News*. I believe cows are the top story. Raghnall MacCrum acquired some new stock. Aye, I couldn't think of a more exciting story to run. I only picked Raghnall because he lives next door.

When did my life become so mundane? I used to love my job. Lately, it feels like a ball and chain attached to my feet, dragging me down, down, down.

Rafe Knight certainly spiced up my life—in a negative way.

Despite my fervent wish to forget about him, memories of Rafe plague my thoughts. His naked body hovering above me. The way he licked his lips as he gazed at my breasts. I'd felt his cock grazing my belly, and the sensation was intensely arousing.

"*Iasg is feòil*! I do not want to think about that man. No, never again. Do you hear me? No more thoughts of Rafe naked. I forbid it."

Arguing with myself might not be the best sign. Maybe I should have a wee chat with Jack MacTaggart. He's a therapist, after all. Aye, that sounds like a good idea.

Since I'm already dressed, I grab my purse and race out to my car. Raghnall waves at me as I drive away, and I wave back. Just knowing I'll have a chat with Jack makes me feel more relaxed and secure. I probably should have rung Jack first or sent him a text, so he'd know to expect me. But I couldn't wait. I'm sure Jack won't mind an impromptu session, especially since this is an emergency.

Aye, I urgently need to cleanse that despicable man from my mind.

I arrive at Jack and Autumn's house faster than usual, though it's possible I might have exceeded the speed limit a wee bit. I park along the side of the street, right in front of Jack's house. When I ring the bell, the door swings open within a matter of seconds.

Autumn smiles at me. "Iona, what are you doing here? It's always great to see you, but Jack's with a client right now."

"I'll wait, if that's all right with you. I have a rather urgent issue."

"Urgent? Oh, no, what's the matter?" Autumn slings an arm around my shoulders, leading me into the house. Just as she swings the door shut, she tightens her hold on me. "I'm sure whatever the problem is, Jack will know what to do."

"Aye, he's a wonderful therapist."

"Let's both sit on the sofa. I just put Michael down for a nap, so we've got plenty of time for girl talk." Autumn studies my clothing. "That's a pretty dress. I've never seen you wear it before."

"I bought it online last week. Only just received the package yester-day." I hunch my shoulders. "Just wanted to…I don't know. Spice up my wardrobe, I suppose."

"Nothing wrong with that." She clasps my hand. "You don't have to tell me what's wrong, but I want you to know you can if you'd like. I'm not a licensed therapist, but I have common sense on my side."

"You're a love, Autumn." I lay a hand over my belly which has begun to grumble. "Do you have any snacks? I didn't realize how hungry I was until just now."

"I'd love a snack too. You sit here and relax while I go rustle up some-thing."

"Thank you, Autumn."

While she heads for the kitchen, I sink back on the sofa and close my eyes. Jack will sort me out for sure. It's only the negative excitement today that knocked me off kilter. The silence in the living room lulls me into a semi-sleeping state, though I can still hear all the little noises like Autumn bustling about in the kitchen. All of that background noise has a lulling effect on me.

"Here you go, Iona. This will ease your worries for sure."

My lids flutter open, and I see Autumn leaning over in front of me while holding a tray of treats and drinks. "Thane Black Label single malt? Every-one's drinking my brother's whisky these days."

"It is the yummiest." Autumn sits down beside me, setting the tray on her lap. "I brought some very decadent goodies to go along with the whisky. We still had some of the turtle cheesecake Jack's mom made for us a few days ago. There's a slice for each of us."

"Chocolate-covered strawberries? Cannae remember the last time I ate those. Salted caramels too? And cashew brittle? My blood sugar will hit the stratosphere. Good thing I'm not diabetic."

"I brought some not-sugary treats too." She points at eight little items. "Savory sandwiches made with honey, cream cheese, and Boursin cheese."

"Ooh, I'd love that. But I'll need to be carried out of the house in a trol-ley if I eat all of this."

Autumn leans closer and speaks in a softer voice. "Go on, have a little fun. I made the sandwiches myself."

"Just now? You're a kitchen whiz for sure. And I certainly wouldn't want to insult my hostess." I gently pick up a wee sandwich square and eat it slowly so I can appreciate its nuances. "Mm, this is absolutely delicious. Jack is a lucky man to have you for his wife."

"I'm lucky to have Jack too. He's a great cook, a great therapist, and so sweet."

"Aye, you two are very lucky."

I hadn't meant to sound disappointed, but I couldn't help it. I'm happy for my friends, Autumn and Jack and all the others. My brother Thane found his perfect match in Rebecca Taylor, but my brother Ramsay hasn't found the right lass yet. Most everyone I know is married, engaged, or soon will be. I've never had a serious relationship. My job and my children came before everything else.

Sometimes I wish I had made more time for dating. Then I might've found my perfect mate, if such a thing even exists. Of course, I know it has happened for so many people, just not for me.

A door opens down the hall, and I hear muffled voices.

"I should leave," I tell Autumn. "Dinnae want Jack's client to be embarrassed that I saw them."

"Don't worry about that. Jack introduced me to his new client."

"Oh. In that case, I'll have another wee sandwich and a few salted caramels."

Autumn grins. "Me too. I adore sweets. They're my greatest weakness."

"I think even the people who claim they never eat sugar sometimes grab a box of chocolates and gobble up the whole thing in one go."

Autumn sits up straighter, her focus on the hall behind us. And she grins. "Honey, your session is over. Come and kiss me, please." She swerves her attention to me. "Iona, have you met Rafe Knight?"

I jerk upright, twisting around to stare in stark horror at the evil man. "Did you and Jack trick me into this horrid reunion?"

"Of course not. Do you know him? Nobody told me it was a secret."

Jack touches Autumn's cheek and gives her a quick kiss. "It's no secret. But I didn't know Iona was here, otherwise I would have warned her and Rafe. They had a rather unfortunate encounter this morning."

And this afternoon. But I will never tell anyone what happened in my hotel room with that *bod ceann*.

Rafe seems uncomfortable. Good. He deserves to feel that way.

I shove two caramels into my mouth, chewing slowly while I glare at the horrid man.

Jack leans in and sets a hand on my shoulder. "I think a joint session might clarify your issues with each other."

I gawp at him. "You expect me to bare my soul to the man who tried to knock my door down? You're off your head, Jack."

"Would you be more comfortable with the idea if Autumn joined us?"

"No. I cannae be in the same village with him, never mind the same house."

I grab two more sandwiches, then march out the door. I do call out "goodbye" as I'm leaving. My honor demands it.

Rafe Knight has no honor.

As I jump into my car and scramble to get in my seat, I glimpse a figure emerging from the house. A tall, muscular, British figure. All right, I can't tell he's British just by looking at him. I do recognize his face, obviously, so I'm inferring that the figure is Rafe. I resist a powerful impulse that urges me to glance his way.

Instead of going home, I drive to my office. Writing the story about Raghnall's cows takes ten minutes. The rest of the newspaper is filled up with adverts and community news, which is supplied by members of the community. All I do is clean up the grammar and create the headlines. The newspaper is printed in Loch Fairbairn, thanks to generous donations from the community, mostly my friends and family.

Even after I've completed my work, I stay in my office.

Playing solitaire on my computer gets boring very quickly. There must be a story somewhere, just waiting for me to find it. It's time to scout the web for a good, juicy exposé. Not much online that I can mine. I sigh. That means it's time for on-the-ground research.

I head for the café and order a large cinnamon latte. Then I sip it while pretending to read a book, just waiting for someone to say something of interest to the community. It's what any good journalist would do. I'm not simply spying on everyone.

"Could I get you a refill, Iona?"

I glance up at the waiter, a sweet young laddie called Alan. His parents run a wilderness retreat business that brings in quite a few tourists, and I did a human-interest story on them a few months ago. "Thank you, Alan, I'd love another cup."

That's true, but I will probably be wide awake at two o'clock in the morning after consuming this much caffeine.

A man sits down at the table behind and to the left of me. My ears prick up the moment he brings out his mobile phone and dials a number. I can faintly hear the call ringing on the other end.

"I'm here, just where you wanted me," he says. "Now will you give me my first assignment?"

The gent is definitely British, and he's in his mid-thirties, I'd wager. Over the years, I've developed a good nose for sniffing out approximate ages without even looking at the person.

My mystery man laughs, though he keeps his tone sotto voce. "Don't you worry about that, mate. I'm perfectly positioned to catch all the good gossip. You wanted me to visit the café first, then fan out to the other locations. Yes, I know that. Stop treating me like I'm a child. Relax and let me do my thing. Of course. Cheers." The stranger disconnects his call. "What a knob."

Whoever the Brit is, he doesn't like the caller. To label someone a knob is not an affectionate term.

Does this Englishman have any connection to Rafe? Maybe the man on the other end of the call was my despicable Brit.

No, he's not mine. I don't want him. *Shoo, Rafe, go home.*

My reporter instincts are telling me Rafe has nothing to do with the mystery man whose conversation I overheard.

After ten more minutes of listening for anything of interest, I give up and go home.

Chapter Nine

Rafe

*I*ona checked out of the hotel. I know this because, when I emerged from my room this morning, Mrs. Agnew informed me of that fact. "Your girl went home," she'd told me, as if I care what Iona Buchanan does. She is not my girl, anyway. Mrs. Agnew also offered to give me Iona's phone number. I know where she lives—because I stalked her, slightly, just a bit, only enough to…make myself seem like a psychotic arse.

A straight jacket might be in order.

The only place where I can buy food is the café, but I don›t feel like going there again. Everyone knows me by now, of that I'm certain. What I most need to do today is find Toby. Jack gave me some surprisingly useful advice. He suggested that I should make amends with my son and explain to him all the things I'd refused to discuss ever since the divorce.

What a simple, straightforward task. Explain seven years' worth of things I've avoided thinking about. Toby deserves to know the truth, even if my confession results in never seeing my son again.

He won't believe me. How could he? I've done a bang-up job of lying.

But I did it all for Toby.

In the middle of the hotel's car park, I stop and consider my next move. If I don't eat at the café, where will I find food? There must be a supermarket or convenience shop somewhere in the blasted village. But I could wander for hours trying to find one. The map on my mobile doesn't help. Either there isn't a supermarket in this village or for some reason everyone here wants to hide the location.

That seems unlikely.

I wouldn't feel quite so unwelcome if I had someone with me. So, I ring Toby. When he answers, his response isn't what I'd hoped.

"Bugger off, Dad."

"That's no way to speak to your father."

"I heard about what you did yesterday. Harassing Iona Buchanan. Rampaging through the village. It's humiliating to be the son of a lunatic."

No, I won't deny I've behaved abominably. "Please, Toby, I need to see you in person to explain everything. Will you meet me somewhere? Anywhere?"

He says nothing for what feels like forever, though it was only a minute or two. "Yeah, I'll meet you somewhere. Eric will come with me. Wait for my text. Goodbye, Dad."

Even when he's angry with me, my son is still polite. He didn't hang up on me without saying goodbye. He did tell me to bugger off, but I know he didn't mean it.

While I wait for Toby to summon me, I sit in my car listening to a Scottish radio station. Apparently, it's local. I figured that out because I'm a bloody genius. That means I heard the DJ declare its name—"Loch Fairbairn's one and only destination for news, sports, and music over the airwaves." Naturally, they're playing bagpipe music, though I assume the station doesn't exclusively play that sort of thing.

Turns out I was right about that. As I'm listening to an annoying pop song, my mobile chimes. I have a text message. From Toby.

I snatch my mobile off the dashboard, then fumble and nearly drop it on the floor at my feet. I catch it just in time. The message contains only an address and the words "use your maps, old man." At least I'm capable of following those instructions, despite my geriatric status. I find the location on my mobile's map feature.

My brows knit together. Toby must have cocked up the directions. He can't be sending me there. Not unless he intends to start a war. But if I want to see my son, I must follow his instructions to the letter, keeping one eye on the map's directions whilst also trying not to crash into another vehicle. Based on the way the other drivers behave, I suspect Scots pay minimal attention to the laws of the road.

When I reach my destination, I see three cars on the premises. Two are parked along the road directly in front of a house. One car sits in the gravel drive, but there's enough room for another vehicle to pull up behind it. Should I park in the drive too? Toby didn't provide parking instructions. For a moment, I just sit here in the middle of the road, trying to determine the best course of action.

The front door of the house opens, and a beautiful woman with coppery brown hair trots over to my car. She smiles, tapping on the passenger window. When I don't respond, she mouths, "Roll down the window."

I dutifully roll down the passenger window. "Ah, I'm not sure if I'm in the right place."

"Of course you are, Rafe. Toby gave you directions." She thrusts her arm into the car to offer me her hand. "I'm Rebecca Taylor, soon to be Rebecca Buchanan."

I cautiously shake her hand. "Eric Taylor is your son?"

"Yep." She retracts her arm. "Come on, Toby's waiting."

"Who lives in this house?"

She grins. "Thane and I live here, of course."

Bloody hell. Why has Toby brought me here? Perhaps my son has tricked me into some sort of intervention or brainwashing.

Rebecca is still grinning at me.

I blow out a breath and give in. Shutting off the engine, I shove the keys into my pocket and go round to where Rebecca waits for me. As she leads me toward the porch, I begin to feel rather…anxious. What bollocks. I never feel nervous about meeting new people. In my profession, I encounter many strangers and often make new friends. Rebecca and Thane will not unsettle me, if that's their plan.

We've just stepped onto the porch.

Rebecca grasps the door handle and hovers there. "You should know that Toby asked us to help. That's the only reason we're kind of, sort of interfering."

"Is your mate Jack MacTaggart here to brainwash me?"

"No, Jack isn't here. We've kept the number of guests to a minimum." She bites her upper lip briefly. "I'm not supposed to tell you who's in there waiting for you."

Not sure I will like it once I find out who is inside the house.

Rebecca swings the door open, walking in ahead of me. I follow her into the cozy home, and the aromas of food tease my senses. I haven't eaten breakfast yet. Blimey, I could eat a smorgasbord of Scottish foods right now, no matter what they feed me. But they probably won't offer me anything to eat. I am the evil man everyone wants to assault.

Just as Rebecca shuts the door behind us, I finally get my first glimpse of the people gathered here. Toby and Eric, I'd expected. But Thane and Ramsay are here too.

And so is Iona.

I freeze, and I must be gawping at her. Considering the way I've treated her, she has every right to ram her knee into my groin and whack me over the head with a blunt object.

"Dinnae worry, Rafe," Iona says. "This isn't a trick, and the constables are not waiting out back to arrest you. Though I think that's where you belong, you *trealaich tolla-thon*."

Thane chuckles. "She called you an ersehole with a tiny cock."

Naturally, he thinks Iona's jab at me is amusing. I resist the urge to tell Thane that his sister knows full well I do not have a tiny cock because she's felt it inside her. Even I'm not that much of an arse.

Toby approaches me. "Are you going to cooperate?"

"With what? I have no idea why you've brought me here. The last time we spoke in person, you informed me that you're shagging Iona Buchanan. Then you proceeded to rail at me about the divorce."

When I'd mentioned Toby's claim involving Iona, Eric Taylor had winced and shoved his hands into his jeans pockets. He hunched his shoulders too. Why would he do that? Now, he averts his gaze and can't seem to look at me for even a second. It can't be that he—No, that's barmy. I don't believe Eric would shag Iona any more than I believe Toby would.

Still, it is possible that Eric might have wanted to seduce her but failed. Toby would cover for his best mate even if it meant I would blame him for Eric's actions.

I sweep my gaze over the men and women gathered in this house. "May I speak with Toby alone? I won't get angry. Jack gave me excellent advice, and I intend to follow it."

Ramsay, Thane, and Iona exchange glances.

Thane nods. "All right. We'll be out back with the animals."

"Wait," Toby says. "I want Eric to stay. It's a deal-breaker."

As much as I'd rather talk to my son alone, I understand why he wants his best mate here with him. "Agreed. Eric can stay."

"Thanks, Dad."

He seems genuinely glad that I'm going along with his rules. I would do anything for my son, but he has no idea how much I've sacrificed for him.

Thane, Rebecca, Iona, and Ramsay exit the house via the back door.

"Where should we do this?" I ask. "You and Eric might as well take the sofa. I'll find a chair to sit on. But that's only a suggestion."

Toby seems rather surprised by my offer. "Yeah, that's a good idea."

Eric and Toby sit down on the sofa while I hunt about until I find a wooden chair in the corner. Despite the lack of cushioning, the chair is comfortable enough.

Now that I'm facing my son, I don't know what to say.

For a moment, the three of us shift about on our seats and make various uncomfortable expressions.

I suppose it's up to me to get things going. I clear my throat, which has grown tight. "Toby, I know I haven't been the best father—"

"Why would you say that?"

"Because it's true. You think I'm an arse. I've certainly behaved like one." I scratch my hand, but only because every inch of my skin seems to have spontaneously developed poison ivy. "I'm sorry for everything I've done, today and in the past. But I want to make amends."

"You still don't get it."

I dive my hands into my hair, bowing my head. "Our broken family is all my fault, though not for the reasons you must think. Why else would you take up with an older woman?"

Toby winces, just like Eric had done a moment ago. "That's what I need to tell you. I only said those things about Iona to hurt you. It was a bloody stupid, childish thing to do. The truth is that I've never slept with or even kissed Iona Buchanan."

"Then why—"

"Eric is the one who's been trying to win over Iona Buchanan."

I stare blankly at my son. "What? Why would your best mate…"

"Because I didn't want my mom to find out," Eric tells me. "She wouldn't understand how I feel about Iona. She's my dream girl."

Who I shagged yesterday. Even after Toby told me he was shagging her.

I raise my head. "That explains a few things. But I'm more concerned with what you told me yesterday, Toby. You said I broke up our family without a second thought. That's partly true. But you have not become a selfish prick like me, and you never will."

"But why did you leave Mum?"

Should I divulge the truth to him at last? Having kept a secret for so many years, it's difficult to open up about what really happened. "Please, Toby, I'd rather share those details with you alone."

"Eric is my best mate. He's practically my brother. If you can't tell Eric, then you won't tell me either."

"This has nothing to do with him. I like Eric, but he isn't family. You and I should discuss this without your best mate."

Eric begins to stand up, but Toby gestures for him to remain seated. "Either he stays, or the conversation is over."

"Haven't I always been there for you, Toby? Whenever you needed me. I drove you to your first day at university and surprised you with a car of your own."

Toby frowns. "You think all it takes is throwing money at me and everything will be right as rain? I'm not a child. If you're claiming that Mum lied about what happened, then you should tell me your side."

"If that's what it takes, I'll tell you. Right now."

Chapter Ten

Iona

Half an hour after the rest of us left the house, Rafe and the boys walk out the front door. Rebecca and I waited on the front porch, though not to spy. We couldn't hear a blessed thing anyone inside the house said. Thane and Ramsay had decided to stay in the backyard with the animals. Rafe seems quite calm, almost sober. Toby and Eric are relaxed but not quite happy. I reckon the conversation involved some painful revelations, though I have no idea what the men said to each other. I'm guessing.

Eric and his best friend head for Toby's car.

Rafe simply watches while they drive away. Once the car travels out of sight, he shoves his hands into his trouser pockets and bows his head. He still hasn't noticed me or Rebecca, since we're in the shade at the other end of the porch. Watching Rafe, I suffer an oddly powerful impulse to hug him.

Bod an Donais. What is wrong with me?

Rafe steps off the porch and starts toward his car.

"Not yet, Rafe," Rebecca calls out. "We aren't done with you yet."

His shoulders droop, but he doesn't look at us. "I suppose it was too much to hope that my trials were over."

Rebecca and I get up off the porch swing and trot down the steps, but she turns right toward the gate to the backyard. "Take your time, Iona. We'll wait for you two."

"Take my time with what?"

She winks, as if that explains everything.

I walk up alongside Rafe. "Are you all right?"

"Do you care if I'm not? Of course you don't."

"Stop assuming you know what I feel or what I want."

He grunts. "I'm despicable and vile and odious. That's what you believe and feel about me."

"I take it your chat with Toby didn't heal your relationship with him."

He shrugs. "I told him everything he wanted to know. Then he announced that he needs more time to think."

I desperately want to ask him what he and Toby needed to discuss, but it's none of my concern. Maybe Rafe and I had a poke once, but that doesn't give me the right to question him about his life. If he wants to tell me, I'll listen. Aye, that does conflict with my journalistic nosiness. But I can find a way to separate the two things if I feel like it.

"Why don't we go into the backyard?" I ask. "Animals can have a powerful calming and soothing effect on humans."

He raises his brows. "What sort of animals?"

"Come with me, and you'll find out."

Rafe gazes at me for a moment, his expression impossible to interpret. Then he exhales a full breath and nods. "Let's go."

For about one-tenth of a second, I debate whether to hold his hand. Then I make the decision. If he doesn't like it, sod it.

I slip my hand into his palm.

Rafe stares at me with stark panic in his eyes, but it only lasts for a few seconds. Then he clasps my hand. We stroll across the lawn without speaking, and I keep hold of his hand even while I unhook the latch on the backyard gate. Rafe closes the gate after us and even remembers to hook the latch.

We don't get far before Rafe meets his first obstacle.

He stops dead, but he doesn't seem all that surprised. Maybe he has seen this sort of critter before. When the animal approaches him, he…smiles and pats the creature's head.

"Who is this?" he asks me.

"His name is Odin, and he's a llama. Thane treats Odin like a pet, but the beautiful laddie has a job too. Odin protects the homestead."

Rafe scratches under Odin's chin, and the llama licks his face. "I've heard that llamas are quite good as protectors. Does Thane harvest wool from Odin?"

Before I can answer that question, Thane saunters up to us. "Aye, once in a while I'll shear him. I might get a sweater and a scarf out of the wool."

"My parents have had sheep for my entire life. They create all sorts of clothing and household items from the wool, not to mention selling the milk."

"Do they harvest the milk themselves too?"

Rafe smiles as Odin kisses his cheek. "Yes, milk production is a significant portion of their operations. But the White Knight Family Farm is strictly small scale, and we never sell our sheep for meat."

I think I must be gaping at Rafe. I cannae picture him shearing sheep or milking them—or caring about the welfare of sheep. A strange tingle sweeps through me, awakening my nether regions. This is not the right time to get aroused. I vowed I would never have a poke with Rafe again, yet learning more about him is changing my perspective.

Maybe I could shag him again. Just once more.

No, no, no, you bampot. Keep your hands off Rafe.

I should heed that self-provided advice. But Rafe just grinned and laughed, and now I'm getting warm and slick between my thighs.

Rebecca walks over to us and stops beside me. "You okay, sweetie?"

"Um, aye." That was entirely convincing. If Rebecca were a very stupid person.

She gives me a knowing smile.

I slant toward her to whisper, "Dinnae look at me that way. What you're hoping for won't happen."

"Uh-huh, whatever you say." That knowing smile now comes with a knowing tone of voice. "Getting it on with a man who drives you crazy might not be a bad way to pass the time. And if it turns into something more…"

"There won't be anything more. And I will never 'get it on' with him again."

Only after I spoke those words a touch too loudly do I realize Rafe and Thane are staring at me. They must have heard what I said. Ugh, what am I meant to do now? Spout the dumbest possible excuse, naturally. "As I said Rebecca, driving crazily might be one way to pass the time, but if you turn into something, it could be dangerous."

Four mature adults give me a variety of confused looks.

Ramsay puckers half of his mouth and tilts his head slightly to the side. "Iona, are you having an early-onset senior moment?"

"What? No, you *cacan*. Why would you say such a thing?"

Before Ramsay can speak, Thane intercedes. "Rafe, would you like to meet the chickens?"

"Yes, I would."

I just manage to stifle a sigh and stop myself from seeming unusually relieved. The five of us amble across the backyard to the chicken coop. Thane loves to tell newcomers about his animals, and he makes no exception for Rafe. The man who gave me an epic poke listens intently while my brother discusses the ins and outs of having chickens. And of course, he introduces Rafe to his brood.

"This is Wallace," my brother tells him. "He's named after the famous hero of Scotland. The hens are Agatha, Prudence, Ginger, and Henrietta."

"Lovely names," Rafe says.

Rebecca only half stifles her laughter. "Thane named the hens after women he screwed when he was in the MOD."

My brother smiles tolerantly at his fiancée. "I've told you many times, *gràidh*, that I never shagged any of them."

She kisses his cheek. "I'm just teasing you. But you did actually have sex with that horrible Ava Marston-Baines back when she was your handler."

"In the line of duty."

"Uh-huh." Rebecca makes an exaggerated wink. "You didn't enjoy it at all, right?"

He smirks. "Well, I never said that…"

I roll my eyes. "Are you two done flirting? I have a job, you know, and I can't neglect it forever."

Thane lifts his brows. "An article about sheep herding? Or are you finally writing that story about Raghnall MacCrum's cows that you've been threatening to inflict on the village for months now?"

I know Thane isn't being rude. My whole family, and many of my friends, have been teasing me about my lack of meaningful news stories because they know I've fallen into a slump. I did hear something intriguing at the café yesterday, but the one-sided conversation didn't give me much information. If only that British gent would stop in at the café again…

"Our baby sister is getting an idea," Ramsay says with a smirk. "Maybe she's uncovering the history of that vile, despicable, odious Rafe Knight."

Why do my brothers keep smirking at me? It's bloody annoying. And what in heaven's name does Rafe have to do with our conversation? Older brothers are such a nuisance.

Thane smiles with a mischievous gleam in his eyes. "Aye, she must be exposing Rafe."

"It's called an exposé, but that's not what I'm doing with Rafe."

Ramsay adopts the same mischievous expression as Thane. "Are you sure about that, Iona?"

"Yes. I'm positive." But I have no clue what I've just declared that I haven't done. My brothers are confusing me on purpose. "Would you two go away? I've had enough of your childish banter."

Thane smirks again. "This is my house, Iona. Rebecca and I can't go away."

"Leave poor Iona alone," Rebecca says with a look of motherly disappointment. "She's right. You guys are being childish."

Now it's my turn to smirk. "Thank you, Rebecca."

"But your brothers aren't completely wrong. You and Rafe need some alone time to figure things out."

"There's nothing to figure out."

"Is that why you were holding hands a few minutes ago?"

Bod an Donais. I forgot about that. Why couldn't Rebecca forget about it too?

Now Rafe is smirking. That expression is becoming an epidemic.

"Thane and I are driving out to the distillery," Rebecca says. "And Ramsay will be going home in his car, so that means Iona will need a ride from someone."

"I can ride with Ramsay."

"No, ye can't," my brother declares. "I'm driving Finlay to his first day at university, and that's all the way in Edinburgh."

"But Leith could give me a ride."

My brother shakes his head. "Sorry, *gràidh.* Leith is on Skye right now, refurbishing an old house for a young couple who just got married."

Rafe develops the most adorable look of confusion. "Your son is in the sky?"

"No," Ramsay says with a chuckle. "Don't you know about the Isle of Skye? It's one of the northwest islands. That means it's part of Scotland."

"Oh, yes, of course. I knew that. It's only that you didn't call it the Isle of Skye, and that's what confused me."

Rafe seems to be desperately trying not to sound like a British person who has never been to Scotland before or even watched a documentary about it. I don't think he's faking his confusion. No, I'm now convinced that he honestly doesn't know about the northwest islands. How can that be? Even Americans who visit this country for the first time have heard of Skye. But I don't want to embarrass the man, so I take pity on him.

I swerve my attention to Rafe. "I've changed my mind. It would be lovely if you could drive me home."

His deer-in-the-headlights expression is somehow endearing. He shakes it off quickly, though. "I would be happy to do that."

The five of us leave the backyard, making sure to latch the gate behind us. Odin has occasionally escaped from his wee pasture, though only when one of us forgot to secure the gate. The llama doesn't like to stray far, anyway. He has developed an interest in Raghnall's cows, though.

Rafe and I climb into his car and wave at my brothers and Rebecca as we drive away. I twist around in my seat to watch them. All right, yes, I'm verifying that their stories are true. Ramsay does indeed get in his car and leave. Thane and Rebecca climb into their pickup truck and also drive away.

Once their vehicles have gone out of my sight, I face forward and settle in for the brief ride to my home.

Rafe chuckles. "You assumed they were lying about needing to be somewhere, weren't you?"

"The fact that they all drove away doesn't prove their stories."

"Ever the journalist, eh? You need facts and proof of everything."

"What's wrong with that?"

He shrugs one shoulder. "Nothing. It's another tidbit of information about you, though."

"You have many tidbits about me, but I still know very little about you."

Rafe navigates around a corner, heading in the general direction of my home. "What would you like to know?"

"Were you really struck by lightning?"

"Yes."

"*A Dhia.* Cannae imagine what that did to you."

He turns down another street, the one that leads to my cottage. "What does '*a Dhia*' mean?"

"It's Gaelic for 'Oh God.' Would you tell me about your lightning strike? I've heard that sort of thing can create long-term issues."

"Let's wait until we're in your house. I don't want to accidentally drive us into a telephone pole."

Talking about it will upset him that much? Double *a Dhia*.

Chapter Eleven

Rafe

Why on earth did I agree to relate one of the worst moments in my life to Iona? I barely know her. Yet I feel a strong compulsion to share those dark times with her. Most people who aren't scientists find it hard to believe that I was actually struck by lightning. After all, the average person has never met someone like me—a survivor of a powerful discharge. Everyone knows the old idioms "lightning never strikes twice" and "fast as lightning." For most of the human race, those are just things people say.

I wasn't fast enough, but at least I wasn't struck twice.

Fortunately, Iona doesn't question me any further until we've reached her home. Once we're inside, she insists on claiming my hand so she can shepherd me to the sofa. The pigheaded woman orders me to sit down. I try to speak, to tell her I'd rather take the adjacent armchair, but she sets her hands on her hips and gives me a mulish look.

"On the sofa, Rafe. Now."

I make an irritable noise, then obey her command. "Your turn, pet."

"What did you just call me?"

Pet. That's what I said—in reference to her. Bloody hell, I've gone soft. "Ah, never mind that. Just set your lovely little arse down on the sofa, please."

She feigns shock as if she's a cartoon character. "Rafe Knight is being polite? You must have been struck by lightning again this morning, and that's why you're behaving like a normal person."

"I am not normal. And if you'll get your blooming arse on the sofa, I'll explain why."

She drops onto the cushion beside me and grins. "I've never heard anyone say 'blooming' before in that context. It's adorable."

"I cursed at you, and you think it's cute. What a bizarre creature you are." I exhale a gusty sigh and let my head fall onto the sofa's back. "Seven years ago, I was out in the field, watching a mesocyclone while measuring the intensity and lift, hoping for a good batch of lightning within the storm."

"Why would you hope for lightning? And what 'field' are you talking about? Your backyard?"

"No, pet, not that sort. 'The field' means I was out storm chasing in Tornado Alley, which is in the American Midwest."

Iona seems intrigued, but I can't tell if that's morbid curiosity or a genuine interest in my story. She remains quiet, so I assume she wants me to continue explaining.

"I am a lightning researcher. That's why I was outside during dangerous weather, while most people took cover indoors. I'd been traveling with a group of storm chasers."

No, I don't think I'll mention that my wife was the lead researcher on that expedition. Not yet, at any rate. My relationship with my ex is a thorny mess of emotions that I'd rather forget about for now.

I suddenly realize I'm wringing my hands, and I force myself to stop doing that. "We had six vehicles in our convoy, and I was in the lead car. Once we found a good mesocyclone, we pulled over alongside the road and got out our equipment. When it became clear that the storm was shifting track, heading our way faster than expected, our group leader told everyone to retreat into their vehicles for safety's sake."

The woman sitting beside me wriggles about until she's facing me. She doesn't comment on anything I've said. Iona simply sits there watching my face while I go on with the story. Though I can see her only peripherally, I swear I can feel her curiosity burning into me.

I rub my hands on my thighs because my palms have grown clammy. "Being a ruddy stupid arse and a cocky arse as well, I stepped out of the vehicle and shut the door. To get a clearer view of the storm, that was all. I honestly believed I could get the photos and readings we needed before the mesocyclone got close enough to become dangerous."

When I glance at Iona, moving only my eyes, she seems deeply fascinated by my tale. My ex-wife and my son know what happened to me, but I've never told anyone else about it. Well, except for my employees.

"I had miscalculated the storm," I tell her. "What I hadn't accounted for in all my calculations and simulations was the power of positive streamers."

"What are streamers?" Iona asks, then she winces. "I'm sorry. I swore to myself I wouldn't interrupt your story."

"No worries. You can ask me anything you like, even interrupt if you have a question."

Her sealed lips form a sweet little smile. Then she kisses my cheek. "Go on with the story, Rafe, please."

"I'll get to streamers in a moment." I wriggle uncomfortably, and it feels as if invisible fire ants have climbed inside my trousers. "It all began with stepped leaders. Those are the best-known type of lightning because they are quite striking in the night sky or even in the daytime. I didn't hear the crack of thunder, though everyone told me afterward that it was deafening, like a bomb exploding. The camera I'd been holding somehow survived the blast, and that's how I know what happened next."

Iona, the lovely woman, puts her arms around my neck loosely. She continues to gaze at me steadily.

And I grow more anxious as the denouement of my tale approaches. "I was focused on the storm cloud and the stepped leaders. So I didn't notice when upward streamers climbed into the sky, not until they met the negatively charged particles in the cloud. I became a part of the upward streamers. When the energy was discharged, it went right through me."

"*A Dhia*, Rafe. It's a miracle you survived."

"But I died that day."

She draws her head back, eying me warily. "What do you mean?"

"My heart stopped beating for two minutes and forty-eight seconds. Then it just…started up again."

"Someone must have given you CPR."

I shake my head. "No one knew I'd suffered a cardiac arrest until after the storm passed by our team. They were safely ensconced in their vehicles, taking measurements, too busy to realize I was flat on my back on the ground."

"That's horrible."

"It wasn't their fault. Storm chasing is a high-adrenaline activity, and some chasers get caught up in the excitement and are oblivious of everything else until the main event is over." I shake my head again. "And I was that sort."

"How you survived with no one around to provide CPR is a miracle for sure."

"Perhaps it was, but I've never been able to see it that way. My life essentially fell apart in the years after the lightning strike."

Iona slides onto my lap, straddling my hips. "Have you had any long-term effects from the lightning?"

"Oh, yes, plenty. Most aren't visible, but one is." I roll my sleeve up, almost to my shoulder. "This is the scar left behind by the bolt."

She splays her hand over my shoulder, then traces the red lines that branch out all the way to my elbow. "This looks like...a lightning bolt."

"Yes. That pattern is called a lightning flower. People like me who have fairer skin are more likely to have permanent, faint scarring." I dig out my mobile and flick through the photos I've accumulated over the years until I find the one I want. Then I show it to her. "I've kept this image on every mobile phone I've owned since the lightning strike. This was me a few hours post-strike."

She stares at the image, her eyes widening. Naturally, she would be shocked. Any human with feelings would look that way after seeing my wounds.

Then Iona kisses my scars and smiles. "You are even tougher and stronger than I realized."

I lose focus briefly because she has begun stroking my scalp with her soft fingers. I can't blame her for all my distraction, though. "The worst side effect has been my new penchant for flying off the handle. I also sometimes lose focus for a few minutes and can't remember what I'd been doing. Headaches are also a chronic issue."

"At least you've recovered enough to lead a normal life."

I let out a bark of harsh laughter. "Normal life? It's been one tribulation after another."

"All because of the lightning strike?"

"No. All because of me, because I couldn't manage the symptoms as well as I wanted, despite mental and physical therapy." I stare straight into her eyes. "That's why I've been so horrid to you."

She clasps my face with both hands. "No, Rafe, you are not horrid. Aye, ye can be a *bod ceann*. But now I'm finally beginning to understand you."

But I haven't told her the worst parts of my past. I need to know her better before I dump all that rubbish on her lap.

"I must be a devil, Iona. My son hates me, my ex-wife hates me, all your mates and relatives hate me."

She pecks a sweet little kiss on my mouth. "Wait until you've met all of them before you declare they despise you."

"Yesterday, *you* despised me."

"Today, I understand why you acted like a despicable *bod ceann*."

I pull her closer. "What is a *bod ceann*?"

"A dickhead."

"Hmm, I can't dispute that appellation. Even my own family doesn't want me around anymore."

Iona gazes deeply into my eyes. She opens her mouth but stops short of speaking.

"What is it, pet?" I ask.

"You have an ex-wife."

"Is that a surprise? I do have a son, after all."

"Toby is a sweet laddie." She pauses briefly, once again studying me intently. "Do you get along with your ex-wife? Does Toby? Oh, never mind. I shouldn't have asked."

"You have every right to interrogate me. But if you don't mind, I'd rather not discuss Angela yet. Not until I feel certain I can trust you." I squeeze my eyes shut and wince. "Sorry. I know how that sounds, but I don't mean it that way."

Iona places delicate kisses on my closed eyelids. "Look at me, Rafe, please."

With great effort, I obey her command.

Her soft smile begins to thaw the coldness at my core that seems to always remain lodged inside me. "Whatever it is, I can wait until you feel comfortable telling me. Besides, we should get to know each other better before we share our deepest secrets."

"Thank you."

Her delicate laughter tickles my senses. "Dinnae need to thank me."

"Oh, but I do. After the way I shagged you yesterday, I owe you something a bit more sensual and leisurely. Would you like that?" I trace my tongue over her lips, making her suck in a quick breath. "May I take that as a yes?"

"Mm, aye, please do that."

I glance at the picture window, where I can see cows grazing in the distance. "Your house is rather close to your neighbor. I've already scandalized you with wild, uninhibited sex in the hotel. Wouldn't want anyone next door to hear us. Though it seems the farmer is your nearest neighbor, and everyone else is a good distance away. They won't hear, but he might."

"Raghnall? No, he wouldn't pay any mind even if a meteor crashed down in his backyard."

"Good." I flip her onto her back on the cushions beside me. "Then we can fuck right here, all afternoon, and you can scream as much as you like."

"You ripped my clothes off last time. Today, I want to give you a full striptease."

"Maybe I'll do the same for you."

She grins, and I love that expression. Her eyes glitter with humor and lust. "Should I go first?"

"Yes, love, please do."

Iona pushes up onto her elbows and stretches one leg out to tease my cock with her toes. My trousers feel suddenly tighter. The siren walks those toes up my chest to my throat. "You stay right where you are. Dinnae move, dinnae speak, dinnae open your eyes until I say so."

"You haven't told me to close my eyes."

"Oh. In that case…" She walks her toes up my chin. "Close your eyes, Rafe."

I obey her command. Iona Buchanan is the only woman who has ever convinced me to do whatever she wants. My cock is hardening more every second. I need to bury myself inside her body as soon as possible.

A mobile rings. Mine? Hers? I'm too aroused to comprehend the difference in ring tones.

Iona flings an arm out to the coffee table and snatches up her mobile. "*Mhac na galla.* It's Eric."

"Who?"

"Eric Taylor. My unwanted suitor. Didn't you set him straight?"

I feel all my muscles tightening. My fists are clenched, though I had no conscious desire to do that. "Eric is not my son. It isn't my place to tell him anything. Talk to your brother and his woman. Eric is Rebecca's son."

"Aye, I know that." Her mobile is still ringing, and she scowls at the screen. "You're a man. Eric is a man. If you want to shag me again, better set that laddie straight."

"Why is it my responsibility to chastise an adult man who isn't even related to me?"

Iona leaps off the sofa. "You won't get in my knickers today. Get out of my house."

The anger has bubbled up again, and I can't think clearly. I have just one option to prevent another disaster with Iona.

I walk out the door.

Chapter Twelve

Eric

Toby seems happier today, the day after our intense conversation with his father. Rafe isn't a bad guy, but his temper makes me worry about Iona. I mean, the guy basically admitted that he can't control his wild mood swings. Toby never mentioned those to me. The first I heard about it was during the weird therapy session Jack MacTaggart arranged for my best friend and his father. I went along for moral support.

Why would Iona hang around with Rafe? She deserves a hell of a lot better than a British guy with mental problems.

Iona can't like Rafe. She can't want to have a relationship with him.

I decided to hike into town alone since Toby wanted to sleep. I'm starving. Granola bars won't sustain me for long. So, I'm heading out to get supplies, and I plan on bringing food back for my best friend. He'll feel better after a good rest and a good meal.

I stuff my cell phone in my jacket and my wallet in my hip pocket. Ready to go. My hike to the village doesn't take that long. Our campsite is only about a quarter mile away. That means I arrive looking like a tourist instead of a creature in a horror movie.

My food options are minimal—the café or the grocery store. I'm not in the mood for a restaurant, but option two gives me a great idea. So, I schlep down the sidewalks and side streets until I find the grocery store, which I›ve learned is known as "getting the messages" here in Scotland. Yeah, I searched the web for that info. Not sure what I expected, but the Scottish grocery store looks pretty much like the ones in America and England.

There's also a section for locally grown and traditionally Scottish foods.

Should I buy haggis? Nah, I don't need to go totally native just because I'm here for six weeks. Besides, my plan for today is to cook a nice meal for Iona and surprise her with it. I don't want to make anything too Scottish since she must eat that kind of stuff all the time.

No, I plan on crafting a romantic dinner.

But, uh…what would a woman think is romantic food? Back to the internet for more ideas.

An older couple notices me hunting around at the meat counter and approaches me. The man says, "Laddie, what are ye looking for? Maybe we can help."

"Wow, that's really kind of you. I'd love some advice."

The woman clucks her tongue at the man. "How rude of you. We haven't even introduced ourselves. I'm Senga McPhee and this is my husband Ivor."

I shake both their hands. "I'm Eric Taylor. It's nice to meet you, Mr. McPhee, Mrs. McPhee."

"Call me Senga."

"Aye," her husband says. "Dinnae be formal. I'm Ivor."

"Okay. Thanks."

"Let's help you find a romantic meal for your girl." Ivor winks. "Senga knows all about my dinners. They always make her randy."

"Oh, you scamp," Senga says while blushing.

The older couple does give me great advice about how to impress Iona with a fancy dinner, though I didn't tell them who my girl is. Not sure Iona would want everyone to know I made her a romantic meal. I never used to have so much trouble with women. But the moment I first saw Iona, I knew she was the one for me.

Am I crazy? Maybe.

But I want to make Iona feel better after the way Rafe Knight harassed her, and I don't think that's insane.

After leaving the grocery store, I waste a few bucks on a taxi ride to Iona's house. I give the driver a good tip, and he thanks me with a grin. Iona's car is in her driveway, so at least I know she's here.

I knock on her door and wait.

The door swings open—and Iona stares at me like she isn't sure who I am. "Eric? What are you doing here?"

"I came to see you." I raise my bag of groceries. "And to feed you."

"Eric, honestly, I am not your girlfriend. I ate earlier, anyway."

"But how much did you eat? You must be stressed out after the debacle Toby's dad caused."

Iona sighs and shakes her head. "I'm a journalist, Eric. I deal with all sorts of obnoxious people. I broke the story about a local teacher who was embezzling school funds, and that *bod ceann* threatened me with physical harm. If that didn't upset me, nothing can."

"At least let me show you the groceries I bought."

She sighs. "If you insist."

Okay, I'm a little disappointed that she isn't excited about the meal I want to create for her, but I can deal with that. I did surprise her, after all. Aren't women supposed to like romantic surprises? I've always had pretty decent luck with girls. But Iona Buchanan isn't a girl. She's a full-fledged woman who has grown children and is a tough journalist. Still, I'm sure she'll appreciate my gift once everything is cooked.

Iona finally swings the door open all the way to let me in.

But she still seems less than enthusiastic about dinner.

I brush aside my mild disappointment and let Iona lead me over to the open kitchen, where she stops us on this side of the island-slash-bar. "Here you are. Do what you like, and I'll wait in my office. I have work to do."

"Sure, yeah, that's fine. I'll shout when everything's ready."

Iona gives me a tight smile, then disappears down the hall.

Maybe she just can't envision me, an American man, crafting a meal that a Scottish woman might enjoy. But Ivor and Senga gave me great tips and even helped me choose the best cuts of meat, not to mention suggestions about how to make a meal truly romantic by choosing appropriate spices and seasonings. I took notes on my phone so I wouldn't forget everything they said.

Now, I move behind the bar-slash-island and get to work.

Turns out, I love cooking—and I rock the meal prep. The instructions my cooking gurus gave me say it'll take two hours to get everything ready. But it actually takes two hours and forty-five minutes. Yeah, I timed it. Once I've got the table set and the mood music playing, it's time to escort the lady to her table.

I jog down the hall and poke my head into Iona's office. "Dinner is served."

She jumps up and lays a hand over her belly. "Och, it's about time. I'm fair starved. How long does it take to make sandwiches?"

"What gave you the idea I was making plain old sandwiches?" She told me earlier she wasn't hungry, but now she's famished. Women are so confusing.

Iona walks up to me and shrugs. "You're a young man. Laddies your age dinnae want to learn how to cook."

"Well, I'm not your average adult male in his twenties." Okay, maybe I'm kind of peeved that she called me a young man. That makes me sound like I'm a kid with a crush on his hot math teacher. "Come on, before the food gets cold."

I offer her my arm.

She compresses her lips, then sighs and gives in.

As we exit the hallway, she gets her first look at what I've done for her. She'll be impressed, for sure. I went to a heck of a lot of trouble to whip up this meal, which could probably qualify as gourmet.

I pull out a chair for her, and she sits down, politely smiling at me.

Before I can even get started explaining the dishes, Iona stabs her fork into one of the two chicken breasts and starts hacking away at it with her knife.

"That's Caprese stuffed chicken," I announce. "Seasoned and perfectly seared, stuffed with sun-dried tomatoes, mozzarella, and fresh spinach."

Iona mumbles something, but the food jammed into her mouth muffles whatever she said.

"Don't forget your salad," I say. "It's got balsamic honey roasted figs and halloumi. That's a kind of cheese."

Iona mumbles again while stuffing her face.

"For dessert, I made chocolate strawberry shortcake."

The woman I'm trying to impress grunts and continues gobbling up her food like she hasn't eaten in several days.

I give up and sit down at the table opposite her. All I do is pick at the food, too bummed out to really enjoy it. Iona treats her dessert with slightly more appreciation.

Once she's done, she sighs and smiles contentedly. "That was fantastic, Eric. You're a good friend to make a meal like this for me."

And there she goes again with the "friend" bullshit.

Iona rises and yawns. "I'll wash the dishes in the morning. Good night, Eric."

"But—"

She marches over to the door and yanks it open. "I said good night, Eric. I'm jeeked after eating so much."

Iona ate everything on her plate. What else can I do? I leave and trudge back to the tent Toby and I have been sharing.

Women are crazy.

Chapter Thirteen

Iona

Three days and eleven hours have elapsed since my last argument with Rafe, when I'd told him to get out of my house. I might have been hoping, just a wee bit, that he would come running back to beg my forgiveness. That hasn't happened. Rafe is far too stubborn to grovel. Aye, he isn't the only pigheaded idiot in this equation. I've been just as stubborn and combative, though I don't have a good excuse for my behavior. Rafe does.

For the entirety of the past two and half days, I've been trying to imagine what being struck by lightning might feel like and how it might affect a person's mental state in the long term. Rafe told me the details of how he'd been struck, but not how it made him feel, emotionally. His hair-trigger temper is an artifact of that, according to Rafe.

I searched the web to confirm that claim. It's not that I don't trust Rafe, though honestly, I still can't decide if I do or not. I performed that search mostly to get a better understanding of what he went through. But I still can't comprehend it.

Will Rafe ever call me? Or is he waiting for me to make the first move?

The more important question is whether either of us can cede a wee bit of ground in this battle and have a mature discussion.

I need time to think about it. So, I go for a walk down the streets of Loch Fairbairn to clear my head. Along the way, I meet friends here and there, offering them my usual greeting. "Hello, how are you," and the like. They can probably tell that I'm in no mood for a chat, though I'm not being rude.

Soon, I've fallen into my favorite type of self-hypnosis. I'm contemplating stories I might write and people I might want to interview. After seven years of being a journalist, I've found I can walk through the village without accidentally stepping out into traffic or knocking down pedestrians, even while I'm lost in my own thoughts.

Eleven minutes into my walk, according to my watch, I spot someone I recognize. I don't know his name, but I've seen him before—on that day when I'd gone to the café alone. Aye, it's the mysterious British man who had been talking to someone on his mobile while seated no more than a few feet away. I couldn›t resist listening in on the gent's intriguing dialogue, wishing I could hear the other end of the call.

What sort of journalist would I be if I hadn't memorized the dialogue and later written it down? *I'm here, just where you wanted me*, the man had said. *Now will you give me my first assignment?*

To find out what that laddie's assignment is, I'll need to do a fair amount of snooping. I have him in my sight right now. It's time to test my detective skills. I sit down on a bench and pretend I'm reading a book on my mobile phone. As the mystery man wanders past me, I glance at him only via my peripheral vision. Maybe I should contact Magnus MacTaggart, the private investigator who prefers to be called a bounty hunter for reasons I don't understand. It hardly matters.

I'll ask Magnus later. Maybe.

Once my quarry has moved a decent distance away, I casually rise from my bench and slip my mobile into my purse. I keep my walking pace casual too, as if I'm simply enjoying a pleasant stroll.

The Brit hails a taxi.

I purposely drop my purse and kneel to pick it up. That should seem like nothing special. But it does obscure my face. A sideways glance tells me the Brit didn't notice. He's too busy telling the driver the address where he wants to be dropped off.

403 Baxter Caolraid.

That's my home. The British *cacan* wants to see me. Why? I don't know the man, but I will find out soon enough what the reason is for his visit. Fortunately, I know every hidden alley that I can cut through to reach my cottage before the taxi gets there. That means I need to run like a deer being chased by a predator. No one spots me since I'm keeping to the back areas. But when I leap over the fence into Raghnall MacCrum's cow pasture, I do cause a wee bit of a ruckus. The cows run about and moo loudly, though only for a moment or two.

They've already quietened down by the time I burst into my backyard.

I slam the sliding door of my porch shut and race to the front door, peering through the peephole.

No one is there. Yet.

Unbelievable. I outran a taxi. Maybe I shouldn't congratulate myself just yet, since the speed limit in the village is thirty miles per hour. Our local taxi driver, Erskine Melville, never exceeds the limit. It's his badge of honor. The laddie believes in adhering to the law for more than honor, but also for safety's sake.

Today, I'm grateful for that.

While I wait for the mystery man to arrive, I sit down on the sofa with my laptop computer and begin to brainstorm ideas. The man who's coming to see me might become a story, who knows. I've also heard that the school might be getting a new teacher, so I'll need to cover that if and when it happens. It isn't scintillating, but it will do for now.

Thoughts of the mystery man keep distracting me. What does he want with me? I have never interrogated anyone before, but I'm itching to do that now. Maybe I should ring Thane or Ramsay and ask one of them to come to my house. Being alone with a stranger who is clearly operating at someone else's behest isn't the safest thing to do without backup.

I do have a *caman*—a stick used in shinty. Ramsay gave it to me as a souvenir after I wrote about a particularly wild match between the MacTaggarts and the Buchanans. Aye, that *caman* could serve as a weapon.

The soft rumble of a car engine seizes my attention.

I leap off the sofa, almost dumping my laptop on the floor in the process. Tearing the door open seems unwise. Instead, I peer through the peephole that my brothers had insisted I should have installed for safety's sake. But I don't see the stranger out there, only Erskine in his taxi with his head down, probably making a note of how much the fare was. Then he drives away.

What in the world? Where is the mystery man? Skulking around behind my house?

I suddenly wish I'd rung my brothers after all.

Rushing to the patio doors, I search the vicinity for any sign of the potential intruder. Still nothing. I wrap my arms around myself as I continue to survey the area. I have no yard fence. Never needed one.

Maybe I should go out there to get a better view.

A powerful fist bangs on my front door.

A Dhia. Is that the mystery man? If it is, he seems quite agitated. I grab the *caman* and peer through the peephole.

My whole body relaxes as I let out a literal sigh of relief. Then I pull the door open. "Rafe? I wasn't expecting to see you outside my door. Thank goodness it's you."

One side of his mouth kinks upward. "Thank goodness? Can't recall you ever saying that when you see me. Now, if you'd said 'Rafe, you despicable, odious arsehole, how dare you knock on my door,' then I would understand."

"Please just come inside."

"Is this some sort of trick?"

"No, of course not." I seize his arm and drag him into the house, then I shut the door. "Did you see anyone along the street just now?"

His playful smile mutates into a furrowed brow. "Should I have done?"

I shrug.

Rafe notices the *caman*, and he stiffens. "What's happened? I can't imagine you carrying a stick like that around inside your home just for the fun of it."

I lean the *caman* against the wall and hug myself. "I think someone is after me."

"What does that mean? After you?"

"Um...I shouldn't bother you with this problem, not after the way I shouted at you."

His lips curl into a gentle, playful smile. He hooks his thumb under my chin. "I did my fair share of shouting too. We can talk about that later. Right now, I want to know what has you so frightened. If my blustering on the day we met didn't unsettle you, I assumed nothing could."

"Everyone thinks I'm a tough-as-nails journalist. But I've never stumbled onto a seriously dangerous, exciting story before." I hunch my shoulders. "Raghnall MacCrum's cows are the highlight of my career so far. I've always wanted to sink my teeth into a really juicy story. Now that I seem to have stumbled onto one, I'm not sure I can handle it."

"This relates to your need for a strange-looking stick."

"A *caman*, aye. It's used in shinty." I release a long sigh. "This will be a rather long, complicated story. Maybe we should sit down."

Rafe sweeps me up into his arms, marches around the corner of the sofa, and carefully deposits us both on the cushions—with me on his lap. He brushes hairs away from my face. "I want every detail. Leave nothing out."

I relate everything that's happened since the first time I heard that British man talking to someone on his mobile in the café. Sitting here on Rafe's lap, I feel at ease and...safe. How I can feel that way considering his past behavior, I dinnae know. It must be because I understand him better now. His lightning strike left him with many scars, both visible and emotional.

Once I've finished talking, Rafe simply stares at me with curiosity.

That makes me feel uncomfortable. "Well, I've told you the whole story. Aren't you going to say anything?"

"Calm down, pet. I'm thinking."

"Meanwhile, that mystery man is out there. What if he's prowling around, getting the lay of the land?"

Rafe slides me off his lap. "I'm going outside."

"Why?"

"To see who or what is out there." He stands up. "Stay here."

I jump up. "What about me makes you think I'll hide in the house? This is *my* story."

"You don't know if there is a story. That bloke might simply be unhinged, and when he saw you in the café he became infatuated."

"A stalker? That doesn't add up. I told you the stranger is working with someone else."

"Oh, yes, I forgot. Sorry."

Because of his lightning-strike injuries, I assume. They make him forgetful sometimes. "Dinnae fash, *gràidh*. There's no need to apologize."

He gives me the sweetest wee smile. "Thank you, Iona. Perhaps you should come with me. We'll go out there together and see what's going on. Would you bring me the shinty stick or whatever you Scots call it?"

I retrieve the item and give it to Rafe. He slaps it against his palm as his expression grows harder. "Now we'll see what that git wants with you."

"No violence unless it's absolutely necessary."

Rafe starts toward the sliding glass doors. "Stay behind me. If you see or hear anything, tell me. But keep your voice too low for the git to hear."

"Aye."

He slides the door open slowly, careful to make as little sound as possible. We both sneak outside. When I move to shut the door, he shakes his head. Maybe he worries we'll need to escape into the house quickly. I survey the area as we inch further away from the house. I hear Raghnall's cows mooing now and then, but no audible evidence of the stranger. The further we go away from the house, the more anxious I feel. Yet I also experience a twinge of excitement.

Thane had an adventure when a former MI6 agent sought revenge against him. Several MacTaggarts have had their own adventures too. But my life has been dull and unremarkable so far. Will this be my chance at adventure?

Rafe halts abruptly. He swivels his head right and left, gradually, but I don't dare ask what he thinks he might have seen or heard. I noticed nothing. Until...

Crunch.

Someone just stepped on a twig, I'd say.

Rafe's gaze narrows, his lips flatten, and he observes the area while moving only his eyes. He tiptoes forward, and I follow him. Inch by inch, by inch, by inch. Our footfalls remain almost imperceptible. I doubt the intruder can hear them. We're approaching the tree that lies about twenty feet from my cottage.

Crack.

We both freeze. That noise had come from far too close.

Rafe whispers to me, "Stay here."

Chapter Fourteen

Rafe

Iona's brows wrinkle, and she searches my gaze as if she hopes to find illumination there. I have nothing of the sort, not yet. But I intend to get some right now. I leap forward, barreling toward the tree with no concern for who or what might be hiding behind it. Someone is there. I know it. The figure behind the tree, whom I had glimpsed briefly as a sliver of a shadow, must be Iona's mystery man. What he wants with her, I can't say—not yet. But I will wring the truth out of that tosser one way or another.

Iona only follows my command briefly, then races after me.

At least she isn't trying to outpace me.

But I forget all about that when a figure bursts out from behind the tree, sprinting toward the fence line of Iona's neighbor's cow pasture. The prat sprints at a speed that I would label as impressive if he hadn't been stalking Iona. Harassing a woman is beyond the pale. I catch up to the bloke just as he tries to vault over the fence. The git can't quite make it, though, and he gets tangled up in the woven wire. His thrashing results in him bouncing backward onto the ground. He did a fair amount of cursing too.

As I skid to a halt, breathing hard, I snag the back of the man's jacket. I plant one foot on his chest, and he struggles for a few seconds. Then the tosser gives up and glowers at me.

Since I still have the shinty stick—the *caman*, as Iona called it—I thump it on my palm three times. "Who are you? And what are you doing mucking about on this property?"

He lifts his chin. "I got lost."

At least now I know Iona was right about this man. He is British. I snort with derision. "Try again. The truth this time."

The prat puckers his mouth. I assume he thinks that's a defiant expression, but it looks more like something a spoiled child refusing to eat his greens might do.

Iona comes up beside me, staring down at our new friend with a genuinely defiant expression. "Who is giving you orders?"

The prat thrashes, but he still can't get away.

"Tell us what we want to know," I snarl. "You have five seconds to confess, or else we'll ring the coppers. The Loch Fairbairn jail is hideous. You'll be eaten alive by cockroaches and starving rats."

Iona's lips tick up the faintest bit, though I doubt our new mate noticed that.

The git bares his teeth. "You lot will never break me."

"Your mission is that vital?" Iona asks. "Tell us what you want before I sic my boyfriend on you."

Boyfriend? I'm a bit old for that designation. Besides, we haven't discussed what sort of relationship we might actually have. It's beside the point right now.

Enough of this rubbish. I swing the shinty stick up above my head, then swing it back down, aiming straight for the bastard's chest.

"All right, all right, stop!" the tosser shrieks, and I halt the stick inches away from his rib cage. "What do you want to know?"

I set the bottom of the stick on the ground, keeping my hand draped over the top. "You are going to grass on your mate, whoever that person is, if you want to walk away with all your limbs intact." I glance down at his groin. "And I do mean all your limbs."

"Look, it wasn't my idea. The Scot is a prick, and I only took the job for the money."

"His name. Now."

Just as the prat is opening his mouth, someone shouts at us.

"Are ye having a picnic over there, Iona? I could bring potato salad."

Iona's eyes widen, but she recovers from her surprise quickly. "No, Raghnall, it's nothing like that. Go back to your house."

Raghnall stops just on the other side of the fence and scans the three of us. His brows hike up. "What's going on here?"

"Nothing," Iona says. "Go back into your house, Raghnall."

She emphasized those words, clearly trying to convince the old man to walk away.

Our prisoner thrusts one leg up, neatly kneeing me in the groin. Just as I gasp and glare at the tosser, he rolls away from me sideways. Iona tries to catch him, but the bastard is too bloody quick. By the time I recover from the pain of that groin kick, the git is racing past Iona's house. He veers left, out of sight.

I take off after him. Iona follows.

Raghnall shouts, "I'm ringing the police!"

That won't do any good unless we can catch the git.

But as I round the corner of Iona's house, making a beeline across the yard, I realize we've lost our prisoner. I stop and try to catch my breath. Iona grasps my arm, struggling to speak but too breathless to manage it.

I wrap my arm around her. "He's gone."

"Mhac na galla."

"You need to teach me Gaelic, so I'll understand all your curse words."

"Later."

Raghnall emerges from his house, trotting down the porch steps. "The constables are on their way."

We've lost the intruder, so there's no point in calling in the coppers. But I'm still too out of breath to say so.

Raghnall strides over to us. "Dinnae know why, but Fergus asked what Rafe Knight was doing now, and should he bring a Taser this time." The old gent's brows knit together. "Why would he say such a thing?"

"This is Rafe Knight," Iona tells Raghnall. "And what Fergus told you was just a misunderstanding. A sort of joke. You can go back into your house. Rafe and I will handle the constables. Everything is all right."

Raghnall nods and trots back to his home.

Iona and I sit on the porch steps while we await the arrival of the constables. She rests her head on my shoulder. I keep my arm around her. I've known this woman for a few days, yet I already feel protective of her. After my atrocious behavior on the day we met, I wouldn't have expected Iona to...like me.

The constables arrive ten minutes later with lights and sirens blazing.

But they aren't our only visitors. Another vehicle roars up the street, screeching to a halt just behind the parked constable's car. Both doors of the vehicle spring open.

Oh, bloody hell. Of course those two are here. I'm too knackered to deal with them, but they won't give a toss about that.

Ramsay and Thane march up the concrete path, reaching the porch steps only a matter of seconds behind the constables.

Fergus holds up a hand. "Thane, Ramsay, keep your mouths shut while we question the witnesses."

"Raghnall saw some of what happened," Iona tells the constable. "But Rafe and I are the real eyewitnesses."

"She overheard some bloke in the café talking on his mobile," I explain. "He was discussing some sort of job he was being paid to do. It turns out the job involved spying on Iona."

"Aye," she says. "And a wee bit earlier today, I saw that same man on the street and followed him, from a discreet distance. After a while, he stopped and called for a taxi. The address he gave was for my house."

Fergus taps his pen on his little notebook. "He must not have recognized you, aye?"

"Well, as I said, I maintained a discreet distance from the *bod ceann*. When I stopped closer to him, I dropped my purse as an excuse to bend over. My hair shielded my face."

"I see. Did he knock on the door?"

"Of course he didn't bloody knock on the door," I growl. "He was here to spy on Iona."

She lays a hand on my knee. "Relax, Rafe. He's only doing his job."

Just the touch of her hand eases my temper. I still don't understand why, but perhaps it's only that innate mothering instinct women have even when they don't have children. Does Iona have any sons or daughters? I never bothered to ask her.

Fergus now squints at me. "You're the hair-trigger sort, aye? Dinnae like Iona taking up with a man like that."

"I'm sorry for lashing out. It's not something I can control."

"Are ye claiming mental illness?"

"No. But I have old injuries that can cause..." I don't care to explain, and I fear I'll get angry again if I can't tamp down the instinct. "It's personal."

Iona takes hold of both my hands. "Rafe has told me all about his issues. He is not the one you need to be interrogating. Go find the British *cacan* who invaded my homestead."

"We will do that." Fergus looks to Thane and Ramsay. "If you two will stay with Iona and her new friend, Sorley and I can go after the intruder."

I slap my hand down on my thigh. "Stop talking and get your arses in motion. The intruder is moving further away by the second."

"Aye, we will do that. Straight away."

While the constables head for their vehicle, Thane and Ramsay glare at me. I'm about to tell them to bugger off, but I don't get the chance.

"Shoo, both of you," Iona says while flapping her hands at them. "Dinnae need my brothers breathing down my neck. You'll be more useful if you go with Fergus and Sorley."

Thane glances at me, then his sister. "If you're sure this one won't assault you..."

"Rafe has never done any such thing. He shouts occasionally, but that's all."

"And ye won't explain why you accept that from him."

"Later, Thane. Hunt the villain now."

Her brothers exchange glances and shrugs. Then they turn and walk away. Once they've climbed into their pickup truck, they follow the coppers down the road.

Iona rests her head on my shoulder.

For a moment, I simply gaze at her face. Her sweet expression gives me a strange feeling in my chest. "Do you honestly trust me?"

She tilts her head back to look at me. "Aye, Rafe, I trust you."

"Why? I've behaved like a bloody stupid arse ever since the moment we met."

"That's the key phrase—'behaved like.' You've told me about the long-term aftereffects of your lightning strike. Now that I know why you act the way you do, I cannae stay mad at you."

I search her gaze for some sign that she fully understands my problems. "Why would you want to get involved with a man who flies off the handle during stressful moments?"

"You did not fly off any handle today. I was impressed with how calmly you handled the intruder situation." She places a hand over my groin. "And the way you treated that *bod ceann* made me so randy."

Her statement makes me randy. I can feel blood rushing into my groin. "You undoubtedly feel that way only because of adrenaline. Once that high fades, you might wish we hadn't shagged."

Iona flattens her lips and blows a breath out through her nostrils. "For pity's sake, Rafe. I'm a grown woman, a journalist, and a mother. Dinnae treat me like I'm a silly schoolgirl. I want you to fuck me. Immediately. Are you interested or not?"

"What a ridiculous question." I surge to my feet while cradling Iona in my arms. "If you open the door, I'll kick it shut. Then we can shag wherever you like—the sofa, the floor, anywhere."

"Hurry up, then."

I stalk up to the door and wait while she opens it. Then I slam it shut with one boot, never pausing, and stalk into the living room. While I keep Iona in my arms, I survey the house. "Where are the bedroom and bathroom?"

"Down that short hallway. It ends at the door to the master suite."

"Are there any other rooms?"

"Aye, two others that used to be the children's bedrooms."

The open kitchen has possibilities, and the fluffy rug in the living room also looks intriguing.

"*Bod an Donais*, Rafe, hurry up."

"Yes, milady, I shall." But once again, I can't think straight. It's not my temper flaring up again. No, lust has taken hold so fiercely that my mind is a muddle. "Perhaps you should choose the location."

She bites her lower lip while her brows furrow. Then she grins. "The sauna."

"What? You didn't mention that in your inventory of rooms."

"I forgot about it. My family likes to use the sauna once in a wee while, but I rarely do. It feels odd to soak in there alone."

As I imagine fucking her in that sauna, I realize there's a problem. "Something like that takes time to start up."

"Only ten to fifteen minutes." She takes my earlobe into her mouth and suckles it, making me gasp. "I'm sure you can think of a way to keep us aroused for that long."

Extended teasing and almost orgasms before the main event...Yes, I could go for that. "You've won me over. Playtime before the sauna."

Chapter Fifteen

Iona

Rafe sets me down, and I trot out to a building I doubt he'd noticed any of the other times he was here. Probably because we argued on those other occasions. Our only sexual encounter was in the hotel. The sauna is small—cozy, I'd say—but it has enough room for both of us with a wee bit of room to spare. We kindle the fire until it's ready to heat up the sauna on its own. Then we rush back into the house.

But Rafe halts in the middle of the living room while I continue toward the hallway.

When I realize he stopped, I spin around to stare at him.

"Stop right there, Iona. We are going to undress in the living room."

"Oh. I like that idea."

"Then get your sweet arse over here." He crooks a finger at me. "Come, pet."

I sashay over to him. "How about a few sensual delights from the kitchen first?"

"That sounds perfect."

I claim his hand, leading Rafe toward the kitchen and around the far side of the island. I don't fail to notice the fact that he can't resist admiring my erse while I move about gathering the food from the refrigerator. I enjoy the sight of his erse too. Even with trousers covering those cheeks, it's still a sight to behold. I barely got a glimpse of his erse the first time we shagged. That was Rafe's fault. He'd been so riled up that he needed to fuck me like a mad man.

Not that I minded. I loved it, in fact.

Even when he behaves like somewhat of a mad man, I don't mind. Learning about the long-term side effects of his lightning strike has given me a new perspective on Rafe Knight.

He leans against the island, now admiring my breasts, thanks to the plunging neckline of my blouse.

I lean over a wee bit more than necessary as I drop a collection of clear plastic boxes on the island and begin popping them open one by one. "Here we go. I had put these in the freezer until I was ready to eat them, but I thawed them out overnight. So, all I need to do is heat them in the microwave."

"Just the thought of shagging you in the sauna makes me hot enough that I'm quite sure I could heat up these dishes just by blowing on them from afar."

I can't stop the girlish giggle that bubbles out of me. "Thank you for the compliment, but I doubt your breath meets the safety standards for reheating food."

"What safety standards? No one informed me Loch Fairbairn was that strict about meals reheated at home."

I slide all the dishes onto one plate and set it in the microwave. Rafe watches with curiosity as I punch buttons, getting it wrong several times before I manage to hit the right length for heating up our snacks.

Rafe chuckles.

And I plant my hands on my hips. "What is so amusing?"

"You had to try three times before you hit the right button."

"Aye. So what? Microwaves are notoriously difficult to use."

He chuckles again and pinches my erse. "Only for Scottish women."

I pinch his erse. "Would you like to prove that claim by operating the microwave?"

"Later, perhaps."

Together, we set the table that lies at the other end of the open kitchen. Rafe teases me occasionally, and I offer saucy remarks in response. *Bod an Donais*, who knew setting out forks, knives, and napkins could be so erotic? I might drag Rafe down on the tabletop so I can shag him right now.

"Sit down, Rafe. I'll bring the food."

He dutifully obeys my command, but I assume he did that only because he's hungry. Rafe Knight is an alpha male through and through. I never used to like men who behaved that way, but I do now.

I set the microwave dish on the table. "Dig in. There's plenty for both of us."

"You cooked this?"

"Only in that I reheated it. I told you that already."

Rafe studies the food, and his brows wrinkle. "Looks like something lovers would enjoy, full of sensual aromas and spices and seasonings." He spears half a chicken breast and sets it on his plate. Then he inhales deeply. "Definitely sensual. Why would you make a dish like this for yourself?"

"I didn't. A friend made it."

"What mate of yours would cook a lover's meal for you? Only a man who wants to shag you, I'd say."

I sit down on my chair. "Mm, it smells as good as it did the first time."

Rafe squints at the food still inside the microwave dish. "Why are there two unfinished segments of chicken? There should be one whole breast and one half-eaten, since you cooked this only for yourself."

I slap my fork down on the table. "Stop interrogating me, Rafe."

"Perhaps I will if you tell me who ate this meal with you. One of your brothers?"

"No." Why shouldn't I tell him? It's none of his business, but I have no reason to avoid answering his question. "Eric Taylor cooked this food for me."

Rafe stiffens, his spine snapping ramrod straight. Through clenched teeth he hisses, "Eric Taylor was in your home?"

"He's a friend. Dinnae need to explain myself to you. If I want to have dinner with Eric, that's none of your concern." I stab my fork into my chicken and rip a piece off it. "Eric wanted to make a nice meal for me. He's a sweet laddie."

"Who wants to fuck you."

"Aye." I slant toward him. "So do you."

"That's different. I'm a man, he's a pup." Rafe glares at me. "You've been shagging him, haven't you?"

"*Mhac na galla.*" I leap up, causing my chair to tumble over backward. "I've been very understanding of your temper because I know why you have trouble controlling it. But this jealousy…It's intolerable. You have no right to accuse me of sleeping with Eric. I told you I am not doing that. Believe me or don't, it's up to you."

For a moment or two, we stare at each other without speaking or moving. Maybe I should have expected this reaction from Rafe, but I had no idea he would deduce that someone else cooked this meal. Why couldn't Rafe just accept what I told him? I suppose it was sort of a lie. I shouldn't have hidden the truth about the food and who crafted it.

Bloody hell. I'm as stubborn as Rafe.

So, I try for reconciliation. "Let's both calm down and try to work things out together. I should have told you Eric had visited me the other night, since you and I have become closer. But you shouldn't have accused me of sleeping with Eric."

Rafe slumps in his chair. "Yes, you're right. I apologize."

"And I apologize too." I walk round to Rafe's side of the table and settle my erse on his lap. "I would love to reconcile with you in the sauna."

"Might as well finish our dinner first." He winces. "Even if Eric Taylor did cook it for you."

"Are you sure that's what you want to do?"

"Positive."

I brush my thumb across his lips. "The first time I ate these dishes, I devoured them so quickly that my tummy got a wee bit upset afterward. I wanted to get it over with so Eric would leave."

"Hmm. You definitely aren't enamored of him, then." Rafe sits up straighter and grabs his fork, spearing a chunk of chicken. Then he holds it near my mouth. "Ladies first."

I close my lips around the soft flesh, chewing in a leisurely manner, savoring every nuance as the flavors infiltrate my senses. My eyes drift half-closed. I had tasted these exact dishes when Eric made dinner for me, but I swear that today the food seems more succulent and richer than ever before. Warmth sifts through me amid a sensual tingling sensation that dives deep inside me, making me wet.

"This food makes you randy," Rafe says. "I'll need to get the recipe from Eric, even if I have to beat it out of him."

"It isn't the food making me feel this way. It's you." His cock is growing stiffer and thicker by the second. So, I slide a hand down to his groin and gently massage it through his trousers, making Rafe suck in a sharp breath. "Cannae deny ye like this, aye?"

His eyelids flutter, almost as if he might shut them. His head tips backward a wee bit too. "I know you never slept with Eric. But I can't blame him for wanting you so much that he'll go to extreme lengths. You are stunningly beautiful and sexy as hell."

"No other man has ever described me that way, not even my unwanted suitor." To see the evidence of his lust for me so clearly, it arouses me to an almost painful level. Pleasurable pain. "Please, Rafe, make love to me."

He groans deeply as I stroke his length. Even through his trousers, he can clearly feel everything I'm doing. "Fuck, Iona. If you keep teasing me, this will be a replay of our first shag—hot, hard, and insane. You know I have trouble controlling my passions."

"Dinnae want ye to hold back. Unleash all your passions."

"In that case..." He grasps my shirt between my breasts and rips it open. Buttons tumble to the floor. "I'll buy you a new blouse."

"Stop talking, start fucking."

He chuckles, then his gaze drops to my chest. His lips curve into a steamy smile. "Thank you, pet."

"For what?"

"Wearing a bra that closes in front." He plucks the clasps free one by one, all the while cupping my erse with the other hand. "Don't move unless I tell you to. I need to undress you, pet, with my fingers and my teeth and any other part of my body that will work."

A delicious wee shiver rushes through me. Rafe is by far the most erotic lover I've ever had. And I know this time, we'll rock the house—literally. I hope we don't frighten Raghnall's cows.

Rafe pushes my blouse off over my shoulders and tosses it all the way across the room. He repeats the process with my bra, which lands on top of the kitchen island. I sit here, immobilized by everything he does, fascinated by the wild hunger on his face. When I finally manage to get my muscles to respond, I reach for his shirt, determined to rip it open.

But he clasps my wrist to stop me. "No, no, no, pet. You'll get what you want eventually, but not now."

"What I want is you inside me, and I cannae wait."

"You will." He tugs my naked torso against his chest. "I love how desperately you want me."

He lowers his head until it's nestled between my tits. Then he drags his tongue up my chest, snaking it out now and then to flick the tip over my skin. I shudder every time he does that. When he gets to my throat, he gives up licking and rakes his lips upward until they meet my chin.

"Oh, God, Rafe, hurry up. I've never been this aroused in my entire life. Fair certain I'll go insane in the next ten seconds."

He lifts his head, but only to smirk and wink. "Perfect."

Rafe stands up with me still in his arms.

Instinctively, I wrap my legs around his hips, and he winks again. The *bod ceann* is enjoying the chance to torment me, and I won't deny I love every second of it.

He keeps hold of me with one arm, then uses the other to swipe everything off the table, from the silverware to the food. He's making a bloody mess, and still, I dinnae care. He can wreck my house as long as he makes me come so hard that I scream.

The man I desperately need to fuck me disentangles my legs from around his hips and takes hold of my jeans. Fortunately, I prefer the sort that has an elastic waistband so I can slip them on and off easily. When Rafe notices that fact, he grins like the devil himself and yanks the jeans down to my ankles.

Rafe tosses them past my head, and I hear a slap that must be my jeans hitting the glass doors. "Glad you're barefoot, pet. I won't need to waste time on removing your shoes."

The only sound I can make is a whimper.

He grasps my knees and shoves them apart. "Time to devour you, love."

Chapter Sixteen

Rafe

I've needed all my self-control to stop myself from ravaging her like a wild beast, but I can't hold back any longer. Iona Buchanan's luscious body is laid out before me, and I allow myself a moment to admire her beauty. Those plump tits and their swollen nipples. The delicate curve of her waist. Even her navel turns me on, and I can't resist ducking my head to swirl my tongue inside it. She doesn't have the body of a twenty-year-old, but I love that about her. Even her tiny stretch marks make me want her.

She's a real woman, through and through.

As much as my lust commands me to ravish her wildly, I refuse to rush. At least for the moment. Soon, I won't have enough control left to accomplish what I mean to do to her right now.

I thrust my face between her thighs and devour her.

Every time I scrape my tongue over her clit, she jerks and cries out. But when I pet her folds, she thrashes and shouts and bangs her fists on the table-top, making it jounce across the floor. Bloody hell, I haven't even fucked her yet and she's already going crazy. Am I that good? Iona certainly makes me feel that way. I swear I could keep going for days as long as I'm inside her.

But I won't go there just yet.

I nip at her clit, thrusting a finger inside her. The second she cries out, I push another finger into her opening, loving the velvety slickness and heat of her body. She grips the edges of the table hard enough that it must hurt, but she doesn't seem to care. My cock throbs. How much longer can

I torment her before I risk coming all over the floor without even being inside her?

Long enough. I have unbreakable willpower.

I latch on to her nub and suckle it so hard that it must hurt, but rather than smacking me, she begs me to keep going. Not with words. Neither of us can speak right now, of that I'm certain. Her pleading gaze tells me all I need to know. So, I nip and lick and suckle her clit until she explodes.

"Rafe! Yes! Oh, God, yes!"

I consume her flesh until she finally collapses, her entire body slack and slicked with sweat as if she ran a marathon. The weight of lust has done that to her. I can't deny the sight of her naked, spread out before me with her glistening flesh exposed, might just drive me irretrievably insane.

And I don't give a toss if it does.

Iona lies there with a dreamily dazed expression. Her eyes appear darker thanks to her pupils dilating. Her skin is dappled with pink here and there, another sure sign that I've satisfied this woman completely.

And we aren't even done yet.

I lean over her, setting my hands at either side of her shoulders. "Ah, my sweet Scots lass, you are stunning in the throes and immediately after. I'd love to taste you over and over again, but we do have plans."

"What? Plans?"

"Yes, pet. I vowed to do this for you, and I never renege on a promise."

I strip naked. But before I can fuck her, I need a condom. Shoving my hand into the pocket of my trousers, I dig out one of three packets I've been carrying in my pocket ever since the first time we had sex. As quickly as is reasonably possible, I roll the condom on.

Then I thrust my cock into her as deeply as I can go—and then I stop. For a moment, I allow myself to revel in the feel of her soft, slick flesh molding to my shaft, and the enticing scent of her desire for me. My ex-wife only ever wanted a quick orgasm and never cared what I wanted. Iona isn't like that at all. She could climax repeatedly for hours if I had the stamina for that.

"Do something, Rafe. I need you to come inside me."

"Not yet." I shove my arms beneath her body and hoist us both up and off the table. "Wrap your legs around me and hold on hard enough that you won't lose your grip."

She complies instantly.

I stagger toward the glass doors, bumping into the table and a chair along the way. With a bit of effort, I manage to push the door open. Iona clings to me more firmly while I stagger across the yard and over to the sauna's door. In the furthest recesses of my mind, I wonder if Iona's neighbor, the cattle farmer, might see us and wonder what the bloody hell we're doing out here. Raghnall might call the police, I suppose. But I rather doubt it. Who wants to ring the police station to report a barmy couple shagging in the backyard in the nude?

Three times, I try to open the bloody sauna door, and three times I fail. I almost drop Iona on the final attempt. Yet somehow, my cock remains lodged inside her.

"Let me do it," Iona says, her tone breathless.

"Hurry, then, and do it."

She twists sideways and snakes her arm out, feeling around until she finally grasps the knob and turns it. The door eases open, creaking faintly. I rush inside and kick the door shut. Luckily, it has a latch that closes automatically. Our entrance has let some of the steam escape.

"Bend your knees a wee bit, Rafe."

I obey Iona, and she stretches her arm out to grab the ladle out of the water bucket and dump the water onto the hot rocks. That sends up more steam, filling the sauna. But that movement to the left also has the side effect of triggering her inner muscles to tighten around my shaft.

"Bloody hell, woman, you'll make me come too soon if you don't stop squeezing my cock."

The Scottish lass in my arms bites her upper lip. "I'm so sorry, Rafe."

"Don't apologize. Just loosen up a bit, would you?"

She releases her hold on my cock.

And I surge toward the nearest wall, slamming into it. Iona wraps her arms around me fiercely, crying out as I pump into her with brutal force.

"Harder. Please, Rafe, harder."

I pull out almost all the way, then pound into her like a maniac, over and over, shouting with every lunge. Iona's tits are mashed to my chest, and their rigid tips rub against my skin. The lovely lass abruptly freezes, a sure sign that she's about to come.

But I don't want to let her do that just yet.

And so, I freeze too. "Did I say you could come yet?"

"Huh?"

The pure confusion on her face is the most charming thing I've ever seen when a woman is in the throes.

I brush damp hair away from her face. "Let's wait just a moment. Then I'll allow you to do something for me."

"You are an arrogant sod, aren't you?"

"And that's what makes you want me so desperately. Isn't it?"

She smiles with devilish sweetness. "I reckon it is, you despicable, odious, vile bastard."

A chuckle rumbles out of me. "If you were trying to insult me, pet, better practice your tone of voice. Your sultry timbre made it sound like a come-on."

"Maybe it was." She squeezes her inner muscles around my cock. "Dinnae give up now. It was just getting good."

I nip her bottom lip. "Ever since the day we first shagged, I've given you nothing but bloody fantastic sex. You should thank me. Or perhaps give me a medal."

She kicks my arse. "Get on with it, Rafe."

"Yes, milady."

I stagger over to the back wall of the rather small sauna. Not much room to work with here, but I can innovate. Once I've reached the edge of the bench, I spin around and drop down on the wood surface. Then I turn sideways, lying down with my knees bent. Iona has remained in my arms, but now she lies atop my chest with her chin propped beneath mine.

Iona gazes at me with delight glittering in her eyes. "Are we about to have a wee lie-down?"

"No, you cheeky lass. You are going to fuck me." I slap her arse. "About time you did some of the work. And make it a hard come, would you?"

"Is there anything else you require?"

"No, that's all." I wink. "For now."

Iona pushes herself up onto her hands on my chest and begins to rock back and forth. The gentle motion seems certain to give me a heart attack, considering how aroused I am. But I can't deny I love watching her tits as they sway to and fro. I love the sight so much that I lunge my head up to catch one peak between my teeth, laving it with my tongue. Then I twist myself into a near pretzel position to smack her arse.

"Oh! Rafe, you scamp." She slaps my chest. "Behave yourself."

"Why? You love my despicable scamp attitude."

Iona never stopped fucking me even while we were speaking. Her desire is clearly mounting, and she speeds up her pace more with every stroke. I feel as if my cock might erupt at any second. For her, I'll hold on as long as humanly possible. I can't stop myself from grasping her hips to hold her firmly to me while she pumps her hips faster and faster. The steam roiling around us only adds to the eroticism of our lovemaking.

She comes again, more powerfully than before, and throws her head back to scream.

Finally, I can't stand it any longer. To avert a heart attack, I thrust my hips upward to plunge deeply inside her once, twice, three times while electric shocks barrel down my spine, forcing me to spend everything I have inside this incredible woman's body.

Iona and I collapse in a heap on the bench. One of my arms hangs over the edge. We're both fighting to regain our breath. When I can manage to control my muscles again, I brush my fingers through her damp hair in a rhythm I hope will feel soothing to her. After the way I pummeled her body, we both need time to come down from the endorphin high. Since she let me do this to her, I owe the sweet Scottish lass a reward.

Once I've gotten rid of the condom, I hook a finger under her chin, urging her to meet my gaze. "Let me massage you, love. I don't want you to get too sore."

Her eyes widen, but only for a brief moment. Then she smiles with lazy sweetness. "I would love that, Rafe. Thank you."

I pat her arse. "Then turn onto your side so I can move out from under you."

She complies, and I then instruct her to lie on her stomach. Once she's done that, I kneel on the bench beside her legs. Her lids fall halfway shut while I massage her from head to toe, paying maximum attention to her legs and arms, the areas most likely to get sore after receiving such an intense workout. I lovingly rub those areas but also use my hands to iron out any kinks on her back and neck.

Her smile, full of sweetness and total satisfaction, gives me an odd feeling in my chest. It's not a bad feeling. I like it, but I can't quite figure out what it signifies. She enjoys my company, especially when I fuck her. Other than that, I have no idea what Iona wants from me. To suggest I might be her boyfriend seems bizarre. I'm too old for that. But she's more to me than a casual lover, so…I have no bloody idea what we're doing.

Once I've completed the massage, I rise and stretch. "Are you hungry, pet?"

"Mm, starved." She sits up, and her face now lies at the level of my cock. It's no longer hard, but she doesn't seem to care. "We don't have any food, though. It's, um, sort of littering the whole living room."

"You must have some food items in your refrigerator or freezer."

"I do. But before we eat…" She pats the bench beside her. "Let me massage you."

"That isn't necessary."

She rolls her eyes. "Forget about necessity. Lie on the bench and let me rub you down, *gràidh*."

With this woman, I have no willpower. Why shouldn't I let her do what she wants with my body? I lie down and stretch out on the bench with my feet nudging her hip. "Have your way with me. I've never had a massage that wasn't related to physical therapy. This will be a new experience for me."

Her brows hike up. "Are you having me on?"

"No. Why would I lie about that?"

Iona leans over to touch my cheek. "No wonder you're so easily enraged. Didn't your ex-wife do anything nice for you?"

"Well, it was probably my fault. I never could make Angela happy, especially after the lightning strike."

"I'm honored to be the first person to ever give you a massage."

And I'm honored to have a woman like her in my life.

Chapter Seventeen

Iona

Oh, Rafe, that poor man. It's no wonder he has trouble trusting anyone and can't believe anyone might want to have him in their life. I do want that. Being with Rafe Knight makes me realize how lonely my life has been for all these years. So many failed relationships. Just as many failed careers, if not more. But I always made sure my daughters had everything they needed. My ever-changing jobs came about because the companies I worked for went out of business. My children love me and support me, but I wish I'd spent more time with them and less time chasing after jobs I hated.

Then I found my calling. And now I've found a man who just might be…Oh, I can't make myself use that phrase. It's ridiculous.

But Rafe might be my soul mate.

No, it's far too early to declare that.

Since I have Rafe at my mercy, lying in a prone position, I can't give up the chance to put my hands on him. We've had sex twice, but I only got to see him naked this evening. After the sweet and gentle way he massaged me, I need to show him how much I appreciate that—by reciprocating.

I slide off the bench to kneel at his feet and begin to massage him, starting with his soles. The sauna still provides warmth, though the steam has lessened. I could stoke the fire, but I'd rather just keep giving Rafe the loving attention he deserves. While I gradually move my hands up his body, I take the time to admire every inch of him. He has an impressive physique, particularly for a man of his age.

Now that I've grown rather fond of him, I think it's time for us to have an honest discussion and learn more about each other.

But I'll finish the massage first.

Rafe's eyes have slid partly closed, and his lips form a relaxed wee smile. I avoid his cock during my ministrations. As much as I would love to shag him again, that would delay the serious talk we need to have. So, I continue running my hands over his body, enjoying the feel of his muscles which are strong but not as ripped as a bodybuilder. I like that he's a normal man, in terms of his physique. He's quite unusual in other ways.

Once I reach his throat, I stop and press my lips to his. "I love being with you, Rafe."

He seems briefly stunned. "Why would you say that? I'm the man who practically broke down your front door on the day we met."

"I understand you better now. But I'd like to know more about you and share more of myself too." I rise and rest my erse on the edge of the bench. "Will you do that? Please?"

He sits up, clasping my hands. "Yes, I will. Anything you want to know, I'll tell you."

"Let's go inside and find something to eat that hasn't been lying on the floor all this time. Then we'll open up to each other."

Rafe and I shut down the sauna, then return to the house. We hold hands, as we've often done lately. It feels good and right.

Cleaning up the mess we made in the living room takes a wee bit of time, but Rafe and I have fun teasing each other while we work. The sun has begun to set. Has it really been that long since Rafe knocked on my door earlier? Since time has flown by so swiftly, we agree to whip up a snack rather than a full meal. I'm not terribly hungry, anyway. We have fun deciding which foods to choose. Afterward, we cuddle on the sofa to feed each other, sharing a plate and using our fingers instead of silverware.

Now that we're done eating, it's time for that conversation I suggested. "Are you ready to talk now, Rafe?"

He makes a pained face but then blows out a breath and nods. "Interrogate me for as long as you like."

I elbow him in the side. "This isn't an interrogation. We're two adults who've been shagging and now want to get to know each other better."

"Well, when you phrase it that way, it does sound less ominous."

"I'll go first. What would you like to know about me?"

Rafe rubs his chin as if he's giving serious thought to my question. It's pure sarcasm, though. But when he asks a question, he gives up teasing me. "Have you ever been married? Do you have children?"

"I never married. But I do have two children who are adults now."

"Girls or boys?"

"Two beautiful young ladies. Maeve is the oldest at twenty-three while Rowan is twenty-one." I tuck my legs beneath me and rotate slightly toward Rafe so I can see him better. "Maeve and Rowan were adopted. I knew their parents very well. David and Mary were wonderful people and devoted parents. But they had a terrible automobile accident and passed away. I had been best friends with Mary, and she insisted on listing me in their will as the person they wanted to raise their children if something should happen to them. They had no living relatives except for an elderly aunt who had Alzheimer's."

Rafe studies me. "You raised two girls on your own? I'm even more impressed by you now."

"Because I did what my best friend wanted? No, that isn't impressive."

"How old were you when that happened?"

Suddenly, I feel somewhat uncomfortable. I didn't do anything extraordinary. But I answer Rafe's question. "I was thirty years old at the time. Eventually, I adopted the girls."

He stares at me almost as if he's awed. "You, a young and vibrant woman, took in two little girls. You raised them as your own. I'd say that counts as impressive. What are your daughters like now?"

"Maeve is studying to become a teacher. Rowan opted out of going to university and instead took a job working for Evan MacTaggart." I realize I'm smiling now, though I didn't purposely do that. "Evan's long-time assistant, Tamsen Spurling, resigned last year so she could move to Germany with her fiancé, who is German. I suggested Rowan could fill in until Evan found a new executive assistant, but after one week, he promoted her to full time. My daughter works for a billionaire."

"You've raised two incredible young women." Rafe gives me a quick, soft kiss. "I'm hardly surprised. You are a force to be reckoned with, and I've no doubt your daughters learned that from you."

I wrap my arms around myself because I feel a wee bit embarrassed by Rafe's profuse praise. "My daughters are impressive. But I zigzagged from one job to another until I finally found my calling as a journalist. I stayed at each job for at least three years. So, at least I wasn't a career-hopping eejit."

Rafe slips his arm around my shoulders. "I suppose it's time for me to share my past."

I consider saying something to encourage him, but I suspect that would only make him feel more uncomfortable talking about himself. Instead, I'll gaze into his eyes and hope that will ease his discomfort.

He rubs his forehead, then dives in. "I was married to Angela for seventeen years. When we first met, she was a vivacious and clever girl who loved life and wanted to become a lightning researcher. We met at university and quickly became a couple. I'm three years older than Angela. I had already graduated and gotten a job at a research facility by the time she earned her degree."

My journalist curiosity insists that I should ask questions. But I tell that part of my brain to be quiet.

"Angela changed rather quickly after Toby was born. She was a good mother, for the most part, but she grew restless and jealous of me." Rafe lets his head fall back against the sofa and stares up at the ceiling. "You see, I was promoted to head researcher within four years. The gent who had been in charge retired. Angela resented the fact that I was given that position and that she would become my underling."

I begin to wring my hands, though I never do that. Listening to Rafe share his story makes me anxious on his behalf. Maybe I should worry about what that means. I'll think about it later.

"Still, I would have stayed with Angela for Toby's sake," he tells me. "Our marriage essentially ended after five years, but we remained together for seventeen years. Until the lightning strike. Until I realized just how narcissistic my wife had become. Still, she always treated Toby kindly and made sure to attend his university graduation. My behavior after the lightning strike gave her an excellent excuse to have me removed from my position. That means I got sacked."

"That's awful."

"Losing my university position turned out to be a blessing in disguise. It spurred me to start my own independent laboratory, with help from a few wealthy donors."

I'm literally biting my lip in an effort to prevent myself from asking a nosy question.

Rafe notices, glancing at me sideways while still hanging his head back. "It's all right. I won't fly off the handle because I'm talking about my ex-wife. She stayed with me for one month after the lightning strike. Then she filed for divorce and ordered me to move out of the house. That was the event that changed our family irretrievably and nearly destroyed my relationship with Toby."

I'm still biting my lip, but now I'm doing that so hard that it's turned white.

"Ask your question, Iona. You've been dying to do that."

"Well, I, um..wondered why you let your ex-wife poison your relationship with your son."

He bows his head. "I was weak. That's why."

"No, you are not weak and never have been. That lightning strike nearly killed you, and it left you with long-term consequences."

"But I just walked away from my son without even trying to fight for custody."

I climb onto his lap, straddling him. "That's rubbish, Rafe. Your wife walked out on you, not the other way around."

"Don't you understand? I should have fought for my son. He might've been seventeen, but he was still my child, my little boy." Rafe's eyes begin to glisten, and I think he might be on the verge of crying. "Toby drove me to and from my physical therapy appointments and doctor's visits while I recovered. He lied to his mother about that, since he knew she wouldn't approve. I shouldn't have put him in that position."

"He was old enough to decide for himself." I grasp Rafe's face with both hands. "Toby must love you very much to have gone against his mother's wishes. Remember that. But most of all, talk to him again. I'll go with you."

"Toby probably won't speak to me unless Eric is there." Rafe lashes his arms around me. "If you're there, I might get angry simply because I see Eric and remember how he's been harassing you."

"It isn't harassment. He's confused, that's all. Please let me go along when you meet with Toby and Eric."

He shuts his eyes but keeps his arms around me as he takes a moment to digest what I suggested. Then he opens his eyes. "Have it your way."

"Thank you." I kiss his cheek. "Now, let's go to bed—to sleep."

"I'd better ring for a taxi."

"No, Rafe. You are sleeping here tonight, in my bed." I lean in until our eyes are millimeters apart. "That means both of us in my bed, sleeping together."

"You are a stubborn woman. But I can't resist you, so I shall do whatever you believe is appropriate."

"Good." I hop off his lap, now standing between him and the coffee table. "Fortunately, we don't need to undress. We're both still naked."

"Thank you for reminding me of that fact, but I was aware of it already." He rises and stretches, groaning with satisfaction. "I'm ready to go to bed with you, Ms. Buchanan."

"Glad to hear it, Mr. Knight."

We hold hands while we amble down the hall, past the two vacant bedrooms and into the master suite, where I've slept for as long as I've lived in this house. Rafe commands me to wait on the threshold while he prepares the room. He's never been in my bedroom before, so I have no idea what he means to do. I peek around his large body to get a glimpse.

Rafe flicks the switch on the bedside lamp, which emits a cozy glow. Next, he sweeps all the clothes off the bed and carefully turns down the sheets. "You are a bit of a slob, eh? Clothes were strewn all over the bed."

"Aye. Dinnae peek under the bed. It's as messy as the clothes on top."

He looks at me over his shoulder and clucks his tongue. "I need to teach you etiquette."

"Go ahead and try."

Chapter Eighteen

Rafe

After a brief attempt, I gave up on schooling Iona in the art of the turndown. She seems determined to remain a heathen. We fell asleep together, wrapped up in each other's arms. I woke up this morning to her charmingly soft snores. After the wild time we had yesterday, I forgive her for snoring. As long as it doesn't mutate into chainsaw territory, I can live with it.

While she still slumbers, I carefully crawl out of bed and make sure the covers remain over her. Then I amble out into the living room, making my way to the kitchen island. We hadn't bothered to clean up after our evening snack, so the plates and glasses and other rubbish remain in the sink. After washing everything and wiping down the counter, I'm finally ready to consider what to make for breakfast.

A gourmet, I am not. But I can create a decent meal.

What Iona and I did yesterday left me knackered. But after a good night's rest, I feel reinvigorated. And I'm determined to cook a hearty breakfast for the woman who has become my salvation. Perhaps that statement is leaning toward the saccharine side, but I don't give a toss. Not that I plan on telling Iona about my saccharine feelings. I'll wait until we know each other better.

Once I've whipped up our breakfast, I head for the bedroom to awaken the sleeping beauty with my kiss. Yes, I've now stepped completely over the line into sappy romance. My son would never believe it.

Fortunately, Iona rolled over in her sleep. That means I can sneak up behind her, slanting over the bed to plant butterfly kisses on her shoulder. "Wake up, love. Time to rise and shine."

Iona stirs and moans.

When I kiss her shoulder again, adding a slight shake too, she still only moans and vaguely stirs. *Crikey*. This woman is determined to sleep until the next century. I step up my game by sliding a hand down to her breast and cupping that succulent mound. She still doesn't respond. I nuzzle her ear, then suckle the lobe.

Still no joy.

I slide that hand along her belly until I feel the downy hairs on her mound. Then I push one finger between the folds. The scent of her desire makes me want to bury my face between her creamy thighs. But still, she refuses to wake up. Or perhaps she's having me on, and she's been awake the whole time.

One way to find out.

"Well, pet, if you're that exhausted..." I slide my hand up to her belly. "Then I'd better not disturb you."

I am getting hard, though. The aroma of her cream could drive me mad, and it probably will unless I ease the pressure. If Iona wants to go on sleeping, I'll handle the problem on my own.

So, I slide off the bed but remain standing, almost touching the mattress. Iona pretends to snore, though not believably. I unzip my trousers, pull out my cock, and begin to stroke myself.

Iona lazily turns over onto her opposite side, facing me. Her lips curl into a devious little smile.

While she watches, I let my trousers drop to the floor and go on stroking my cock. My breaths turn into grunts and hissing. I keep my gaze locked on Iona even as I pump faster and feel those electric shocks gliding down my spine, about to unleash my come. I'm pumping so hard and fast that I might fall down if I don't come soon.

Iona flips the covers off, exposing her nakedness. "Come all over me, Rafe, please."

"Can't do anything but that."

She massages her tits, flicking her thumbs over the stiff peaks. But that doesn't push me over the edge. No, that happens when she thrusts a hand between her thighs to rub herself.

My back arches, a growl explodes out of me, and I unleash everything I have, spraying it onto Iona. With two more pumps, I'm done. And I release a sigh of deep pleasure. "Better have a shower, love. I've soiled you."

She shakes her head. "Everything you do cleanses me."

"That makes no sense."

Iona thrusts her hands into her hair and rolls her hips. "I'll help you understand what it means if you join me in the shower."

"But I made breakfast. It will get cold."

"Scamper into the kitchen and put everything in the oven on low heat."

I scoff. "Men like me do not 'scamper' anywhere."

"Then I'll shower alone." She cups her mound with one hand. "I'll take care of my needs alone under the steamy-hot water."

Her sensual tone leaves me with no recourse.

I rush out to the kitchen and fling the dish of food into the oven, just managing to restrain myself from accidentally setting the temperature to high. Then I sprint back down the hall to the bathroom, where the door hangs open, ready and waiting for me. Iona stands in the shower amid a cascade of steamy water, her skin glistening, her head thrown back as she thrusts her fingers through those wet locks. The sensuous curve of her spine stops me for a moment, and I can't resist raking my gaze over every inch of her skin.

She notices me watching and smiles. "Step into the shower, Rafe. I want to wash you."

"I've been able to manage that on my own since I was six years old."

"But I want to do it for you." She steps out of the spray, waving for me to walk into the shower. "Dinnae tell me no. I'm very persuasive."

"Yes, you are." I stride into the shower and grab a sponge. "I'll wash you first, pet."

Her lips tighten into a smile that dimples her cheeks.

Yes, she loves it when I tend to her needs.

I lather up the sponge and begin gently swirling it over her shoulders, while the suds trickle down her skin. She moans when I slide my hands over her hips to skim them up her belly to her breasts.

A phone rings in the bedroom.

"*Mhac na galla,*" Iona hisses. "Who would be calling this early? It doesn't sound like my ringtone."

"No, it's mine." I rinse myself off to shed the suds, then step out of the shower to grab a towel and quickly pat myself down. "Pardon me, love, while I see who's ringing me. It might be Toby."

I jog over to the bed and search for my mobile, hunting about underneath it as well as among the covers. As my mobile rings for the fifth time, I finally spot the device lying between the two pillows at the head of the bed. Snatching up the mobile, I tap the screen to answer. "Toby, what's wrong? You never ring me this early. Never wake up this early either."

"Why do you sound breathless? Have you been working out in Iona's house?"

I freeze, and a sudden chill ripples through me. "I don't understand."

Toby makes an irritated noise. "I'm a computer scientist, Dad. Did you really think I couldn't crack the encryption on your mobile phone and access the geolocation data to track you down?"

"What? You had no right to track me."

He lets out a bark of laughter. "You've been tracking me since the day you gave me a mobile phone for Christmas when I was sixteen. Kind of hypocritical of you to get annoyed when I did the same. Soooo, why are you at Iona's house at eight in the morning?"

The sneaky tone in his voice irritates me immensely. But I can tell he isn't angry. Toby seems determined to tease me until I erupt like Mount Vesuvius. He will be disappointed. I don't feel angry at all. My surprise had lasted only a moment after Toby declared he'd cracked the whatever-it-was.

"I'm rather busy at the moment, Toby. Why don't we meet for lunch somewhere?"

"Who will be joining us? You, me, Iona, and her two angry brothers?"

"Only you, me, Iona, and Eric. Assuming Iona isn't busy working on a story. Thane and Ramsay are not invited today under any circumstances."

My son remains silent for several seconds. When he speaks again, he sounds genuinely mystified. "You're okay with Eric joining us? I thought you wanted to pummel him into a pile of dust."

"Were you not listening during our discussion in Thane's house last week? I bear no ill will toward Eric. Provided he doesn't harass Iona anymore."

"You really like her, don't you? That's brilliant!"

I roll my eyes, but Toby can't see that. The woman I fucked last night and sort of fucked this morning has just sashayed out of the bathroom, dry but completely nude. The sight of her body distracts me, and I suddenly can't remember what I meant to say to my son.

"Still there, Dad?"

"Did you say something? I wasn't listening."

Toby snorts. "Yeah, I noticed. What I said was it's about time you found a girlfriend, a nice one who doesn't insult you all the time like Mum did."

"Please don't talk about your mother that way. Our divorce might have been acrimonious, but she is still your mum." I slide an arm around Iona's waist, tugging her close. "Besides, you still spend time with your mum, so I assume you don't despise her."

"No, but she isn't a good person. She was always nice to me, though she treated you like a human pile of rotting rubbish. Why did you let me believe you initiated the divorce?"

"Because I believed it was the right thing to do at the time." I rub my forehead. "Now I realize it was the wrong thing."

"Doesn't matter anymore. But where and when should we meet?"

"Just a moment." I hold my mobile to my chest as a sort of poor man's mute button and glance down at Iona. "Darling, would you mind if we had lunch with Toby and Eric at the café? I know Eric has been annoying you lately, but my son might not come if I ban your unwanted suitor."

"It's fine with me. Eric is a sweet laddie at heart."

"Maybe if he sees us together, he'll give up his quest to win your heart." I raise my mobile. "Toby, we'll meet you boys at one o'clock at the café."

"Brilliant!"

Yes, that is my son's favorite word. "See you then, Toby."

I disconnect the call.

And Iona smiles up at me with dimpled cheeks yet again, seeming inordinately pleased with herself.

I raise my brows. "What have I done now, pet?"

"You called me 'darling.' That's a term of endearment."

"True. But I've also called you 'pet' and 'love.' Why does the word darling please you more than the other terms?"

She hoists herself onto her tiptoes to kiss my cheek. "No one has ever called me 'darling' before."

"I'm honored to be the first." I kiss her forehead. "You've been saying something in Gaelic whenever you feel affectionate toward me. What does it mean?"

"The word *gràidh* means dear or darling."

No one else has ever referred to me as "darling," not in Gaelic or English. Iona and I have become better acquainted lately, but I need to learn everything about this woman. She seems like a sweet, wonderful woman who has a spine of steel and a soft heart. I like all of that. But I've been burned—scorched might be a better term—far too many times to jump into a relationship this quickly. My ex-wife did all the scorching. Even Toby doesn't know the full extent of her behavior.

Angela was granted custody of our son. That's how divorce works. The mother is given greater privileges than the father. Only recently have I begun to feel as if Toby and I are getting to know each other.

Iona clasps my hand, walking backward to urge me to follow her. "You promised me breakfast, and I'm fair starved. Come on, Rafe, let's feed each other."

We do precisely that. It's the first time ever that I've enjoyed a playful breakfast with a woman. Iona isn't like anyone else.

As we're cleaning up the dishes, something occurs to me. "Whatever happened to your intruder?"

She shrugs. "The constables couldn't find him. The *cacan* seems to have gone missing. Magnus MacTaggart and his wife, Piper, offered to work with Fergus and Sorley to track down the mystery man. No luck yet."

I don't like this at all. The git who meant to spy on Iona remains at large, free to enact whatever dastardly plan his handler ordered him to undertake. "Aren't you worried? The prat is on the loose."

"Aye." She shuts off the faucet, turning partway toward me. "I refuse to let fear rule my life. That's why I've gone on with my daily routine as if nothing has happened. I won't let one *cacan* upset me."

"I understand that. But I can't help worrying about you."

Chapter Nineteen

Iona

Rafe Knight has insecurities galore, thanks in large part to his ex-wife, I'm fair certain. Toby is a lovely young laddie, and I doubt he inherited those traits from his mother. Rafe might believe he's a bastard, but I intend to expunge all that self-loathing from his psyche no matter how long it takes. Aye, he has become important to me. I despised him at first. But now, I've gotten to know him so much better. He deserves his happily ever after.

Whether I can give that to him is an open question. But I'm willing to try.

So, I clasp his face with my damp hands and kiss him. "You're so sweet, Rafe."

"I can honestly say no one has ever used that term to describe me." He pulls me into his arms and nuzzles the top of my head. "Your hair smells like fragrant flowers, and it's quite soothing to my senses." He lifts his head and clears his throat. "Getting back to the problem at hand, I would feel better about the situation if you let me stay with you for the duration of…whatever might happen. I can sleep in another room or outside in a tent, if you like."

I stare at him blankly for a moment, then burst out laughing. "Oh, Rafe, you absolutely are the sweetest man in the world."

"But you think I'm barmy and don't want me to stay here."

"I never said any such thing."

"Then, do you want me here?"

Cannae help laughing again. "Aye, Rafe, I want you here in every sense. And of course we'll share my bedroom. Dinnae think Maeve or Rowan would want a man sullying their beds. They do come home occasionally."

"They won't be horrified if they come home to find a strange man sleeping in their mother's bed?"

Laughter bubbles out of me again. "No, you silly man. They'll be as thrilled as Toby was when he heard you were with a woman."

"Your laughter is the most beautiful sound on earth and the best balm for any gent's soul."

None of the men I've ever dated would say such a thing to me. They would've been too embarrassed. But I love that Rafe has no shame when it comes to complimenting me. I wonder if he ever feels shame about anything. After all, he did storm into my life like a bolt of lightning and kissed me through the bars of his jail cell. Then he stormed into my hotel room to have a poke of monumental proportions with me.

Aye, it's likely he has no shame whatsoever. And that brings up a question. "Rafe, were you always as shameless and vocal about your feelings as you are now?"

His brows knit together, and his lips tighten. "No one has ever asked me that question, so I've never thought about it."

"Try to think about it now. I'm curious."

He leans his hip against the counter while his gaze goes distant. He doesn't even move a finger for at least thirty seconds. Then he nods his head slowly. "I believe my shamelessness existed before the lightning strike, but it was far more muted. It ballooned after the strike—after my near death at the hands of a bolt of lightning."

"I reckon it makes sense that if the lightning affected your emotions, it would also change your attitude about…everything."

"Angela accused me of becoming a different person, as if I were an alien wearing a human disguise."

"Does Toby feel that way? Or did he at the time?"

Rafe hunches his shoulders. "I don't know. Never asked him. I suppose I was afraid of what he might say."

"I doubt he thinks you're an alien."

Our discussion ends there. I didn't want to press him to talk about himself anymore. Rafe has been through enough in his life, and I can wait until he feels up to exploring his own feelings.

Since we have a few hours to kill before our lunch with the laddies, I convince Rafe to visit Thane's distillery. He makes a pained face when I suggest that. But then he agrees that it could be fun and it will give him a chance to prove to at least one of my brothers that he isn't a horrible man. Rafe suggests that helping him isn't my only goal, and that I'm probably more worried about my intruder than I've let on. A trip to the distillery might help me forget about that incident, at least for a while.

Rafe is a very clever man.

I drive, since he has no idea where the distillery is. It's a wee ways off the main road and hidden behind trees. But there is a driveway, so we aren't careening into the darkness of the unknown, as Rafe quips. I point out it's daytime, but he just smiles. I'm happy to see *him* happy—and relaxed, ready to face the world proudly. He doesn't even seem concerned about having lunch with Toby and Eric.

Everything will work out for Rafe and Toby. I'm certain of that.

But Eric on the other hand…I wish he'd find a girl his own age and give up on pestering me. Then we could be friends.

As we pull into the distillery's car park, I'm surprised to see so many people already filing into the main building, ready for a tour of the facility. Thane's clientele are mostly tourists who prefer to do their sightseeing in the afternoon. But I know he and Rebecca have worked hard to lure in more visitors from more demographics. Clearly, their strategy has paid off. I see adults from their twenties into their seventies or perhaps even older.

I've just parked the car when Rafe speaks. "You're quite proud of your brother's accomplishments, aren't you?"

"How did you know? I didn't say a word."

"True. But you started smiling the moment we reached the distillery complex. And when you glanced at the main building, you lit up even more."

I open the door on my side, but I haven't gotten out yet. "Is there something wrong with feeling proud of Thane?"

"Of course not. But I like seeing you this way. No one would be proud of me, especially since my mum and dad moved to Shropshire to enjoy their dotage in a quaint little cottage. They have no idea what my life is like now, and I mean to keep it that way." He gazes down at his hands and wrings them. "At least they never saw what I was like after the lightning strike. I only told them about it months later, and even then, I downplayed the aftereffects."

"Why would you do that? Don't you get along with your parents?"

"Yes, but—" He lifts one shoulder in a slight shrug. "What's the point of telling my parents everything? It would only upset them and make them worry about my health. I'm their only child, and they had me rather late in life. Mum is eighty-two. Dad is eighty-five."

"Oh, I see. Are they in poor health?"

Rafe flashes me a dark look. "Could we get out of the car? I'm bloody sick of being stuffed inside this tin can."

His anxiety has reared up again, so I'll cut him some slack. Once we've climbed out of the car and start walking toward the main distillery building, Rafe seems less anxious, at least enough that he answers my question.

"My parents are in reasonably good health," he tells me. "Slightly above average for a couple their age."

"I'm glad to hear that."

He throws me a teasing sidelong glance accompanied by a similar smile. "May I know about your mum and dad?"

"I'm happy to tell you about them." I hop onto the pavement, then explain. "My father, Keith, is now seventy-two. My mother, Elsa, is seventy-one. They haven't retired because they love their professions. Da is a leatherworker, and Ma does needlework. They earn a good living, though they have slowed down a wee bit as they got older. Not because they're feeble. It's only because they want to spend more time with family."

"The Buchanans must be a close-knit family. Your brothers are extremely protective of you."

"We are close, aye. Isn't your family like that?"

He chuckles. "My parents would never threaten to beat me into submission, literally, simply because I chose to get involved with someone they didn't like. My parents had no great love for Angela, but they let me make my own decisions." He winces. "Perhaps they shouldn't have. I made a ruddy awful decision when I married Angela. But I can't regret it. She gave me Toby, after all."

"The laddie takes after his father, clearly, and not his mother."

We've just reached the main doors of the distillery, and Rafe holds one side open for me. "It's a miracle Toby turned out as well as he did with two fucked-up parents."

Once we're inside the main hallway, I lay a hand on his arm, stopping us both. "You have a valid reason for being fucked up. Angela is nothing more than rotten a *phitean*."

Rafe grins. "What in the world does that Gaelic word mean? I assume it is Gaelic."

"Aye, it is." I cross my arms. "And it means she's a C-word."

He chuckles again. "You are adorable, Iona. The tough journalist can't speak the C-word."

"You didn't either."

"In solidarity with you, naturally."

"Hmm." I squint at him. "You are full of shite."

Rafe slings his arm around me to crush me to his body. "I am most definitely full of shite, always, every day, until I'm dropped into my grave."

Someone coughs loudly behind Rafe. I cannae see who it is, what with Rafe's large body blocking my view. But then he turns to the side, and I finally can see.

"Are you two done with your foreplay yet?" Thane asks. "Or would ye rather have a poke in the hallway?"

I squint at my brother now. "Rafe and I were having a conversation. And you should be ashamed of yourself for eavesdropping."

"This is a public hallway, Iona. If you want secrecy, go into the restroom and block the door." He rubs his chin. "Come to think of it, Rebecca and I have already done that at least once."

Rafe seems highly amused by my conversation with my brother. "Can't keep track of your naughty interludes, eh? Maybe you should put up a sign warning tourists about that."

I make an irritated sound. "Thane, go back to work. I want to give Rafe a private tour of the facility."

The man in question lifts his brows. "I thought you wanted to show your brother that I'm not a raging arsehole."

"Yes. But Thane is probably too pigheaded to accept the truth, not unless the American Wives Club gets involved. Honestly, it might take a blow to the head with a *caman* to do that."

Rafe's brows draw together over his nose. "The American Wives Club? What in the world is that?"

"Why don't you two come into my office," Thane suggests. "We can grab Rebecca and Fiona along the way, then have a serious discussion about your intruder, Iona."

Thane leads the way, though I know how to find his office. He's my bossy oldest brother, though, which means he believes he's in charge of everything. Even here at the distillery that isn't true. Two strong-willed women handle most of the behind-the-scenes work.

"Who is Fiona?" Rafe whispers as we're following Thane.

"Fiona Sterling is the distillery manager," I say in an equally soft voice. "She used to be Fiona MacTaggart before she married Domhnall Sterling last year."

"How many MacTaggarts and Sterlings are there in this part of Scotland?"

"A normal amount of Sterlings, but a prodigious number of MacTaggarts."

Rafe has been holding my hand, but now he raises it to kiss my knuckles. "Should I expect to be assaulted by every Scotsman in the vicinity of Loch Fairbairn? I assume they all adore you."

"Dinnae fash, *gràidh*. No one will steal me away from you."

Only after the words left my mouth did I realize what I said. Calling him "*gràidh*" doesn't fash me. But declaring that no one will ever steal me away from him…I can't believe I spoke those words.

No, I cannae have strong feelings for a man I hardly know.

We've just reached Thane's office and walked inside, so that at least gives me a distraction from thinking about my potentially strong feelings for Rafe Knight. Thane and Rafe go down the hall to grab two more chairs, then return with them—and with Rebecca and Fiona.

Thane insists I should sit beside Rafe.

For my brother to do that could mean only one thing. He's sure I've become fond of Rafe Knight, and I can't deny it's true. But I am wondering why Thane arranged this meeting.

Everyone just sits here, silent, as if waiting for someone or something.

"What are you waiting for, Thane?" I ask. "We need to be in the village by one o'clock to meet Toby and Eric."

"I know that, but one person hasn't arrived yet." He gazes at me with his usual calm expression, unlike the way he'd behaved on the day Rafe stormed into my life. "Still no news about the intruder yet?"

"The constables couldn't find him. I know Fergus and Sorley are trying, but there just aren't any clues to help them. Couldn't you tap into that black box Ava Marston-Baines gave you?"

"Afraid not. It was for one-time use only, then it self-destructed by erasing all its memory and releasing a capsule that melted all the components."

I slump in my chair. "Too bad. It would've been so helpful."

The door bursts open, and my brother Ramsay stalks into the room.

Chapter Twenty

Rafe

Ramsay Buchanan glowers at me in a very convincing manner, as if he means to throttle me and then toss me to Thane so he can finish me off. But I rather doubt either man wants to assault me. Iona would beat them to death with a *caman* if they tried it. My ex-wife would never have stood up for me if someone leveled insults at me or threatened to murder me. After the lightning strike, she wriggled out of driving me to my physical therapy sessions. Angela also categorically refused to offer any sort of comfort.

Blimey. My heart stopped beating for two minutes and forty-eight seconds. A spouse should stand by their partner in bad times, not run away to find a new lover.

Oh, yes, Angela did that too.

Ramsay stalks up to my chair and glowers at me again. Actually, he never stopped glowering. "Why should we believe Iona's problem isn't your fault?"

"What problem would that be?"

"You know which one, ye *baltan*."

I must seem confused because Iona tells me, "Ramsay called you a C-word."

"Oh, that would make sense considering his rancorous tone. But I still have no idea what 'problem' your brother is referring to."

Thane jumps out of his chair to grasp his brother's arm. "Calm down, Ramsay. This is a strategy meeting, not a cage fight. Maybe Rafe honestly doesn't understand what problem you're talking about."

I fold my arms over my chest as I gaze dispassionately at Ramsay Buchanan. "It might help if you named the issue. I'm not clairvoyant."

"We're talking about the intruder."

Iona lays a hand on my shoulder. "I assume you mean the *cacan* who spied on me, and who Rafe detained."

Ramsay snorts derisively. "Detained? You let him get away, ye eejit."

"He kneed me in the groin. I defy either you or your brother to remain able to fight off an attacker under those circumstances."

Thane studies me with curiosity, his head tipped to one side. "I would've thought such a violent event would be ingrained in your mind. Yet you seem to have completely forgotten it."

"No, I didn't completely forget." I look to Iona, and she seems to understand what I'm trying to ask her without speaking. She kisses my cheek. I take that as confirmation. So, I sigh and face her brothers and the others. "Seven years ago, I was struck by lightning. It was an upward streamer that used me as an auxiliary vein of the bolt itself. I suffered a cardiac arrest, clinically dead for several minutes before my heart miraculously came back to life and brought me with it."

Ramsay stares at me with his upper lip curled. "Dinnae understand what that has to do with why you forgot about the intruder's attack."

"Here's how it's related." I stand up and face Ramsay head-on. "I've suffered long-term issues related to the strike. One of them is forgetfulness, another is my hair-trigger temper."

Ramsay glances back at his brother. "Do you believe his story, Thane?"

"I do."

Ramsay looks at Iona. "What about you? How can you be sure this *bod ceann* won't hurt you when he's in a rage?"

"Because I've gotten to know him. Rafe is a good man who's had terrible things happen to him." She lifts her chin in a defiant expression. "Rafe never hurts anyone but himself—unless someone is attacking him or another innocent person."

The Buchanan brothers exchange a look that I can't decipher. Fortunately, they offer to explain. Thane does the talking. "We trust our sister, and that means we trust you. Iona would never let an abusive man into her life. Besides, Toby told us what a good man you are."

I'm briefly stunned by his declaration. "My son told you that? He's been angry with me lately, so I assumed—"

"Stop assuming. Get the facts before you reach any conclusions."

"Yes, that's good advice." I lift one brow. "Does this mean you and Ramsay won't be shouting at me anymore or threatening to kill me?"

Thane shrugs. "Cannae promise that."

Ramsay chuckles. "I think the Brit is afraid of two burly Scots."

Iona scowls at her brothers, though it's clearly sarcasm. "Don't insult Rafe. If you want him to prove his mettle, challenge him to a shinty match or a round of Highland games. I'm sure he would wipe the field with you two."

Thane and Ramsay stare at their sister for a moment, then start laughing. When they finally stop doing that, Thane pats his sister's arm. "Dinnae worry, *gràidh*. We already know Rafe is no scared rabbit. He chased that intruder away."

"Was there a point to this little meeting?" I ask. "Iona and I do have a lunch appointment."

"Aye, and you'll get there on time," Thane says. "We'll make sure of that. But here's the point of this meeting. We want you to take Iona to England with you for a wee spell, at least until we can capture the *cacan* who's been spying on Iona."

The woman in question springs out of her chair, hands on her hips. "I am not a frightened wee lassie who faints at shadows. I am a journalist, and I can find the *cacan* myself."

"No need for that. Magnus and Piper are already on his trail."

I spring out of my chair. "If your mates are going after the bastard, I need to be there with them."

"No, Rafe. Your job is to take care of Iona." Thane raises a placating hand toward his sister, though she seems less than placated. "Please, *gràidh*, we need to know you'll be safe. Let Rafe take you to England."

The more I listen to the three siblings arguing, the more convinced I become that Thane is right. "Iona should go on holiday in England if only to give those blokes Magnus and Piper a chance to hunt down the intruder."

Everyone goes silent for about three seconds. Then they erupt into laughter.

"What is so bloody funny?" I snarl.

Iona touches my arm. "Piper is a woman and Magnus's wife. I mentioned her to you once."

"Oh, yes, of course." I knife a hand through my hair. "Sorry."

"No apologies necessary. Everyone here knows about your lightning strike injuries now, so they won't harass you about it—much."

The alarm on my watch chimes, reminding me of where I need to be and when. "We should get going, Iona, or we'll be late for lunch with the boys."

We say goodbye to everyone, then I try to drive to the café. Iona swats my hand away when I reach for the handle of the driver's door. I consider arguing the point or perhaps stuffing her in the boot but change my mind. Her mulish nature is part of her charm.

As we pull out of the car park, my mobile chimes. That means I have a new text. Iona reaches into my jacket pocket to retrieve the device. She hands it to me, since there are no other vehicles in the vicinity. I pull up the text. "It's Toby. He says we should meet them in the outdoor section of the café."

I toss the mobile back to Iona.

When we arrive at the café, we spot the boys immediately, before we've even stepped out of the car. Wrought-iron railing surrounds the outdoor patio, so we need to walk through the indoor section and wend our way around tables and chairs to reach the patio.

Toby and Eric both rise halfway from their chairs to greet us. I pull out Iona's chair for her. Toby smirks as if he thinks it's amusing that I would be polite to a woman. Or perhaps my son is simply glad to see me spending time with someone outside of work.

Once we're all seated, we order our food. Then, the interrogation begins.

Toby grins at me. "Can't believe you finally met the right woman. It's about bloody time. By the way, how did your interview with the Buchanan brothers go?"

"Fine. We understand each other."

Eric hasn't spoken except when he greeted us. Now, he uses the excuse of sipping his water to avoid joining in the conversation.

"What about the git who's been spying on Iona?" Toby asks. "Thane and Ramsay can't be happy about that."

"Naturally, they want to pummel the wanker. So do I. But we can't do that until someone finds him." Iona slips her hand into mine under the table, and that simple touch eases my tension. "Thane and Ramsay want the two of us to go to England for a spell. They have a husband-and-wife private detective team on the git's trail."

The boys look at each other and grin, speaking the same words at the same time. "Magnus and Piper."

Both boys make a strange hand signal that I don't understand. It seems to indicate something good, considering the fact they're smiling. I can't keep track of the trends young people invent.

Toby turns to me, still grinning. "Don't worry, Dad. People your age just can't understand the younger ones. We were trying to say it's awesome that Magnus and Piper will be helping you guys. We haven't met them yet, but they sound like badasses."

"Hmm, I see. The children of the world have all gone collectively insane."

"Come on, Dad. We aren't children. Eric and I both have well-paying jobs, and we graduated from uni four years ago."

"What does that prove?"

He rolls his eyes. "That we're full-fledged adults."

I swing my attention to my son's best mate. "Not sure you've been be-having like an adult lately."

Eric winces. "Yeah, I know. But I'm, uh, coming to the conclusion that I've been a complete ass."

"Then you won't be harassing Iona anymore."

"Yeah." He glances at Iona. "Saying sorry isn't really enough, but I can't think of another way to make amends."

Iona's brows shoot up. "You've given up on winning my heart?"

Eric nods. "Toby and I had a long talk about that. Then my mom and Thane gave me a talk of their own. The gist of it is that I realize I've been an ass, and I won't do that anymore."

"Same for me," Toby says. "I shouldn't have gone off on you the way I did, Dad. I pretended to be the one who wanted Iona, so Eric's mum wouldn't find out he'd been bothering her. That's all over now."

Our food arrives, and we and spend the next half hour eating and engag-ing in casual conversation, none of which involves Eric's infatuation with Iona or her stalker. We laugh quite often. I'd been slightly anxious about this meeting, yet it's turned out to be a positive experience. But in the back of my mind, I can't stop thinking about the git who got away from me.

Iona is coming home with me, temporarily. She'll be safe because I will make certain of it. I still have niggling doubts, though, about the whole situation.

"Wake up, Dad," Toby says. "You missed a great joke. A Scottish one Iona told us."

"Sorry." I force myself to focus on the present, rubbing my eyes and tak-ing a deep breath. "I've been thinking about the stalker situation. We have no idea how long that wanker had been surveilling her or how far-reaching that surveillance was."

"What are you suggesting we should do about that?"

"Go to England. The four of us."

Eric's eyes flare wide. "Why me? I'm not a family member. That creep has nothing to do with me."

"Are you certain of that? Iona saw him in at least two separate parts of the village, which suggests he could have been monitoring her for who knows how long." I lean forward, hoping to impress Eric enough that he will listen to me. "You've been to Iona's house multiple times. Her stalker has likely seen you. Please come with us to England. I'll ring Rebecca to discuss the issue with her first, of course."

"Let me call my mom. She'll freak out less if I break the news."

"Don't you live in England, anyway?"

"Yeah." He brings out his mobile and dials a number. "Hey, Mom, it's me. I heard you guys had a big summit this morning at the distillery. Rafe thinks I should go with him and Toby, Iona too, in case that creep is still after her. No, I'll be safe, trust me. Toby and Rafe aren't wimps, and neither am I." He laughs faintly. "Yes, I will come say goodbye before we leave."

I glance at Toby, but he's fixated on his best mate.

Eric laughs outright now. "Mom, I'm not going to be assassinated by anybody, promise. Magnus and Piper will find the guy. Uh-huh." He rolls his eyes, then lowers his voice to whisper. "I love you too, Mom. Jeez, you're so embarrassing."

He says goodbye, ending the call.

"It's set, then?" I ask.

"Yep. We're having a slumber party at the Knight house."

Toby seems excited now, as if he can't wait for that. There will be no "slumber party," but I won't bother pointing that out. I'm glad the boys are in a good mood and the tension between all of us has abated.

We enjoy a Scottish dessert called *cranachan*, then drive to Iona's house so she can pack for the trip. Toby and Eric stay with her whilst I drive to the hotel to retrieve my bags and check out. When I return to Iona's home, three more vehicles are parked along the side of the street, directly in front of Iona's yard.

The persons inside those vehicles have clearly gone into the house. I don't see any evidence of anyone lingering outside.

Just as I mount the steps onto the porch, the door swings open.

Iona flings herself at me, kissing my face repeatedly. I see no reason for her to behave as if I've been gone for ten years. It was only half an hour. Eventually, she takes half a step backward, seizes my hand, and leads me inside.

How and when will the stalker issue be resolved? Sooner or later, we will learn the answer. Will the news be good or bad? The only thing I know for certain is that I will protect Iona and my son at any cost.

Chapter Twenty-One

Eric

While Iona and Rafe stand on the threshold of the front door, kissing like there's no tomorrow, I try to remember the reasons why I thought Iona Buchanan was the only woman for me. The reasons were super important. I remember that much. I believed she would eventually realize nobody else could make her happy.

Uh, why? Not sure anymore.

Iona pulls her lips away from Rafe's and beams at him like he's the sun and the moon and the stars all wrapped up in one gruff British package.

She met him last week.

I spent months trying to find a way to convince Iona we belong together. Every chance I got, I drove to Scotland to see her. Okay, maybe I should've taken the hint every time she called me a "sweet laddie" and suggested I should find a girl my own age.

Rafe and Iona walk into the house hand in hand. When he sees me, Rafe whispers something to Iona and then approaches me. "I'm sorry, Eric. We shouldn't flaunt our relationship in front of you."

"Why not? I deserve to get flaunted." That's not the same thing as flogging, is it? Better look that up on the Merriam-Webster online dictionary later.

Rafe clamps a hand on my shoulder. "Don't feel bad. Iona despised me when we first met. If I could overcome that obstacle, you can find a woman your own age who will appreciate you."

"Yeah, I know. I finally figured that out, and it didn't even involve you beating the crap out of me." I slump my shoulders and stare down at the wood floor. "I finally realized I was just banging my head against a brick wall."

"We'll be good mates, eventually. You can count on it."

I cannot believe how nice he's being after the way I acted—like a total lunatic, that's how I was behaving. When did Rafe turn into a good guy? The asshole who stormed up to Iona's house and raged at her so hard she got him sent to jail.

Things often aren't the way they seem at first. I've learned that lesson the hard way.

Now that Rafe has come back, we're ready to start our journey. But just as we're opening up the trunk—the boot, as Brits and Scots like to say—Thane drives up in his fancy pickup truck. The glare on the truck's windows makes it hard to see who else might be in there, until both doors are thrown open. Thane, my mom, and another guy I don't recognize all pile out of the vehicle, clomping straight up to our little flock.

Iona knows the new guy, though. She smiles and kisses his cheek. "Magnus, how wonderful it is to see you. But I didn't expect you to see us off. Piper didn't come with you?"

"No," says the enormous, musclebound Scottish guy who has the deepest voice I've ever heard. "Piper is at home with the wee one. I'm delivering the message on my own."

"What message?"

"It's about your stalker." Magnus eyes me and Toby upside-down and sideways, like we're members of SPECTRE or something and he might need to crush us into pulp with his bare hands. "Who are these ones? I assume the tall man is Rafe Knight, but these two I don't recognize."

"I'm Eric Taylor," I announce. "And this is my best friend, Toby Knight."

"Then your friend would be Rafe Knight's son. Aye?"

"Yeah. So, what's up with Iona's ghost man?"

Magnus glances at Thane. "Should I tell them? Or would you prefer to do it?"

"I suppose it might be easier coming from me, since the laddies and Rafe already know me." Thane hugs my mom to his side, and they exchange whispers that I can't make out. Then the whisky man aims his attention at Iona. "You shouldn't travel by car, *gràidh*. It would take at least nine hours."

"Why does that matter?"

"Because we still haven't found your stalker, and I dinnae like having him running around in the Highlands in secret. He has a mobile phone, but he must have masked it somehow, so we can't track him that way either." Thane walks up to his sister, grasping her shoulders. "Please, Iona, let Rafe and the others take you to England, to his home. I trust him to protect you if that *cacan* manages to find you there."

She kisses her brother's cheek. "I'll do what you say, Thane."

I raise my hand like a kid in school, not sure why. Maybe because Toby and I are the youngest people in this group. "May I ask a question?"

Thane chuckles. "Of course, laddie. This isn't primary school."

"Well, I'm wondering how we're going to get to England if we don't drive."

"On a jet, that's how."

"I hate airline seats. They're so cramped and uncomfortable. Driving would be better than that."

Thane gives me a tolerant smile. "Did I mention commercial airlines? No." He shakes his head at me. "You're flying private, laddie. Lachlan MacTaggart is lending us his jet."

"Wicked!" Okay, I probably shouldn't have shouted that. Oh, who the hell cares? I'm stoked. "That'll get us there in no time, huh?"

"Don't get too excited, sweetie," my mom says. "You'll have to drive about an hour and a half to reach Inverness, the closest airport. Then it'll be about an hour or so of in-flight travel."

Two and a half hours total, approximately. Yeah, that's not bad at all. "Uh, where exactly are we going in England?"

My best friend elbows me in the side. Then he whispers out of the corner of his mouth. "To Dad's house, moron. We already went over that."

"Not all of it. Where does Rafe live, exactly?" I forgot to whisper, so now Toby is giving me a disgusted look. He'll get over it.

Rafe speaks up. "My home is just outside Norwich. But my research lab is a bit further away, situated on a rather large plot of land."

I prepare to ask more questions, but I don't get the chance. Thane and Mom need to say goodbye to Iona, then me. My mom gets embarrassingly gushy, hugging me and kissing my cheek while blubbering about how much she'll miss me. Jeez, I live in England. She's shacking up with Thane in Scotland. That means she doesn't see me all the time.

Toby doesn't need to say goodbye to his dad. Rafe is coming with us.

"Listen up, laddies and lasses," Thane shouts. "Rebecca and I will lead the way to Inverness, but we'll be dropping Magnus off along the way. Then, it's on to the airport and London after that."

Magnus managed to steer clear of the gushiness by jumping into the backseat of Thane's truck. I wish I could do that. Mom is going overboard big time.

Finally, Thane and Mom climb into the truck with the gruff private eye who masquerades as a bounty hunter. But they still don't leave. Only after the rest of us have piled into Rafe's car do we finally get on the road. Thane veers around our vehicle while grinning at us. He's a weird guy, but I've gotten to like him way more than I expected. Sometimes I even wish Thane were my dad, since my real one is a jackass.

During the ride to the Inverness airport, we play the kind of silly traveling games my family had never really been into when I was a kid. We didn't travel that much, actually. Now I get to play games with my best friend, his dad, and Iona. They're all amazing people.

We drop Magnus off in Ballachulish along the way.

By the time we reach the airport, I'm getting excited about seeing Rafe's "rather large plot of land." It's an intriguing mystery, just like the man himself. Lightning researcher? I'll need to quiz him about that in flight.

Turns out we don't even need to go through security at the airport. Flying private has its perks, for sure. On the tarmac, we say our goodbyes again since my mom insisted on walking to the jet with me like I'm a six-year-old who needs his mommy to hold his hand. Thane had wanted to just turn around and drive away without leaving his truck.

Yeah, like Mom would let him get away with that.

Another goodbye, then we're on board and in the air.

This is going to be the best vacation ever.

Except for that niggling worry we all have about Iona's stalker. Maybe I don't want to marry her anymore, but I still care about her safety. And I'll do whatever it takes to ensure nobody hurts her—or any of my friends and family.

Chapter Twenty-Two

Iona

What a whirlwind my life has been over the past week. My quiet life as a journalist who writes about cows and school plays has exploded, and now I'm on the run from my own home. At least I have good company. Since Eric has given up on his quest to win my heart, we've become friends—in the past few hours. It's hard to remember what my life was like only a week or so ago. The new world I find myself in offers so much more than I could have imagined.

As soon as the jet reaches cruising altitude, which I know because the pilot announced that over the intercom, Eric begins to quiz Rafe. He seems sincerely fascinated by the man. Rafe has fascinated me since the day we met, even when I thought I hated him. But my interest in him is nothing like what Eric wants to know about the man.

We've all been sitting around a table that has chairs at either side of it. That allows us to see each other quite well. Eric sits beside Toby, while Rafe and I relax in the chairs opposite them.

Eric now leans forward, setting his elbows on his thighs. "So, Rafe, what did you mean when you said you've got a 'rather large plot of land'? That's kinda vague."

"I enjoy being vague. It keeps everyone else on their toes." Just as Eric seems about to complain, Rafe winks. "I was joking. The large plot belongs to my company. Unlike most lightning research firms, I do not work for a university or any other sort of educational endeavor."

"You're independent, huh?"

"Exactly. My company resides on that rather large plot—five thousand acres, to be precise. All our research begins there, though we also do field work outside of the UK."

"Your work sounds awesome. But does the UK really get much lightning?"

Rafe raises his brows. "You've lived in the UK for years. Haven't you seen any thunderstorms?"

"Well, uh…no? That makes me weird, huh."

"Never worry about being 'weird,' Eric. Being normal is very blasé. Why do you think I gravitated toward fulminology years before I was struck by lightning?"

I can't help interjecting. "Fulma-what?"

Rafe smiles. "Fulminology, pet. It's the study of lightning."

Eric's eyes light up, and he leans forward more, grasping his knees. "So, you're a fulminologist?"

"Yes. That's why my research group is based in southeast England, where the most lightning occurs in the whole of the country." Rafe smiles with a deviousness that makes me want to drag him into the bedroom. "I even built my own Tesla coil."

"Holy shit!" Eric grins. "You're my new hero, man. You are so based."

"I would thank you for the compliment if I knew what it meant."

Toby shakes his head. "Dad, you are so old. But Eric is right, you are totally based."

Rafe's brows wrinkle. "And that means…"

"You're super cool. Is that what you elderly people would say?"

"Watch your mouth, little twat. You'll be old soon enough."

The men go on teasing each other with generational insults, but I lose track of their conversation. My mind insists on letting me see only one thing—Rafe's face. Every time he smiles, at anyone, I feel warm and soft, and I want to crawl onto his lap. Naturally, I want to ask him questions, but not in front of the laddies.

My hopes of getting Rafe alone before the jet lands are dashed when the pilot announces we'll be touching down at Norwich in five minutes. I assumed we would need to land at one of the London airports and drive to Norwich, but I was wrong. I'd only been to England a few times in my life before now. It's hardly surprising that I know so little about the region.

Once again, we don't need to pass through security when we exit the plane. I wish I could always travel by private jet, but unfortunately, I don't have that sort of money. Billionaires like Evan MacTaggart might need their own jets to whisk to and from international meetings, but a lowly small-town journalist like me has no need for outrageous amenities.

A car is waiting for us on the tarmac.

The moment the co-pilot opens the door, Toby and Eric shout excitedly and slide down the handrail of the air stairs. Rafe holds my hand as we carefully make our way down the stairs. Only young laddies would slide down them. When we reach the ground, I realize why those two were so excited. The limousine parked on the tarmac has a passenger who's waiting for us beside the car.

And it's Courtney Taylor, Eric's fraternal twin sister.

He and Toby take turns hugging the lass firmly. They chatter away too, but I'm not close enough to make out the words yet. As Rafe and I amble toward the trio, I have to ask about something.

"I didn't realize Toby was good mates with Courtney too."

"Oh, yes, she's one of the gang. Courtney has the thankless job of trying to wrangle the boys and inject some small measure of sanity into their antics."

"I've met Courtney once. Dinnae think I'll get much chance to speak to her before she leaves."

Rafe halts, turning slightly toward me. "Leave? I gather no one told you. I assumed you'd overheard the conversation we gents had on the jet."

"Clearly not. I fell asleep for a wee while."

"I thought so. But your hair fell over your eyes, and I couldn't be sure."

"So, what did I miss?"

Rafe smirks. "Courtney is joining us at my home. That's the information you missed during your cat nap. Eric received a text from his sister whilst we were in flight."

"That's wonderful. I'd love the chance to spend time with the lass."

Someone whistles, and even here in the outdoors the piercing noise rattles my eardrums. I glance around and see Eric is the perpetrator.

"Hurry up, guys!" he shouts. "Get your butts in the limo. Some of us want to get to Rafe's place before New Year's twenty-thirty. Oh, wait, you old farts will be dead by then."

That cheeky laddie. Now that he's given up winning my heart, he's become terribly sarcastic.

"Watch it, tosser," Rafe calls out. "I might throw you out the window as we're speeding down the road."

Rafe lifts me into his arms and jogs toward the limo. Eric swings the rear door open as Toby waves his arm in a grand gesture, beckoning us to jump inside. Somehow, Rafe manages to keep me in his arms while he climbs inside the vehicle. He also sits down on the bench seat without releasing me. Now, I'm sitting sideways on his lap.

The laddies wait for Courtney to get inside the vehicle before they finally jump in too. What chivalrous men. I had no idea young laddies could show this much respect for a woman. That makes me wonder about Toby's mother. She sounds like the worst sort of narcissist, and I cannae understand how she could be loving toward her son yet treat Rafe like the enemy. Toby must take after his father. He's a sweet laddie.

And so is Rafe. Well, he's not a laddie. But he is a sweet man underneath all his blustering.

We arrive at Rafe's home in the early evening. It feels like no time at all has passed since we left Loch Fairbairn. The limo driver drops us off and offers to carry our luggage into the house, but Rafe shoos the man away. He does give the driver a sizable tip, so the gent doesn't mind being gotten rid of, not at all. In fact, he waves goodbye and smiles as he drives away.

At last, I turn toward the house. And my jaw drops. "*Pit air iteig*, Rafe. Your house is enormous."

He tucks me under his arm and chuckles. "Didn't I warn you? Sorry. I meant to give you just enough details that it would be a lovely surprise when you lot saw my home. But it isn't as palatial as you're implying with that exclamation of shock."

I jab my elbow into his side. "You sneaky *riatach*. Were you afraid I would get my hooks in you and steal all your money?"

"Of course not." He kisses the top of my head. "Let's all go inside. I'm a bit peckish, despite the meal we enjoyed in flight."

"Yes, it was kind of Lachlan MacTaggart to lend us his chef."

When did Lachlan hire a chef? The one time I flew on his jet, the only food available was a fine selection of prepackaged snacks.

Lachlan must have grown his wealth lately.

Rafe digs his car keys out of his pocket and tosses them to his son so Toby can unlock the door. Then he, Eric, and Courtney rush into the house ahead of us, laughing and joking. We can hear their laughter even before we reach the concrete walkway that leads up to the door. Thankfully, Rafe does not insist on carrying me over the threshold, though it wouldn't have surprised me if he tried. I prefer to walk under my own power.

Once Rafe has shut the door, I let him lead me into the living room before I begin my inquisition. The youngsters have gone into the kitchen.

"Cook enough for all of us," Rafe shouts toward the kitchen. "Elderly people like us need more food than you children do."

Laughter erupts from the kitchen.

Rafe shepherds me over to an L-shaped sofa and drops onto it, his weight causing a *thump* sound. Then he pats the cushion beside him. "Sit beside me, darling, please. I need the feel and scent of you around me. I've become addicted to your presence."

I dutifully settle onto the cushion right next to him, cuddling closer. "You aren't the only one with a fixation. Dinnae think I can sleep or go anywhere without you anymore. You are my human security blanket."

"Whether that's a compliment or not is hard to say." He lifts my hand to his face and kisses each knuckle one by one. "But I can tell you with absolute certainty that I never want to be without you."

That statement, along with my "human security blanket" remark, seems to contradict what I've been telling myself for days now. I feel happier and safer with Rafe than I do with my own family.

He rubs his cheek against mine. "You always smell like every sweet, savory thing imaginable. I could devour you right here on the sofa with the children in the kitchen."

"We shouldn't call them children, should we? They're adults."

He makes a derisive noise. "They aren't acting like it today."

The children—um, young adults—emerge from the kitchen carrying plates of food. Toby has a tablecloth tucked under one arm, and he now spreads that out on the coffee table. Courtney and Eric lay the food items out, with each plate or bowl holding one dish. They've done a splendid job of setting the meal, and I'm impressed. Rafe seems equally amazed.

And the food is as impressive as the presentation.

The fare might not be restaurant class, but it's delicious and recharges all of us after our journey. Though Eric, Toby, and Courtney have their own flats, none of them live nearby or even in the same vicinity. So, they suggest staying here would be the best option. Thane did say we should stay together. I've lived alone for so long that it's hard to remember when that wasn't the case. I had my daughters with me for quite some time—until they went away to university.

Aye, I'd been alone ever since then. But I am not alone anymore. I have a big, sexy Brit in my life.

Our evening meal leaves us all feeling relaxed and rather sleepy. Rafe's house might be larger than mine in Scotland, and larger than most houses I've seen in Loch Fairbairn. He has enough rooms for everyone with four upstairs bedrooms and two downstairs. Toby quips that only his father and I should remain downstairs, otherwise everyone else might be "kept awake until dawn by the old farts shagging."

As it turns out, Rafe and I go to bed a few minutes later—and all we do is crawl into bed and drift off. Aye, we do sleep naked. Strictly because we're too exhausted to open up our luggage and find our nightclothes.

I wake up in the morning feeling oddly good considering the circumstances. Though I don't believe that *cacan* who assaulted Rafe will be able to track me down here in England, I still suffer from a wee bit of anxiety. That feeling crumbles away as soon as Rafe awakens and rolls onto his side to smile at me sleepily.

Then he yawns loudly.

I tousle his hair with my fingers. "*Madainn mhath, gràidh*. How do you feel?"

His brows lift. "That depends on whether you explain the alien language you were spouting. You've told me *gràidh* means 'darling.' But the rest is gibberish."

I feign offense. "Gaelic is not gibberish, you Sassenach."

Rafe chuckles. "Do Scots really still call us Sassenachs?"

"No, not unless a Brit annoys us. But you wanted to know what I said to you. *Madainn mhath* means 'good morning' in Gaelic."

"Fascinating. You must be trying to indoctrinate me into the Scots cult by feeding me Gaelic when I'm only half awake." He rolls on top of me, though he carefully holds his body a few inches above mine so he won't crush me. "Time for a morning shag. If the children hear us, they might faint. Shall we risk it?"

"Oh, aye, right now."

Chapter Twenty-Three

Rafe

Do elderly people shag first thing in the morning? Naturally, we do. Our children jokingly like to tell us we're ancient and bound for a nursing home, but Iona has the stamina and strength of a lass half her age. I've discovered a new vigor since I met her. That means I can shag her until sundown, and neither of us will expire from dual strokes. Worries about the git who had spied on Iona linger in the back of my mind twenty-four hours a day, sunup to sundown. But I won't allow those concerns to ruin my day.

Or my morning.

I gently rest my full weight on Iona, briefly, only so I can push my arms under her body and flip us both over. Now I'm beneath her. "Go on, darling, shag me for as long and as hard as you like."

She tickles my lips with her fingertips. "Are you sure you can handle me? After all, you are older than I am, and you've been struck by lightning. I wouldn't want to give you a heart attack."

I smack her arse. "Cheeky chit. If I could survive a lightning strike, nothing you do could possibly harm me."

"Good to know." She sets her hands on my chest and pushes up into a sitting position astride my hips. "How much do you trust me?"

"Completely, irrevocably, one hundred percent."

Her sweet little smile gives me another one of those odd pangs in my chest. But I've come to realize that's a good thing. A pang like that means I have deeper feelings for her. My affection for Iona will heat up our shagging.

She walks her fingers up my chest slowly. "What if the children come running down the stairs while we're having a poke?"

"I don't give a flying toss."

The beautiful lass laughs.

And I thrust my hips up, making her emit a sharp squeak. "Get it on with getting it on, would you? I might fall back asleep if you keep delaying."

Her lips curl into a deviously sexy smile. She wriggles backward until she can shove one knee between my thighs to part them for her. Will I fight her wishes? Never. Iona can do anything she likes to me.

Iona wriggles again, shimmying backward until her face lies directly above my cock. Then she lies down, holding her head up by resting her elbows on my hips. The temptress raises her head just enough to make certain I see it when she drags her tongue across her lips, wetting them.

Suddenly, my breathing grows heavier.

The temptress flings her head side to side, grazing her hair over my cock with every swing. The delicately sensual sensation drives me mad. I want to flip us both over so I can fuck her right now. But I agreed to her suggestion, and whatever else I might be, I am not a liar. I'll endure Iona's delicious torture for as long as she cares to keep going.

The curtain of Iona's hair envelops her face, leaving me unable to watch her expressions whilst she goes down on me. First, she drags her tongue up my cock from the base to the crown, moaning as if she loves doing this to me. I fucking love it, that's for sure. When she wraps her tongue around my crown, I fist my hands in the sheets. But when she sinks her mouth down over my length, sucking gently along the way, a shout explodes out of me.

"Bloody hell, Iona, you're driving me mad."

She flicks her eyes up to glance at me even as she begins to pump my length with her mouth. But when she adds one hand to the mix, I'm lost. Speechless, mindless, I grip the headboard and unleash grunts, growls, and hoarse shouts.

What if our children hear what's going on in this room?

I don't give a damn.

She slides her other hand beneath my cock, pushing it forward until she finds the skin behind my bollocks. Her soft fingers massage my perineum. It's the most erotic and unbelievably arousing sensation. No woman has ever done this to me. My back arches whilst she gives up my erection so she can pull one of my balls into her mouth and suckles it.

My entire body jerks. "Ah!"

Iona raises herself up on her elbows. "What's your pleasure, Rafe? Blow job or fucking?"

Since I can't speak, still breathless from what she's done, I simply shake my head weakly.

"My choice, then?" she says. "All right. This is what I choose."

She swallows my cock and sucks it as if I'm a giant lollipop, grunting repeatedly, massaging my bollocks the whole time. I gasp for breath but can't get any air. All I can do is grip the headboard even harder and arch my back, releasing strangled noises.

Then the rapid spasms begin, racing down my spine like bolts of mini lightning, and I can't stop myself from coming. Not that I tried. No chance in hell of that. The spasms reach my cock at last, and I erupt inside her mouth.

She swallows over and over, devouring everything I have, then sits up and licks her lips. And she smiles. "Ye taste almost as good as *milsean*. I could spend all day doing nothing but devouring you."

"And what is *milsean*?"

"Sweets or dessert."

"Gaelic is an intriguing language. Or perhaps I find it fascinating because you speak those foreign words in your sexy voice." With a bit of a struggle, I manage to sit upright. Then I reach up to cup one tit. "Your turn, pet. Lie down for me, please."

Iona crawls on all fours and lies down on her stomach.

"Your arse is lovely, darling, but I mean to use my tongue on you. Can't do that when you're lying on your stomach."

She glances at me over her shoulder. "You are the most creative lover I've ever had. Surely the great Rafe Knight can figure out how to make this situation work."

"'The great Rafe Knight?'" I can't help chuckling. "That's one phrase I've never heard before. But I'm afraid you'll need to turn over."

She wriggles her arse. "Dinnae want to move."

"If that's how you feel..." I slide both arms beneath her and flip the cheeky woman over so she's now lying on her back. "There. That's better."

She gives me an exaggerated pout.

"Time to pleasure you, pet." I lie down between her thighs and spread her labia gradually, using two fingers and gliding them down to her folds. I've left plenty of room for what I have planned. Phase one, teasing her labia. I use my thumb to do that, lightly tracing the nail up and down whilst she wriggles. "You like this, don't you? I've only just gotten started, and I have so many other ways I want to touch you before I finally let you come."

"Oh, yes, Rafe. This feels wonderful."

I haven't even touched her clitoris yet and already she's biting her lip. The scent of her juices wafts around me, a heady distraction that's hard to ignore. Self-control has never been my strongest attribute, not even before the lightning strike. But I will do my damnedest to give her the ultimate in cunnilingus.

Lowering my head, I touch my lips to her clit, just barely.

Iona jerks. A sharp little cry spills from her lips, and her breasts begin to heave. The sight of those tits rising and falling distracts me for only a second or two. Then I resume teasing her. I nip her nub, then pull my mouth away. She issues the most adorable noise of sheer frustration. Her tongue pokes out between her parted lips as she follows my every movement.

As I glide my fingers up and down her labia, avoiding her folds, I resolutely refuse to let her come yet. Instead, I nuzzle the hairs on her mound. When I blow a gently heated breath onto those hairs, she tries to thrash her legs. But I prevent that. My body is pinning her down.

She unleashes a desperate string of what must be Gaelic. It isn't the King's English, that's a certainty.

I slide my fingers down to her folds and massage them slowly.

Her back arches again. "Oh, God, Rafe. Please make me come, please."

"No." I take her clit into my mouth and suckle it fiercely, over and over, as she issues incomprehensible sounds that I suspect are meant to be words. In what language, I can't say. "Are you asking me to make you come, pet? Is it too intense for you? Nod your head if that's what you want."

Iona nods, biting down on her lip.

"All right, then."

I dive in fully this time, using one hand to hold her labia open and pet them whilst I go down on her in earnest. Her panting breaths and faint whimpers tell me she is desperate for a climax. I seal my lips around her nub and suck hard, flicking my tongue. When I glance up at her, the sight steals my breath away. Her chest is dappled with pale, rosy pink—her cheeks too. Her lips are swollen from her highly aroused state.

That sight alone sends blood rushing to my groin.

I give up on holding her labia open and thrust two fingers inside her channel. She cries out. But she doesn't come until I roughly pet her inner walls whilst consuming her clit. That's when Iona explodes like a thermonuclear runaway supernova.

No, I did not make that up. It's a real type of stellar explosion.

Iona's body tries to fold itself into a pretzel, but my weight prevents her from doing that. She screams with enough volume that our children must have heard it from upstairs. By the time her climax fades, she's covered with a light sheen of sweat and the aroma of her cream fills the air. That scent amps up my lust. My cock has thickened, but not enough for me to fuck her yet.

So, I sit back on my heels and gaze down at the beautifully satiated woman lying in front of me. "Bloody hell, Iona. You look like sin incarnate, lying there that way. I want to shag you right now, but I'm not a young man anymore. Can't get stimulated again as quickly as I'd like."

"I have a secret weapon that might speed things up."

"And what is that? A shot of methamphetamine?"

She crawls toward me on her knees and rests her hands on my chest. "No illicit substances are involved. If you trust me completely, as you said earlier, then you will give my secret weapon a try. Unless ye dinnae want to have a poke after all."

"Oh, no, I intend to fuck you right now, here in this bedroom, even if I have to wait an hour for my cock to rouse."

She wags a finger at me. "I told you it won't take that long."

Iona hops off the bed and kneels to open up a compartment in the bottom portion of the nightstand. She brings something out of the depths but hides it behind her body. "Close your eyes, Rafe."

Well, I did vow that I trust her implicitly. I stepped into her sexy trap, and I will not back out no matter what barmy thing she does.

I close my eyes.

The bed jostles, a sure sign Iona has crawled onto it again. Then I hear other noises I can't identify. "Open your mouth, *gràidh*."

Dutifully, I obey her command. Then she touches something cool, smooth, and hard to my lips. What on earth? That object now tips upward slightly as liquid streams into my mouth. More of the fluid passes over my tongue, and the rich flavors of it tease my senses. Once Iona has pulled the bottle away, I take a moment to sort out what I'm experiencing.

"Is this whisky? It doesn't taste like Thane Black Label."

"Because it isn't." She lights a soft kiss on my lips. "You can open your eyes now."

I gaze at the bottle she holds between us. "Is that Thane's whisky? I've already tasted that. You know I don't care for single malts."

"But you only tried Thane Black Label, the least exciting of his single malts. The second tier is Sensual Secret, a whisky that's even smoother and more interesting than the Black Label version." She raises the bottle. "But the newest variety, Dùndubhan Masterpiece, offers more than simply a delight for your senses. It's magical too."

I peer deeply into her eyes. "Hmm, your pupils aren't dilated any more than is normal after an orgasm. That means you must have fallen off your rocker hard enough that you have a concussion."

"Let me demonstrate for you." Iona takes a sip of the whisky. Her lids flutter shut, and she moans with satisfaction. Then her lids open. "Don't you want to at least try Dùndubhan Masterpiece?"

She holds the bottle to her chest, between her breasts, and pushes those mounds together as if she's cradling the whisky. As I stare at her tits, she thrusts one finger into the bottle, and it emerges drenched in whisky. It's drizzling down her one tit.

"Yes, all right, I'll try it, you little vixen." I snatch the bottle away from her and swig a mouthful. And I burst into a fit of coughing. "Blimey. That rot is deadly."

"Wait until it pulses in your veins."

"You didn't mention any vampiric aspect to this whisky. I'll submit myself to that ritual only if you're the one who bites my neck."

Iona leans in, places her teeth on my throat, and nips my skin.

What else can I do? I down another mouthful of Dùndubhan Masterpiece, then I pounce on her.

Chapter Twenty-Four

Iona

Rafe leaps on me like a panther, growling softly like one too, and bares his teeth. "The beast needs to feed, pet, and you are my nourishment. There's nothing like a good, hard fuck to reinvigorate our elderly bodies." He winks. "But I don't feel old at all when I'm with you. Certainly not when we're 'having a poke.' I love that you use that term. But now, I need to pounce on you."

I giggle like a schoolgirl. A mature woman shouldn't do that, but I dinnae care what anyone thinks of me. Rafe likes everything about me, and I feel the same about him.

Now he literally pounces on me. His hands and knees land at either side of my body. He growls again, slightly louder this time.

I reach up to hold his face in my hands.

Rafe kisses my palm, licking it like a cat might do.

And then someone knocks on the bedroom door. "Dad? Is everything all right in there? Sounded like a large animal was threatening to attack you. Maybe Eric and I should rescue you and Iona."

Naturally, there was a significant amount of sarcasm in Toby's voice.

"Oh, leave them alone," Courtney says. "If a puma rips them apart, we'll have the whole house to ourselves."

"And Rafe's car," Eric adds. "I saw his Audi A6 in the garage. That's a wicked four-door sports car."

Rafe sits back on his heels and sighs.

I sit up and hug him as I murmur, "It's their way of showing affection."

"Yes, I know." His tone is equally soft. "But I was looking forward to fucking you like a wild animal."

"We can do that later."

Rafe slides off the bed and shouts toward the door, "We're coming, once we've gotten dressed. You lot have ruined our morning entertainment, so you should be the ones to make breakfast."

Laughter ensues, followed by footfalls clapping down the hall.

Rafe and I take our time getting dressed. Why hurry? The children will be making breakfast for us. Besides, I need to rifle through my bags to find what I want to wear today. Our swift departure from Scotland didn't give me much time for neatly packing. Rafe hastily stuffed everything into his bags. I don't feel slovenly after watching him pack.

When we walk into the living room, Rafe and I both halt and stare. Why? Our children are singing a song I don't recognize, probably something very modern, and they're dancing too. Every so often, they give each other high-fives in unison. Then they go back to singing and dancing—while whipping up a meal for all of us.

Rafe holds my hand, as usual, when we approach the kitchen island. He gazes at the youngsters while shaking his head, seemingly baffled by the display going on in front of us. "You lot are barmy. Are all young people off their trolleys these days?"

Toby grins. "Chill, Dad. You'll ruin your rep as a totally based old coot if you keep acting like a senior citizen."

"I'm fifty-one, you git, not eighty."

"Are you sure about that? I mean, you and Iona went to bed early last night, just like senior citizens do." Toby glances at Eric and grins. "See? I told you this house is an old folks' home. Dad and Iona couldn't stay awake past ten."

Eric laughs. "The insults are flying, Knight family style."

Courtney elbows him in the side. "Shut up, Eric. You and Toby are such babies."

Rafe bars his arms over his chest. "Is there actual food here? Or are we meant to pretend we're eating?"

Toby's jaw drops in a thoroughly sarcastic expression. "I'll have you know we've been slaving away over a hot stove to feed you nursing-home residents."

"Enough old-people humor. It's getting quite annoying."

I slide my arm round his waist. "Relax, *gràidh*. We should be happy that the children are having a good time instead of worrying about my intruder."

Eric grins. "Aw, you called Rafe 'dear.' Isn't that sweet? I know about '*gràidh*' because Thane uses the same nickname for my mom."

"Aye, he does. It's a common Gaelic endearment in the Highlands."

Now that the children have calmed down, we all sit at the dining room table to enjoy our food.

I study the dishes, rather confused by what I see. "What have you cooked for us? Dinnae recognize most of these foods."

Toby aims a tolerant smile at me. "That's because you're the older generation. Younger men and women like to switch things up."

Rafe squints at his son. "Switch things up how? I'd rather have a good fry up."

"Yeah, I know. But the kids made breakfast, so deal with it. You could express a little bit of gratitude."

Rafe glances at the foods again and then nods. "You're right. Sorry. I'm sure whatever you've cooked will be lovely."

"Aye, it will," I say. "But we might, um, need explanations of what these dishes are. Since we're very elderly."

Toby chuckles. "Sure, Iona. We can do that."

Eric clears his throat. "We figured you guys would need a breakfast road map, and I've been assigned the task of explaining."

I look at Rafe, who shrugs, then face the children. "We're ready."

"We'll start with the dish that's closest to you guys and go from there." Eric sits up a wee bit straighter, seeming to enjoy his emcee duties. "First up, we have egg curry, a perennial fave at the frat house Toby and I lived in during our college days."

Rafe's brows wrinkle. "What is a 'fave'?"

"It's short for 'favorite.' Capisce?"

"Yes, I've watched mafia movies on the telly."

Eric continues. "Toby and I had an argument about what to call this while you two"—He mimes a cartoonish wink— "were 'getting dressed' earlier. But eventually, we agreed on the name." He points to a plate of…something. "This is British-American eggy bread. Still think 'eggy' sounds dumb, but whatever. Anyway, this consists of two pieces of bread drowned in a sweet egg mixture and folded over. The sandwich is filled with three kinds of melted cheese."

Rafe's lip curls. "That sounds ruddy awful. Did you get this idea by hunting through dumpsters?"

"Ha-ha. This is a popular breakfast item among our friends."

I lay a hand on Rafe's thigh under the table, giving it a wee squeeze. "We'll try it, won't we? And there will be no lip-curling."

Rafe nods, though it's a somewhat resigned expression.

"I'm sure you'll like this one, Rafe," Eric says. "Toby told me this is the Knight family way of toasting bread—almost burned. So, we made burnt toast with three different toppings to choose from, or you can put them all on one piece of bread. You've got avocado, two kinds of jam, nut butter, and syrup. Courtney insisted on making mini pancakes with wheat germ and pecans. It's kind of too normal for me, but whatever."

Toby nudges Eric in the side. "You forgot to tell them about the spicy hash browns."

"You just told them, so I don't need to."

I smile. "Thank you, all of you, for creating this wonderful breakfast. I can't wait to try these dishes. You can't wait either, can you, Rafe?"

"Oh, yes, I'm thrilled beyond measure."

Despite the sarcasm in Rafe's tone, I have a feeling he'll change his mind once he tastes the food. And as it turns out, he does develop an appreciation for the unusual delicacies these young adults favor. We both try every dish. I whisper into Rafe's ear to let him know all the naughty things I'll do to him later if he refrains from criticizing the food. These three lovely young people spent a good deal of time concocting a fine breakfast for us. We express our thanks once the meal is over, and the youngsters' faces light up.

Even Rafe smiles. He appreciates what Toby, Courtney, and Eric have done for us. So do I. It was a very sweet gesture.

Rafe and I insist on washing the dishes and cleaning up after our breakfast. The children sit on the sofa to play a board game, something called Telestrations. I have never heard of it, and neither has Rafe. But apparently, it's been around for a good while. Since it sounds like a children's game, I doubt Rafe or I will join them.

Just as we finish cleaning up, Toby throws his arms up and exclaims, "I am the king of Norwich Telestrations! That's not much of a prize, mind you. No one will ever know I've won for the entire town."

Courtney and Eric jump off the sofa and bow down to their friend. "Toby Knight is the king, Toby Knight is the king…"

"Enough," Rafe grouchily shouts. "Do you want to go on playing children's games? Or would you rather visit my research facility? If you're very, very good, I might let you touch my Tesla coil."

Oddly, that statement sounds erotic to me. Rafe can touch my Tesla coil anytime, not that I have a clue what one looks like or how it works. Rafe could say any unusual phrase, and it would make me randy.

Toby leaps over the back of the sofa. "You're really going to show me your mad-scientist laboratory? I've begged you to give me a tour for years, but you always had excuses why you couldn't."

Rafe comes around behind the sofa and sets a hand on Toby's shoulder. "I'm sorry. I shouldn't have done that. It's just that—Well, never mind."

"Come on, Dad. You can't stop mid-sentence."

"I know." Rafe glances at Eric and Courtney. "It's only that your mother made me swear I'd never take you to my lab."

Toby bows his head and sighs. Then he looks up at his father. "Yeah, Mum can be kind of…rigid. She made me swear to the same thing. I shouldn't have gone along with that."

"You were a teenager. Our marital problems shouldn't have bled into my relationship with you." Rafe gives Toby's shoulder a squeeze. "From now on, no secrets."

Toby nods.

I can't help feeling a wee bit excited. "Are we going to your lab, then, Rafe?"

He chuckles. "Yes, pet. You are adorably excited about it. Are you planning to write an article about me?"

"I hadn't thought of that. Your work, and what it's cost you, would make an excellent story." My mobile phone chimes, and I check the text message by rote. "This is from Maeve. She and Rowan are standing outside this house right now."

"Come inside!" Rafe shouts. "The door is unlocked."

The door bursts open, and my daughters rush over here to hug me. They talk so fast, and talk over each other so much, that I cannae understand any of it. Finally, the lasses calm down enough to speak.

"Are you all right, Mam?" Rowan asks. "I know I was supposed to stay with Evan and Keely in Inverness, and Maeve was told to stay at school, but we just couldn't do that. You're in danger."

I hug both my daughters at the same time and kiss their cheeks. "Dinnae fash. I'm in good hands with Rafe. He would never let anyone hurt me."

Rowan and Maeve peer around me, and their eyes widen.

"Who is that?" Rowan asks, sounding slightly breathless. "He's gorgeous."

"Oh, aye," Maeve concurs. "Is he your new boyfriend? About time you found someone."

Rowan's gaze grows almost flinty. "Is this Rafe, the beast we heard about? The *bod ceann* who assaulted our Mam?"

I can't help reverting to my mother voice. "Rafe never assaulted me. His behavior early on was a misunderstanding."

"So, I won't need to ask Uncle Thane or Uncle Ramsay to batter him?"

"Absolutely not. Rafe is a good man." If I want to convince my daughters that I haven't been brainwashed, I'll need to step up my game. "Did you know Rafe is a lightning researcher? If you're sweet to him, he might let you go with us to his laboratory. He has a Tesla coil, which sounds fascinating, don't you agree?"

The lasses exchange glances, then shrug simultaneously. Maeve speaks for both of them. "We want to see that. I doubt Rowan has any idea what a Tesla coil is, being a simple assistant to a billionaire, but I can explain it to her." She switches to a baby-talk voice as she looks at her sister. "A Tesla coil is a big machine thingy that makes electricity go crackle and snap like baby lightning."

Rowan rolls her eyes.

"Are we set, then?" Rafe asks. "A group tour of my lab is on tap?"

Everyone voices their agreement with varying types of noises and the occasional mumbled word.

Before we leave, though, I need to make sure my lasses are well fed. "Did you two have breakfast yet? There are some leftovers in the refrigerator if you're hungry."

"Ooh, that sounds yummy," Rowan says while rubbing her palms together. Her tongue pokes out a wee bit too. "We left so early this morning that we didn't have time to eat."

Maeve puckers her lips. "You little liar. The on-board chef cooked breakfast for us on Lachlan's jet, in flight. You are not hungry."

Rowan's lips tighten into a sneaky wee smile. "Well, if no one else wants the leftovers, I might as well have them. Can't let food go to waste."

Before the lasses can start fake-arguing again, I step in. "There's enough left to give everyone a wee snack while we're driving to Rafe's lab. I'll put everything in a tote bag. If you dinnae mind the food being cold."

Another round of group assent seals the deal.

Rafe helps me gather the food and carefully pack it. Then I realize we have a slight problem, and I turn to Rafe. "We won't all fit in your car, *gràidh*. Our entourage has expanded."

Chapter Twenty-Five

Rafe

"Oh, we can figure it out, pet. I excel at organization." Does she not believe me? Iona's brows have wrinkled, her nose too, and she bites down on one side of her bottom lip. I pat her arm. "Don't worry. Once we get to my laboratory, everyone on my team will attest to my organizational skills. I might suffer the occasional brief memory lapse, but that's all. You can trust me to coordinate this little foray."

"Oh, I don't doubt your skills." Iona lifts herself onto her tiptoes to whisper into my ear. "For some strange reason, your declaration that you excel at organization has made me randy."

I just manage to stifle a laugh.

She drops onto her feet again. "I'm dead sure you can organize anything, Rafe. But we only have one car."

"Hmm, I hadn't thought of that. Seven people in my car. Not sure how that will work out…Ah, of course." I smirk. "Eric and Toby could ride in the boot."

Before the boys can complain, I wink at them.

"Good one, Rafe," Eric says. "You almost had me."

"Dinnae worry," Maeve says. " I hired a car at the airport for myself and Rowan. Did you think we hiked here from the Norwich airport? Lachlan insisted on paying for our car."

Iona rubs her forehead as if the logistics of it all pains her mind. "How will we split up the drivers and passengers?"

"The answer is simple." I kiss her forehead. "You're with me, darling. And I will drive."

Courtney raises her hand. "Please let me go with you and Iona. Toby and Eric will want to play toddler car games like 'I Spy.' But I'd rather talk to grown-ups."

"You are welcome to join me and Iona in the adult car."

Maeve sides with the adults too, and we now have one full vehicle.

Rowan waves her hand. "I'd like to go with Eric and Toby in the car Maeve hired for us."

The boys concur, and once we climb into our vehicles, we are away. Now I am alone with three women. Can't recall the last time I found myself in a situation like this. Actually, I don't think I ever have been in this situation. Should I worry about what these women might say when they're alone in this car? It might turn into an epic chinwag. Maybe I should've brought earplugs.

For the first few minutes of our journey, the ladies appear to be enjoying the scenery. Norwich is a beautiful city. We drive by the cathedral, and I attempt to tell them a bit about its history, but the women seem more interested in where to find the best shopping. I suppose that's to be expected. Maeve and Courtney are young women, after all. Iona doesn't seem as interested in talking about shopping. I try to start a conversation with her, but the girls in the backseat are having such a good time that I doubt Iona would hear anything I said. Let them have their fun, I say.

The journey from my home to the north side of Norwich takes about twenty minutes. Halfway through the trip, someone's mobile chimes, indicating a new text.

"It's mine," Courtney says. "Ooh, Phillip texted me."

Whilst she browses her message, I turn off the main road. My laboratory is out in the back of beyond on that rather large tract I own. Iona sits forward a bit and studies the landscape. She must approve of my home region since her lips curl into a soft smile.

"Amazing news!" Courtney virtually shouts. "Phillip wants to meet us at the lab, if that's okay with you guys."

"Fine with me," I tell her. "What about you, Iona?"

"I'd love to meet the laddie. He's British like you, but that's all I know."

Courtney emits a softer exclamation of joy this time. "Better text Phillip to let him know it's a green light."

I let out a sarcastic groan. "If our entourage grows any larger, we'll need to rent a caravan to accommodate all of us."

"Will there be tents and camels in your caravan?"

"No, Courtney, there will not. Americans call it an RV."

"Yeah, I know that. I was teasing." Courtney's mobile chimes again, and she claps her hands. "Yay! Phillip should arrive only a few minutes after we do."

I cannot express how excited I am about some bloke called Phillip joining our entourage. Next, Iona's brothers will probably text her to announce they'll be joining us too. Large groups can be difficult to manage. I should know since I lead tour groups through my laboratory. They're always other scientists. I have employees who handle the tourists.

Iona commandeers the car stereo, plugging her phone into the contraption so she can listen to her own music. Maybe I did sort of expect that she'd blast bagpipes for the entire trip. Instead, she offers us a variety of musical styles, everything from classical symphonies to eighties pop tunes to blues music and, yes, even one or two bagpipe songs. I actually enjoy the bagpipe medleys and find myself both tapping my fingers on the steering wheel and humming along softly.

We turn down the gravel drive that leads to the laboratory complex. Within a moment or two, the trees thin out to reveal the large, flat acreage that stretches out behind the building. One car already awaits us. I know it isn't the vehicle with Eric, Toby, and Rowan in it. Just as I shut off the engine, I see a young man getting out of the mystery car.

Courtney leaps out and races toward him, flinging her arms around the gent.

That must be her boyfriend, Phillip.

Eric, Toby, and Rowan have stopped their car, but they seem to be engaged in a discussion—about what, who knows. Courtney leaps out of our car and races toward her young man. When she throws herself at him, he deftly catches her. Then they begin to kiss passionately.

I blare the horn.

"Such a grumpy man, aren't you?" Iona says in a mock scolding tone. "It's been at least eighteen hours since Courtney and Phillip saw each other. That's nearly an eternity."

"Eternity?" I huff. "What rubbish."

"No, it isn't rubbish."

Maeve leans into the front seat and wags a finger at me. "Mam is right. Dinnae act like a grumpy old man, Rafe. I might have to ban you from dating my mother."

I twist my head around to aim a squinty look at the girl. "Dating? Iona and I just met."

"You don't believe in love at first sight? What about lust at first sight? Rowan texted me while we were on the road and told me how loud you elderly people got this morning." Maeve's smile is full of self-satisfaction. "It's about bloody time our Mam got some action."

Iona's eyes flare wide, and her jaw drops. But when she tries to speak, the only sound she can make is spluttering.

That leaves it up to me to set the wee lassie straight. "Yes, your mother and I have shagged several times. But you shouldn't embarrass Iona by discussing our sex life."

Maeve's brows lift. "You're protective of her, aren't you? Good. That means you won't let that scunner harass her anymore."

"I will do anything to protect Iona. That's why I agreed to your uncle's plan. That 'scunner' will never get close enough to harass her, not as long as I'm alive."

Maeve studies me for a moment. Then she nods. "I give you my permission to marry Mam."

Iona slaps her daughter's arm. "Haud yer wheesht, ye *smuilceag*."

The young lassie laughs. "Oh, you're definitely in love. Why else would you call me a chit? In Gaelic, no less."

Maeve sits back in her seat. But her self-satisfied smile deepens.

Oh, yes, children can be quite annoying. But I wouldn't give up my son for anything, and I'm sure Iona feels the same way about her daughters.

Courtney waves at us, flapping her arm vigorously while grinning. She must want us to go over there, so I step out of the car. Then I lean over to tell Iona, "Don't move. I will open your door for you."

Iona smiles sweetly.

And Maeve smirks.

I hurry round to the other side of the car, pulling the door open, and offer Iona my hand. She accepts it. But as she steps out of the vehicle, she pauses to kiss my cheek.

"Thank you, *gràidh*."

"Ah, yes, you're welcome."

Maeve leaps out of the car and slams the back door shut. And of course, she grins. "A wee bit embarrassed, eh, Rafe? Dinnae fash. Mam doesn't feel comfortable with showing affection either."

"I am not embarrassed."

How did I wind up saddled with a gaggle of women? I suppose I've just mixed a few metaphors, but I don't give a toss.

Toby and Eric finally got out of their car. My son helped Rowan climb out, and she smiles shyly. If my son wants to date a Scottish lass, I won't stand in his way. But Rowan lives and works in the Highlands whilst Toby has a job in England. That's the same dilemma Iona and I will face if we want to continue this...whatever it is between us.

I did vow I would protect Iona at any cost.

That doesn't mean...Oh, bollocks. Who am I fooling? Only myself, most likely.

I lead the youngsters across the gravel drive, heading for Phillip's car. Iona clasps my hand, threading her fingers with mine, and I curl my fingers to clasp her hand. I didn't even think about what I was doing. It felt right, and so I did it.

A realization hits me like a bolt of positive lightning, and I stumble to a halt. Iona halts too, since I'm still holding her hand. The younger ladies and gents trot onward. Why have I frozen? Because my epiphany stunned me, though only for a moment. But I can't share it with Iona, not yet. It's much too soon.

"What's wrong, Rafe?"

I smile down at Iona. "Nothing, pet. Everything is perfect."

She seems bemused but doesn't question me.

We finally approach the rest of the gang.

Courtney wraps her hands around Phillip's palm. "Everybody, this is Phillip Marlowe. Phillip, meet everybody—Iona Buchanan, Rafe Knight, Maeve Buchanan, and Rowan Buchanan. You already know Toby Knight and my brother Eric."

I clear my throat deliberately. "Now, shall we all go inside? I texted my team earlier to alert them to expect visitors. Follow me, ladies and gents."

When our group reaches the glass doors, Toby and I swing them open and hold them there until everyone has moved inside. Then I ask the group to wait so I can explain what we do here.

"On its face, the building seems rather nondescript," I say. "That was a purposeful choice. The location of this facility is kept secret. We have two primary reasons for doing that. Firstly, this building houses a good number of potentially dangerous ongoing experiments. Secondly, we don't want an outsider to slip inside and learn too much about our work."

Phillip raises his hand. "Is all your work top secret? I mean, do you work for the government?"

"I can't tell you that." I wink. "It's top secret. If I told you who pays the bills, I'd have to kill you."

Several people chuckle.

"I'm sure you lot are wondering what sorts of jobs my team have." I lean back against the U-shaped desk where a receptionist always waits. "The lovely woman behind the desk is Helena Goodheart—and yes, her surname is quite appropriate. Say hello to my mates, love."

Helena smiles. "Good morning. It's wonderful to see such a large group of Rafe's mates coming to visit his pride and joy, otherwise known as The Knight-Whitherington Center for Storm Research."

Eric raises his hand. "I thought you were a lightning researcher."

"I am. But lightning never comes out of nowhere. Atmospheric conditions lead to the storms that often trigger lightning."

"You should be a teacher, Rafe. The lecture you're giving us could be something you'd see at a university."

"That's kind of you, Eric. Thank you." I claim Iona's hand, then lead the group down the longest corridor in the building. "Follow us, ladies and gents. You're about to meet my crack team of researchers."

Toby jogs up beside me. "What kind of jobs do they have? You're my dad, but even I don't know exactly what goes on in this place."

"I'm sorry, Toby. I should have shared this part of my life with you much sooner, but your mum didn't want me to do that. Still, it's my fault. I shouldn't have gone along with what she said."

"Never mind that. I'm chuffed to see what you and your people do."

I halt a little ways down the corridor, reluctantly releasing Iona's hand so I can face the group. "The men and women who work here have various types of specialties. Precipitation remote sensing, controlled lightning experiments, thermal imaging, spectral analysis, post-strike analysis, computer modelling and simulation, transient luminous events, lightning mapping, and many other related topics."

"When can we see your Tesla coil?" Toby asks.

"Right now. Follow me."

Chapter Twenty-Six

Iona

Rafe takes command of my hand once again while we walk down the corridor, heading for wherever he stores his Tesla coil. I vaguely know what one of those is. But I've never seen one in person, only on TV programs about Nicola Tesla. Maeve, Rowan, and I used to watch documentaries together. I've missed sharing those experiences with them, and it isn't as enjoyable to watch television by myself. Rafe would love to watch documentaries with me. I'm dead sure of that. He is a scientist, after all.

Rafe halts at the end of the corridor, where two other hallways branch off at either side. Double doors directly ahead of us remain closed. But Rafe pulls out of his trouser pocket what looks like a key card for the door in front of us. He thrusts the key card into a slot, and the door lock chunks.

He must have unlocked the door.

"Is that where your Tesla coil is?" Toby asks.

"Yes, it is." Rafe spreads one arm in a wide gesture. "Come inside my laboratory, the lair of the mad scientist."

Rafe reclaims my hand as we stroll into the large, high-ceilinged room with a railing that separates his contraption from the people wanting to see it. Rafe gives tours of the building, and I'm sure the Tesla coil is the highlight. I tip my head back and realize this chamber has more than a high ceiling. It's enormous. I had noticed, when we were still outside, that one portion of the building stood taller than the rest of the structure. The Tesla coil must be the reason for that.

Once everyone has filed into the chamber, Rafe shuts the doors. "What you see before you is a Tesla coil I designed and built myself before I acquired enough funding to create this research facility. The coil is dormant at the moment. But I am going to demonstrate it for you."

I tip my head back further, trying to grasp the enormity of this room. "Which parts are the coils? Is it the ring near the bottom?"

"Yes, that's part of it. You're very clever, pet. That's the primary coil."

"I'm sure everyone realized what that was."

Our group says "no" at the same time, shaking their heads.

Rafe claims my hand. "You see, Iona, you are the cleverest one in this room."

"Aside from you."

He kisses the top of my head, then proceeds to explain the components of the Tesla coil. I can't focus on every word he says, though, because I'm too busy gazing at him. He sounds quite commanding and sexy when he discusses the spark gap, which involves electrodes or something, and then the transformer. Honestly, the technical aspects of the device fly straight over my head. I pay attention mostly because Rafe is such a dynamic speaker when he's in his natural element—science.

Rafe winks at me, then moves on to other parts of the device.

I must have been mooning at him. I feel as if I were doing that, but I cannae help it.

"And this is the primary coil," he announces while placing one hand on the rim of the whatsit, which reminds me of the heating elements on a cooking stove. "Above that, you'll see the secondary coil. It resembles a round tower."

"Aren't there capacitors?" Eric asks.

"Oh, yes, you are correct." Rafe seems rather sheepish. "I forgot about that. But it isn't my fault. Iona's expression of rapt wonder distracted me from my speech."

I might be blushing. No, I'm too old to behave like a teenage lassie.

"Getting back to the capacitors," Rafe says, "there are two. One is near the bottom. The other is on top of the device, and it's called the top load. If there are no more questions, it's time to demonstrate the Tesla coil."

He flips a switch, and lightning erupts.

Well, it looks like lightning. But I doubt it's the real thing. Despite the arcing bolts of electrical energy that seem just like lightning, Rafe appears relaxed and even a touch smug. He's earned the right to feel a wee bit conceited. The man just created lightning, for heaven's sake.

"Is it safe for us to stand so close?" Courtney asks.

"Yes, pet, it is," Rafe assures her. "But you shouldn't touch the bolts of electricity. The voltage is too high. If this were a smaller coil, it would be safe to briefly touch the bolts." He gestures toward the large device. "What you're seeing is plasma given off by the coil."

Maeve raises her hand.

"Yes, pet? You had a question?"

"Aye. Why have a device like this if you don't do anything with it?"

"I built this coil five years ago as a proof of concept, but also as a therapeutic lesson." Rafe pauses, compressing his lips, then takes a big breath and lets it out. "I was struck by lightning seven years ago and almost died. The bolt that hit me stopped my heart for nearly three minutes, then I revived without any medical intervention. I was hospitalized for several days, however, and I required physical therapy."

He shared his secret at last. Rafe seems much more relaxed now that he's told all of us.

"Building the Tesla coil became another type of therapy for me," he confesses. "I would, and still do, visit this chamber to watch plasma arcs. They approximate lightning."

"What a brave and strong man you are," Rowan says. "No wonder Mam likes you so much. She's just as brave and strong."

Rafe once again seems a wee bit uncomfortable. But when he looks at me, all the discomfort vanishes, and he smiles at me with affection. Then he turns to his audience again. "Shall we move on to the next laboratory?"

Everyone agrees that we should, and we're all quite excited about learning more.

Rafe leads us down one of the side corridors toward a room that's labeled "Precipitation Remote Sensing." I remember he mentioned that at the beginning of the tour. But now he takes us inside the lab to talk about how various types of precipitation can influence a budding storm. I know what remote sensing is, but I had no idea it could be used in this manner.

"My team employs two techniques," Rafe tells us, "to estimate, detect, and measure precipitation. For rain, we use pulses of electromagnetic radiation which bounces off raindrops. But for hail, we rely on satellite microwaves."

When I glance around at our group, not one person seems the least bit bored. On the contrary, their expressions prove they're fascinated by Rafe's work. I am not simply fascinated, though. I adore watching and listening to Rafe. Seeing him like this makes me feel…proud. He went through a harrowing experience and never let it stop him. That lightning strike seems to have made him even more determined to continue his research rather than chasing him away.

Now it's on to the next lab.

In this room, his team analyzes the results of controlled lightning experiments, a technique they've only begun to experiment with recently. For the time being, their experiments are nothing more than computer models. But a successful attempt by a team in Switzerland not long ago proved it can work in the real world. I have no doubts Rafe will do even more with controlled lightning than anyone else might.

Aye, I'm quite biased on the topic of Rafe's brilliant mind.

He takes us to a few more labs where his team does all sorts of things, such as spectral analysis and lightning mapping. But the last stop on our tour might become my personal favorite—transient luminous events.

At first, it doesn't sound terribly exciting. When we walk into the room, I see banks of computers where experts are doing who knows what. Something to do with lightning, I assume. A large screen occupies one wall, but that screen is dormant right now.

Rafe leads us toward the big screen, then turns around to face us. "I believe we have enough chairs over there, stacked up in the corner, for everyone to take a seat. You lot must be tired of standing."

Eric, Toby, and Phillip rush to find the chairs and set them down for the rest of us. Once we're all seated, Rafe begins his lecture.

"Raise your hand if you know what transient luminous events are."

No hands are raised.

"Sorry, Dad," Toby says. "Even I don't know what that rubbish is."

Rafe smirks. "You won't call it 'rubbish' anymore once you've seen this presentation."

"Go on, Rafe," Eric says. "Impress the hell out of us."

The man I desperately want to drag into a closet and shag turns halfway toward the large screen. He picks up a remote-control device, and the screen lights up with his introductory slide—"The Beauty and Mysteries of Transient Luminous Events or TLEs, Presented by Rafe Knight, PhD."

He has a PhD? Why hadn't he mentioned that to me?

I forget about that question once he begins his presentation. He is dead sexy when he's in his element. Well, he's dead sexy all the time, but especially when he gives a lecture on unusual whatsits.

Rafe picks up an old-school pointer stick made of wood, using it to enhance his presentation. "Transient Luminous Events are also known as upper atmospheric lightning or ionospheric lightning. They're called that because they exist primarily in the ionosphere which is another term for the upper atmosphere. But I won't bore you with every little detail. I've brought you to this room to show you what those terms refer to, rather than talking about them."

Eric raises a hand. "I hope you aren't going to show us cartoons to illustrate what you're talking about. My old geology professor loved to do that, but it's really lame."

"I agree, and I never employ cartoons." Rafe waves a hand toward the left side of the room, where a young man sits in front of a computer fiddling about with it. "Everyone, meet our top man on the ionospheric phenomena team. Eddie, please give a quick hello to the group."

"Hey, guys, I'm Eddie Barstow from Lancashire, and I've been working at this laboratory for three years. You're going to love Rafe's presentation. It's wild in the best way."

"Would you start the show, please, Eddie? We didn't need your life story." Rafe turns toward our group, raising his pointer once again. "Now, watch this video and see if you can catch what's going on."

The video plays, but I'm not sure what I'm seeing. It can't be what it seems. That's impossible. But if there's one thing I've learned from Rafe, it's that I shouldn't take anything at face value without investigating. That doesn't apply to my family or close friends. But my journalist instincts often kick in when I'm unable to sort out something I see or hear.

Rafe taps his pointer on the screen. "Did any of you catch that?"

"Catch what?" Toby says. "All I saw was clouds. Looked like a thunderstorm with a few flashes of lightning."

"That's all you gleaned from the video."

"Yeah. Was I meant to see Santa Claus?"

Rafe shakes his head and sighs. "No, Toby, this isn't a Christmas show on the telly. Does anyone else have an idea what we just witnessed?"

No one responds.

So, I raise my hand.

Rafe smiles at me sweetly. "Yes, love, what did you see?"

"Well, um, it looked like blue flashes. Higher up, I thought I saw quick tendrils of red coming down from above the clouds. And…" I hesitate, because what I think I noticed couldn't be. It's too bizarre.

"You saw something else, didn't you? Go on, pet, I haven't known you to be shy."

"I'm not. But it sounds mad because I swear I saw a green ring, briefly, surrounding the red tendrils."

"That is precisely what you saw, Iona." Rafe speaks to the entire group now. "Those transient luminous events are also known as blue jets, elves, and sprites. They exist so briefly that the human eye can rarely spot them. Sprites also have sub-variations known as jellyfish, column, and carrots. You might be able to see a sprite now and then."

Maeve bumps her arm into my shoulder. "Mam is the smartest person in Scotland, if not the world."

I roll my eyes. "Dinnae be ridiculous. I'm hardly a genius. Rafe is far more knowledgeable than I am."

The man in question shakes his head at me. "Don't underestimate your-self, love. Maeve is right. You are the smartest person I've ever met. No offense, Toby."

"None taken, Dad. Iona is awesome. When can I officially become her stepson?"

Rafe ignores Toby's question. "Most of these events are born from posi-tive lightning that shoots upward from the top of a thundercloud. These phenomena are rare and, as the name implies, highly transient. It's unusual for these events to be seen by the naked eye."

He continues with his presentation, telling us about all sorts of un-usual and interesting phenomena related to weather. But I have trouble focusing. Aye, every word he says is fascinating. The problem is that I can't stop thinking about what Toby said. He wants to become my stepson. I don't know everything about Rafe's relationship with his ex-wife, though it's clear from what he has told me that she denigrated him every chance she could.

Did she treat Toby that way? At least he has his father, who loves him and would do anything for him. The same goes for Rafe. He knows Toby adores him and would protect him at any cost.

I would do anything for Rafe too.

Chapter Twenty-Seven

Rafe

The way Iona keeps gazing at me as if I'm the greatest genius in the history of the world makes me somewhat uncomfortable. But every time she smiles at me lovingly, I forget all about that for at least twenty-two seconds. All right, I don't know if it's precisely twenty-two seconds. I'm guessing, because my attention remains glued to her beautiful face.

"What have scientists learned about?" Toby asks. "You trailed off mid-sentence."

"No, I did not." Actually, I'm quite certain I did trail off. Iona had smiled at me again, and all the thoughts in my brain crumbled away. Now, I clear my throat and try to reassemble my wits. "Scientists have learned a great deal about Transient Luminous Events, yet they remain an enigma. It seems likely that we might never fully understand them. Their transient nature and the high altitude at which they occur make studying them quite difficult."

My mates ask a few more questions, then it's time to leave the TLE lab.

Iona walks beside me as we peek into various other labs, but I don't take the group into those rooms. It's nearly lunchtime, and I'm technically still on holiday—extended personal leave, as I prefer to call it. That does sound suspiciously like I invented that phrase to excuse my abominable behavior. I wish I could say that hunting down Iona hadn't been an insane impulse. But I won't lie, not even to myself, not anymore.

Those days are over.

Our tour ends at my favorite room. I halt in front of the closed door and face the group. "This is our last stop. Welcome to the Post-Strike Analysis lab. Shall we pop in and see what the team is doing today?"

Everyone mutters their agreement.

I push the door open and hold it there until all my mates have walked inside the room. Then I stride past them, waving for the group to gather behind me. "Now that we're all here, I'd like to introduce you to the direct effects team. They study post-strike analysis via the contraption you see behind me. It can deliver up to two hundred thousand amps of electricity."

The group needs a moment to study the machine behind me. Then it's time to make lightning.

I glance at the blonde woman seated at a bank of computers. "Melissa, would you give our guests a demonstration?"

"Yes, sir."

She taps buttons on her keyboard—and a miniature bolt of lightning flashes.

My mates display an appropriate amount of awe.

Iona approaches me, laying a hand on my arm. "That was so hot, Rafe, literally."

A chuckle rumbles out of me. "Hot? That was two hundred thousand amps of electricity, enough to kill someone."

"But you survived a lightning strike. That must have shot even more energy into your body than this machine does."

"In fact, this machine produces more amperage than lightning does. An average bolt releases about thirty thousand amps compared to the two hundred thousand in that simulator. That's approximately five times higher than a natural lightning strike."

She slides her hand down to my wrist, then threads her fingers between mine. "I'm sure I speak for everyone here when I say you are a remarkable man with enough strength and intelligence to accomplish anything. Even lightning couldn't stop you, when most others would stay away from the thing that nearly killed them."

"I'm no braver than anyone else."

"*Na dèan beul dhe do thòn.*" She rises onto her toes to give me a stern look. "That means 'bullshit,' Rafe. No more downplaying your strength. You are amazing."

I suddenly realize the others are watching us with varying expressions of amusement. Why do they find anything we've said to be humorous? The thought of a direct hit from a lightning bolt should frighten them, not make them smile.

And I can't help it. I get grumpy again.

Waving my free arm, the one Iona hasn't commandeered, I growl, "We're done here. Come with me to the cafeteria."

I stomp out of the room with Iona trailing slightly behind me. With some effort, I slow my pace to let her stay beside me. Once we walk into the cafeteria, the tension inside me eases enough that I'm no longer growling at anyone. Even while I was behaving that way, Iona kept smiling at me sweetly.

She is barmy.

But so am I. Maybe we do belong together.

The cafeteria has good food. I made sure of that when we built this laboratory complex. We can't all sit at one table, so I suggest the others should choose to sit wherever they like. Iona and I take chairs beside each other at one of the rectangular tables. Maeve, Rowan, and Toby join us with all three on the opposite side. Courtney, Phillip, and Eric choose the adjacent table which unfortunately means they're close enough to listen to and participate in our conversations.

Maybe I don't mind that as much as I claim I do. A bloke has to keep up his reputation, mine being the persona of a raging arsehole. I whispered that to Iona, and she laughed.

"Oh, Rafe, you aren't the villain I thought you were at first. Now I know how kind and sweet and brave you are."

Maeve and Rowan twitter like wee birds.

Bloody hell. I've just employed a Scottish word.

I scowl at the girls, rather halfheartedly. "What are you two laughing about?"

"We weren't laughing at you, Rafe," Maeve says. "We just cannae believe our mam is gushing over a man. It's refreshing. She had spent twenty years or so avoiding men except for the occasional fling."

"Fling?" Iona nearly shouts, her voice higher pitched than usual. "I dated occasionally. There were no flings."

I rest my hand atop hers. "Relax, pet. Maeve is teasing you."

She sighs. "Aye, I know that. I reckon I'm a wee bit sensitive about my awful track record with men." She kisses my cheek. "Until I met you. That changed everything."

Maeve and Rowan simultaneously coo, "Awwww."

I might as well chime in and potentially shock these two lovely lasses. "Meeting your mum has changed my life too. She's both sweet and tough with just enough feminine charm to make her irresistible." I lift Iona's hand to kiss the back of it. "And I believe she just might be the soul mate I've always longed for but never found."

All three women seem stunned.

Yes, I figured that declaration would do the trick. No more twittering at me. But I meant every word of what I said about Iona and my feelings for her.

From the adjacent table, three male voices begin to sing the tune of the wedding march in a ridiculously soppy tone. Toby, Eric, and Phillip are the culprits.

And I growl at them on principle. "Shut your bloody mouths, you twats."

Courtney laughs. "You go, Rafe. Punch their lights out, they deserve it."

A realization slams into me. I actually enjoy bantering with these young people. They are clever, cheerful, and capable.

Once lunch is over, we drive back to my home in Norwich so I can resume my extended leave. It pays to be the boss. No one would dare criticize me for taking such a long holiday. Of course, I permit everyone on my team to go on holiday occasionally. The rules of taking leave from work are mandated by law for my employees. I have no such rules. I'm the CEO.

It's late afternoon, so Iona and I go out to the small swimming pool in my backyard for a bit of relaxation. The pool is heated. That's a good thing since the weather has been a bit cooler today. Iona doesn't have a bathing suit. I have trunks, of course, since this is my home. But none of the young women brought any swimwear of any sort.

When I suggest she could wear her bra and knickers instead, her face becomes the picture of horror. Someone might think I suggested a serial killer should come have a dip with us.

"My underwear will be see-through when it's wet," she whispers to me. "What if the laddies see me?"

"I hadn't thought of that. Are you sure your undergarments will become see-through?"

She rolls her eyes. "Yes, Rafe, a woman knows these things before she leaps into a swimming pool. It's instinct."

"Really? Women all possess this type of supernatural understanding?"

"Nothing supernatural about it. I'm sorry, Rafe, we can't swim today."

"Couldn't we visit a clothing store this afternoon?"

She flattens her lips.

I assume that means she disapproves of my idea. "No swimming, then. Correct?"

"Aye. I've had enough car travel for one day, and I'm jeeked from today's excitement." She yawns. "A wee nap sounds heavenly."

"Oh, I see. Well, if you're that tired, I suppose I'll…find something else to occupy my time while you're sleeping."

"No, Rafe." She grasps my shirt collar to pull me close, then hoists herself up onto her tiptoes. "The nap is for both of us."

The sensual tone of her voice convinced me. "A nap it is, then. For both of us."

I pick her up and carry her toward the hallway amid twittering from the girls and chuckling from the boys. As I turn down the hall, I shout, "Wait until you meet the love of your life. None of you boys will be laughing then."

I pause and turn halfway toward the young hooligans.

No one is laughing anymore. They gawp at me as if I've grown five extra heads. Only Iona is immune to that reaction, though she does gaze up at me lovingly.

"What's wrong with you lot?" I ask in what sounds like a grumpy tone even to my ears.

Toby is equally shell-shocked, but he finds his voice before the others. "Dad, you just announced that Iona is the love of your life."

"Yes. What of it?"

"But you—it's just—Well, I never thought I'd hear you say that. Don't think you ever called Mum the love of your life."

Oh, bollocks. I shouldn't have blurted that out. "I'm sorry, Toby. I didn't mean it as an insult to your mother."

"No, that's not what I meant." He grins. "I'm so bloody happy for you, Dad."

"You are?" I suppose I could have sounded more baffled if I tried very hard. "Well, ah, thank you."

Maeve chimes in too. "Never seen Mam this happy either. Rowan and I know you'll treat her well and make her so happy for the rest of her life."

Iona is grinning, though she hides it somewhat by burying her face against my chest. She does peek out now and then.

"All right, children. Iona and I are going to have that lie-down now."

The children seem to think that's a good excuse for harassing us. Maeve and Rowan inform us that "no one will interrupt" our "wee lie-down." Their cheeky tone makes it clear they're teasing us again. Toby winks and grins in the most idiotic manner, like a cartoon character or a comedian. Eric has enough sense not to behave that way, particularly considering the way he tried to win Iona's heart by harassing her. Politely, according to Iona. I no longer feel odd about being friendly with Eric, though I do wonder what changed his mind about Iona.

Maybe later I'll ask him.

I turn away from the irritating young adults and march straight into my bedroom. *Our* bedroom, for the time being at least. Later, I'll worry about where we might live or how often her brothers might hunt me down to glower at me and issue empty threats. I'll become accustomed to that, I'm sure.

My suggestion of a lie-down appeals to me even more once I've carried Iona into the bedroom and set her down on the mattress. A wave of exhaustion crashes over me. I wipe a hand over my eyes and yawn.

Iona wriggles around to make room for me beside her. "Lie down, Rafe. You look exhausted."

"That's because I am exhausted. Didn't realize how much energy I'd expended on giving everyone a tour of my laboratory."

"You enjoyed doing that, though. Or were you pretending? No, I don't believe that."

I climb onto the bed, slinging an arm around Iona to pull her close to my side. "Yes, I genuinely enjoyed showing the young people my laboratory."

"You enthralled them."

A half-suppressed laugh splutters out of me. "Enthralled? You're over-doing it just a bit, love."

"Just accept the truth, *gràidh*. You are magnetic."

If she believes that, who am I to argue? Iona is the most intelligent person I've ever met. "All right, you've convinced me. I am magnetic, and so are you. Now, may we please have that nap?"

"Mm-hm." She snuggles even closer, resting her head on my chest, and yawns. "Getting sleepy already."

Soon, we both drift off into the world of dreams. I dream about her, naturally, naked in the pool. In my fantasy, she is the sexiest, naughtiest mermaid. Perhaps sometime we could enact that dream in real life. But not until the snarky young people have gone home. We'll need total privacy.

A couple of hours later, we emerge from our slumber and return to the living room. The children have, once again, crafted a meal for all of us. Until this week, Toby never cooked for me unless it was my birthday or Father's Day. Even then, he would whip up something simple and easy like omelets or hamburgers.

It's nice to know the younger generation knows how to treat us elderly gents and ladies.

The next morning, we receive a nasty surprise.

Chapter Twenty-Eight

Iona

At seven thirty in the morning, a fist pounds on the front door. *Bod an Donais*, who would come to Rafe's house this early? I'd been awake for a while, resting my cheek on his chest while I waited for him to rise and shine. He must have been even more jeeked than I realized. But the pounding that echoes through the house has roused him at last.

He groans and rubs his eyes. "What the bloody hell is all that racket?"

"An unfriendly guest, I assume. Time to get up, Rafe." I poke him in the side. "Right now."

"Dad! Some bloke is trying to knock the house down!"

At the sound of his son's voice, Rafe leaps off the bed and scrambles to find his clothes. We had both slept naked last night. I jump up too and gather my clothing. But he gets ready first and races out into the living room. I arrive just as Rafe tears the door open

"You?" he snarls. "How dare you assault my home and frighten these women."

I don't think any of we women are terrified. Anxious and confused, aye. But not frightened. Maybe that's because we know Rafe Knight would take whatever measures are necessary to protect everyone in this house.

Rafe seemed to recognize the visitor, but I've only just reached the doorway. Rafe's body had blocked my view until just this moment.

A chill races through me, raising gooseflesh on my arms. "It's the *cacan* who stalked me in Loch Fairbairn. How did you find us?"

The villain warps his mouth into a snide smile. "As if it was so bloody difficult to track you down. My boss knew how to find you, and he sent me to deliver a message."

Rafe glowers at him. "How long have you been spying on us?"

"Since before you stormed into that dowdy little Scottish village."

I scowl at the *cacan* too. "Dowdy? Loch Fairbairn is lovely and full of good, friendly people."

The stranger sniggers. "Those 'good friendly people' will tar and feather you once my boss is done with you, Ms. Buchanan."

He made my surname sound like a vile insult.

No one denigrates my family name. We Buchanans are a proud, strong, loyal lot. But I don't get the chance to tell the *cacan* that.

Rafe seizes the man's shirt and hauls him closer, to within millimeters of my stalker. His voice deceptively soft and filled with menace. "If you do anything to harm or even annoy anyone in this house or in Loch Fairbairn, I will tie you to the back of my car and drive down the street at high speed. I hope you enjoy the taste of asphalt and blood."

The *cacan*'s eyes widen a wee bit.

Rafe gives him a rough shake. "Tell me your name. Now."

When my stalker refuses to respond, I kick him in the shin. "Tell us."

He looks at something behind us, and I glance back to see what it is.

Toby, Eric, Phillip, Courtney, Maeve, and Rowan stand there with their arms crossed while glaring at the *cacan*.

Oh, my, I've never seen them looking so fierce.

Rafe shakes my stalker again, making the man's head snap backward and forward. "Who are you? This is your last chance to cough up the information."

"I, ah…" The *cacan* winces and blows out a breath. "My name is Hubert Frye."

"And you work for…"

He squeezes his eyes shut. "Graham Oliver."

Everything inside me goes cold, as if icy water has been injected into my veins. When I speak, my voice comes out hushed because I cannae believe what I'm hearing. "Graham Oliver? The man who once owned the Loch Fairbairn newspaper?"

It was a scandal sheet, at best. But I won't divulge the details in front of the children.

"Yes," Hubert says. "Graham claims you stole his livelihood. After Rory MacTaggart chased him out of Scotland, he couldn't get a good job, and he blames you for that. I don't know anything else. I've done what he paid me to do."

Rafe bends his head down to glare into Hubert's eyes. His nose bumps into the *cacan*'s. The dark tone of his voice gives me hot shivers. "I want to know exactly what Graham Oliver paid you to do. Every detail."

I lay a hand on Rafe's arm. "Set him down, *mo chridhe*. I'm the object of Graham's hatred, so I should be the one to interrogate this *cacan*."

Rafe's lips quirk. "Yes, I suppose you should have that honor. But I will remain by your side every moment."

"Of course. Now, please drag this *bod ceann* into the living room and detain him on the sofa."

The younger generation watches as Rafe hauls Hubert away, and I shut the door. The man I love hoists Hubert off his feet, dropping him on the sofa like a sack of potatoes. The *bod ceann* has ruffled hair, wrinkled clothes, and a look of terror on his face. He bloody well deserves to feel that way.

Rafe leaps over the sofa's back, plopping down right beside Hubert.

I walk around the end of the sofa to settle down on a cushion. Rafe is beside me. He seems unlikely to release Hubert since he has his arm wrapped around the man's throat—gently but firmly.

The children gather around us. The lasses take the chairs at the dining room table while the laddies take up positions behind and at either side of the sofa like sentinels. I believe they would step in if Hubert tried anything.

Maeve and Rowan cross their arms, aiming flinty stares at the intruder.

I love those lasses to the moon and back. Buchanans are a steadfast lot.

"Your turn, pet," Rafe says. "Interrogating this bastard is your domain."

"Thank you, *gràidh*." I shift about so I'm half-turned toward Hubert—and Rafe, who refuses to allow me to be between him and the *cacan*. "How much do you know about your boss, Hubert?"

The man shrugs. "He hired me and gave me my orders."

"And those orders were to do…what?"

Hubert's face takes on a pinched expression, and he bows his head. Then he mumbles what must be words, though I can't understand them.

"Speak up, Hubert."

The *bod ceann* sucks in a big breath and looks at me. "I was to scope out the village and uncover as much dirt as possible on you. My job was harder than I expected."

"In what way?"

"Well, based on what Graham told me, I assumed you were a sleazy tabloid reporter and a liar." Hubert wriggles a wee bit as if he's uncomfortable. He bloody well should be. "Graham wouldn't tell me everything, and he would never let me near his ruddy satchel."

Now things are getting interesting. The adrenaline from this man's arrival had waned somewhat, but now it's ramping up again. I feel like a real journalist, at long last. "What about his satchel? Do you have any idea what was in it?"

"I told you he never let me see it. The thing is old and tattered, yet he insists on carrying it everywhere. I wouldn't be surprised if the bloke sleeps with it under his pillow."

More gears turning in my mind, more tantalizing hints.

I hesitate, though only long enough to formulate an idea and try a new tactic. "Tell me, Hubert, where does Graham live?"

"What? I can't tell you that. He'd murder me."

"Graham is that unhinged?"

Hubert rubs his arm. "I didn't mean it literally. He might be a complete tosser, but I doubt he has the nerve to kill anyone."

Aye, I'm well aware of how cowardly Graham has always been. Even the events he triggered years ago were executed in a gutless fashion. He has no stomach for real peril.

But things are taking an even more fascinating turn. "Tell me, Hubert, how did you become involved with Graham?"

"I, ah, just got released from prison a few months ago. I'd been given a five-year sentence but got out a bit earlier on parole."

Rafe grunts. "Not for good behavior."

"Actually, it was for good behavior, I'll have you know. Not much to do in prison except try not to get murdered or become the favorite toy of some burly bloke. Fortunately, no one liked me, so they left me alone."

I'm not sure I believe that story. But we have more urgent issues to discuss. "What did Graham offer you that made you want to risk violating the terms of your parole?"

Hubert grasps his arm firmly. "He said he'd pay me ten thousand pounds to do the job. One thousand in advance, and the rest once I finished my end of the deal."

"What crime did you commit?"

He winces. "Identity theft."

Rafe squints at the laddie. "Whose identities did you appropriate?"

"Elderly people, mostly. They're the easiest to, uh…"

"Trick into giving you their personal information so you could divest them of their life savings?"

Oh, what lovely company Graham keeps. But then, he is a con artist just like his new friend.

I continue my interrogation of this degenerate bawbag. "Why were you walking round and round the village for…how long? Days? Months?"

"Only six days at the time you and this bloke"—He rolls his eyes toward Rafe—"caught me outside your house. But I learned quite a lot during that time and after."

"Such as what?"

The *cacan* lifts his chin in a defiant expression, though his lips tremble. That suggests he's trying to con us into believing he knows more than we think he does. Hubert is a professional con artist, after all. Maybe I should ring Alex Thorne for suggestions.

But no, I doubt we have time for that. I feel as if we've breached the castle walls, and we're on the cusp of routing out the enemy once and for all.

Rafe gives Hubert a rough shake. "Tell her what she wants to know."

The growly tone of his voice makes me want to drag him into the bedroom and shag him like mad.

Hubert's eyes flare wide. "Calm down, mate, I'm going to tell you, I swear."

I squint my eyes the way Rafe did a moment ago. "That pathetic little village has a police station, but the two constables are morons. They spend most of their time helping to catch livestock that escaped from their homes, or perhaps the occasional kitty stuck in a tree. Oh, but those coppers do serve one vital purpose. They make everyone feel safe as houses."

Maybe we have been lax about security, but no one could have guessed that Graham Oliver would do...whatever it is he's trying to accomplish.

"Once and for all, Hubert," I say, "what is Graham's endgame?"

"Sorry. Can't help you there. I told you he keeps everything locked inside that satchel."

"But you must have met with him at least a few times. Where did those meetings happen?"

"In a park. Always a different one every time."

Mhac na galla. I'm out of ideas. That satchel might help us, but we have no clue where Graham is hiding out.

Hubert clears his throat. "There is one more thing I can tell you." He smirks. "Graham Oliver is going to ruin your life, Iona. Everything you've worked for will be burnt to ashes."

"Why does that please you? We're strangers to each other."

"You set the sodding coppers on me back in that sweet little village. I don't appreciate that." He glances sideways at Rafe. "And I'd love the chance to get a bit of payback for what this lout did to me. Rot in hell, I say, for the both of you."

Hubert bites down on Rafe's arm, distracting him just enough that the *cacan* can wrench free of Rafe's grip on his neck. The vile toad springs off the sofa, leaping over it like an Olympic hurdling champion, and flings the front door open before any of us can react.

I scramble off the sofa and race for the door just as it swings open and whacks into the wall.

"No, Iona!" Rafe shouts.

But I'm already sprinting past the threshold. Up ahead, I see Hubert barreling down the drive. He avoids our cars, probably because trying to hotwire one of them would take too long. The pounding of heavy footsteps assures me Rafe isn't far behind me.

"Stop, you bloody-minded woman!"

I run faster, faster, faster, until I'm gaining significant ground in my pursuit of the con man turned enforcer. Hubert glances at me over his shoulder. His eyes widen, though he keeps going. Is he shocked because I'm catching up? Or because it sounds like Rafe is close behind me? Dinnae care. Stopping that identity thief from getting away is my only goal.

My ears have started to ring. I'm pushing too hard, I know, but I can't slow down until Hubert gives up.

Rafe blazes past me and tackles Hubert to the ground, much like he'd done back in Scotland when the vile toad spied on me. Rafe sets one foot on Hubert's chest.

When I catch up to my hero, I can hardly pull in a full breath. "Are you—all right—Rafe?"

"Yes." He sounds almost as breathless as I am. "Did he—hurt you?"

I shake my head. The *cacan* didn't get close enough, but I need a few more good breaths before I can tell him that. My pulse races too fast for me to do anything more than gasp, until I finally regain my normal breathing. Rafe seems to have caught his breath too.

Hubert attempts to slither out from under Rafe's foot. Aye, the daft, wonderful man raced out of the house barefoot. And I suddenly realize I'm barefoot too. No wonder my feet hurt.

Rafe plants his foot on Hubert's chest more firmly. "I wouldn't recommend moving. If I shift my foot one inch higher, I could crush your ribs." He bares his teeth and chuckles. "On second thought, please do move. I'd love to watch while your chest caves in."

A tingle of excitement just rushed through me. I do love it when Rafe turns into a feral beast.

Hubert's lips are quivering. His eyes gape as if he's seen a ghost. When he looks at me, he swallows hard enough to make his Adam's apple jump. "What are you going to do to me?"

I glance at Rafe.

He smiles. "You decide, pet. This bastard has been stalking you, after all."

What should I do? The *cacan* might still have information he hasn't shared with us. "I think we should take him back to Scotland. My brothers and their friends have skills that might become useful."

"As you wish, love." Rafe lowers his gaze to Hubert. "Although perhaps we should take him to my laboratory first."

Chapter Twenty-Nine

Rafe

I can think of nothing I'd rather do right now than beat this man to death with a large brick. But I'll reserve that impulse for later, if necessary. Though I might sometimes behave like a caveman, I do have standards. One is that I do not commit murder in front of my son. I won't do that in front of Iona's daughters or Courtney and Eric either. If I truly wanted to beat Hubert's brains out, I'd haul him into the deep woods first to take him out in private.

Never in my life have I even considered such thoughts. Meeting and falling for Iona has changed me. I would commit any crime to protect her.

But I doubt that will be necessary.

"Why do you want to visit your laboratory?" Iona asks.

"So I can hook him up to the Tesla coil and give him a good shock. Or perhaps the lightning simulator would be better. It provides thirty thousand amps of electricity, after all, and creates a blinding spectacle."

"Aye, that sounds perfect."

Hubert's face has gone pale, so I assume he doesn't agree with Iona's pronouncement. Still, the tosser pretends he's tough. "You don't scare me, Rafe Knight."

"I've been struck by lightning, you wanker. That event changed me, turning me into a raging beast whenever someone irritates me." I hoist Hubert off his feet and leave him dangling above the ground with only my hands fisted in his shirt to keep him from falling. "Would you like to know what a lightning bolt feels like when it hits your body? A flash of intense heat will rush through you so fast you barely have time to register it. You'll notice the aroma of singed hair. And if the bolt smacks down on a hard surface, you might experience cracked vertebrae."

The horror on Hubert's face assures me I'm getting somewhere now.

I set the man's feet on the ground and thrust one arm out toward Iona. "Please roll up my sleeve, pet. Hubert hasn't seen the visible effects of a lightning strike."

She quickly rolls up my sleeve, exposing the web-like scars.

Hubert's eyes bulge to the point that I expect them to pop out of their sockets at any second.

I pull the tosser close and snarl, "Ready for the lightning simulation chamber yet?"

Hubert bursts into tears. "Please, no, don't do that to me. I want to go back to Scotland and be arrested. Send me back to prison, please."

I pat his head. "Good boy, Hubie."

A mobile phone rings, behind me somewhere.

"It's yours, Mam," Maeve declares. "I was keeping it for you."

"Toss it to me, would you?" Iona says. "Thank you, *gràidh*. Hello? Thane? Oh, aye, we're all fine. We were planning to do that anyway, but we have a guest coming home with us. It's the *cacan* who stalked me. We'll do that. See you soon, Thane." Iona turns to me. "There's been a change of plans."

"We're flying to Scotland, I gather."

"That's right. We'll need to tie up this *bod ceann* to make sure he won't do anything naughty like trying to run away."

"Oh, no, I'll never do that again," Hubert blurts out. "I swear it. Never, never, never again."

I groan. One "never" would have been sufficient.

While I keep hold of my best mate Hubie, the others race into the house to gather our belongings. I hadn't even bothered to unpack my suitcase when we arrived at my home. Toby volunteered to pack for me, but that simply means he'll stuff all my belongings inside the bag, and I'll be wearing rumpled clothes for several days. I've never been any good at ironing.

Everyone bustles about, preparing for our imminent departure. But it only takes ten minutes, according to my watch, for the gang to get ready and climb into our vehicles. Eric finds a length of rope in the shed behind the house, and we use that to secure our prisoner. The bastard has the gall to complain about my use of the diminutive Hubie, but he changes his mind after I spear him with a hot glare. Yes, he's quite docile now.

Perhaps it's wrong for me to enjoy tormenting that git, but I don't care. He deserves it.

Half an hour later, we're in the air and flying toward Scotland on a posh private jet that comes with a chef. It's a different jet than the one we'd flown on the first time. The billionaire Diana Sangster provided the jet this time, strictly to speed up the process. Diana is British, after all, and she lives in England with her American husband. Traveling on her jet will mean a one-way trip instead of waiting for Lachlan's plane to come and pick us up.

The longer I'm in Hubie's presence, the more likely it is that I'll snap and punch him in the gut. Best get to Loch Fairbairn as quickly as possible.

No one feels like talking during the flight. Some listen to music, while others nibble on food. I do neither of those things for the simple reason that I have taken charge of Hubie. He sits right beside me, tied up with ropes and gagged with a handkerchief. Fortunately, it's a quick flight.

Thane and Ramsay are standing on the tarmac at the Inverness airport to greet us, and two vehicles wait for us, ready to whisk our group away to…wherever we're going. No one told me our final destination.

I trudge across the tarmac with one hand strapped around Hubie's upper arm and the other holding Iona's hand. We halt at the vehicles.

"What have you done to our sister?" Ramsay demands. "You were supposed to protect her."

"And I did. Here's your proof." I nod toward the bound and gagged Hubie. "Graham Oliver's little friend will tell us everything we want to know."

Thane bars his arms over his chest. "That's good news. But it's a bit late to worry about Graham."

"Why?"

"Because he's already enacted his evil plan. Come, get into the car. We'll be heading for Dùndubhan."

"Dun-what? I've never heard of that."

Iona nudges me with her elbow and whispers, "Don't you remember? The whisky you drank was Dùndubhan Masterpiece. It takes its name from the castle, which Rory MacTaggart owns."

"Oh, yes, of course." I forgot, thanks to my memory lapses. They're worse during stressful times. But the sweet woman reminded me. "Yes, all right, let's go to the castle."

Iona and I ride in the backseat with Ramsay and Thane. Our driver is an older chap who rolls up the partition without being told to do so. Discretion is a vital skill for any limo driver to acquire. We don't speak during the trip, though. Hubie huddles in the corner, pretending that he's looking out the window. Iona cuddles up to me. Her brothers don't squint or scowl at me, which seems like a significant improvement in our relationship.

Thane even smiles faintly.

Phillip came with us too. Courtney assured him he didn't need to come along, but he's clearly quite devoted to her. The bloke refused to stay home. The longer limo behind our vehicle accommodates all the rest of the gang—Maeve, Rowan, Toby, Phillip, Courtney, and Eric. I'm sure the younger gents and ladies are feeling as sober as we are given the circumstances.

The ride to Dùndubhan takes an hour and a half. Iona tells me the castle is rather remote and has a genuine medieval wall around it, though the structure has been refurbished occasionally over the centuries. There have been at least two recent battles there. *Crikey.* If we need to hide out at a remote castle known for being impregnable, our problems must be worse than I thought.

After about an hour, we turn off the highway and head toward a mountain peak I can see in the distance. That's Beann Dealgach, Iona tells me. Rory MacTaggart and his wife, Emery, own the mountain and the castle. Iona also informs me that the couple have taken their twin children to Germany to visit with Emery's parents and sister. They're American, despite living in the land of Wiener Schnitzel.

The closer we get to Dùndubhan, the more Iona relaxes. Thane seems to remain relaxed no matter what is going on around him. I wish I had his composure. Ramsay doesn't quite share Thane's calm demeanor, though he manages to sleep during our car journey.

Poor little Hubie gets no rest. Maybe that's because I'm sitting right beside him. Every time he glances at me, the git quivers from head to toe.

I'd never terrified anyone before today. But this twat deserves it.

Finally, we turn down a dirt road that Iona assures me will take us directly to Dùndubhan. The road has a strip of grass going up the middle, and I don't yet see anything resembling a building of any sort. Just as I'm about to ask if these people actually know where they're going, we come upon a metal gate that spans the road. The gate hangs open as if it's been waiting for us.

Once both our vehicles have crossed through the gate, it closes again on its own.

As we're transported down an ever-darkening road, I realize the track has become gravel now. Within a matter of minutes, the road ends at…the castle. I suppose I hadn't quite believed what Dùndubhan was like, the way Iona described it. I've been a bloody fool. Her description is spot on, though she didn't give me the full picture, having left out the turrets, the walkway atop the wall, the wooden gates, and other things I'm sure I haven't seen yet.

Dùndubhan is majestic.

Once both limos have parked, everyone climbs out of the vehicles. I keep hold of our prisoner with one hand clamped around his upper arm once again. Iona walks beside me. Her brothers take up positions behind and at either side of us as if they are our self-appointed guards. The rest of the gang emerges from the larger limo, seeming rather too cheerful under the circumstances. It's probably just my grumpiness rearing its head.

Will there be food? Soon? I'm hungry.

Iona laughs when I say those words aloud. "Of course we'll feed you, Rafe. Mrs. Brody is already here. She worked for Rory and Emery for several years, but now she mostly serves as housekeeper to some of the MacTaggarts, Buchanans, and Sterlings."

"With all of us here, won't Mrs. Brody be overwhelmed?"

"No, *gràidh*," she says with a sweet little laugh. "She has help, believe me. Her daughter will be here, I'm sure, and so will her husband, Tavish. Besides, I rather doubt everyone I know will show up."

"Oh, I see. That's good to know."

Iona smiles up at me with a touch of sarcasm in her expression. "You are the sweetest angry *bod ceann* I've ever met."

"Thank you, pet. I'll accept any compliment from you, even a barmy one."

But I am not the only angry male on the premises. The door to the castle has opened, and Iona's brothers are now marching toward us. Or toward me, at any rate. I doubt their scowls are aimed at their sister.

Iona leads me toward them, as if she can't wait to find out whether Thane and Ramsay mean to lock me in the dungeon. Does this castle have one of those? I'll find out soon enough.

The brothers halt directly in front of us.

Ramsay straps his arms over his chest and squints at me, while Thane simply stands there with a seemingly casual posture that doesn't match his facial expression.

"Good day, gents," I say in my most cheerful tone. "We survived another flight on a borrowed private jet. At least you two didn't try to crash the plane simply to annoy me."

Ramsay grunts. "We wouldn't do that when our sister was on board, or her daughters."

"But you're fine with everyone else dying in a terrible accident."

Thane shrugs. "I'm sure there were enough life jackets for everyone except you."

Naturally, Eric Taylor would be on their list of passengers deserving of rescue. He is the son of Thane's fiancée, after all. The same goes for Courtney. And I'm positive Toby also gets a pass on fiery-crash death since Eric is his best mate. Not sure about Phillip Marlowe. I suppose that depends on how the Buchanan boys feel about a British man dating the daughter of Thane's fiancée.

Iona snaps her fingers in front of my eyes. "Wake up, Rafe."

"What? I am awake."

"But not cognizant. Aye? You were off in Rafe-land again."

"How did I acquire my own country? I don't recall buying Lithuania." But I did drift away to another state of consciousness. Iona knows I do that occasionally because of my lightning-strike injuries. But I have a question. I lean toward her and whisper, "Have you told them yet? About my issues?"

"No. Did you want me to tell them?"

"It's your decision."

A deliberate, loud throat-clearing causes us both to face her brothers again. Ramsay made that noise, to garner our attention, I presume.

But Thane is the one who speaks. He tips his head to the side to study me for a moment first, though. "We heard what you did to protect Iona. And we appreciate it."

"What did I do?"

"Beat up the *bod ceann* who harassed our sister and got information out of him."

"Oh, that, yes. It was an impulse, and I'm not terribly good at fighting my impulses."

Ramsay chuckles. "Is that right? I never would've guessed."

"May we go inside now?" Iona asks. "We need to tell you about our new friend Hubert Frye and hopefully get more information out of him concerning Graham Oliver."

In lieu of a response, Thane shoves two fingers into his mouth and blows a piercing whistle to get the crowd's attention. "Let's go inside, please, everyone."

With ten of us on the premises, it becomes rather difficult to enter the vestibule. But we settle on going through that space in pairs, heading into the downstairs hallway to gather there. The six younger people amongst us go first. Once we elders enter the hall, it's time to explain our plan.

I will go with Iona and her brothers into the office upstairs that apparently belongs to Rory MacTaggart. I haven't met that bloke yet. But we adults need a private place where we can interrogate Hubie. The younger generation doesn't want to be left out of the fun, but we convince them.

Except for Eric. He waits until the others have started for the sitting room, which lies in an annex of the castle. Then he shoves his hands into his jeans pockets and faces us. "I'd like to stay, if that's all right. This has nothing to do with my dumb-ass attempts to win over Iona. But I am kind of involved in the current situation, even if I'd rather not be."

I glance at Iona, and she nods. "All right, Eric, you are welcome to join us. You did assist in subduing Hubie, after all."

And it's time to interrogate him.

Chapter Thirty

Iona

My life has become a surreal painting that should hang on a museum wall, not come to life before my eyes. I can't believe everything that's happened today. But I am grateful, more than I can even express, for the love and support of everyone I know. My brothers, and even Eric, have rallied around me. But it's Rafe who has given me the most support, the kind that only a man who loves me deeply could provide. Just knowing Rafe will be by my side today, tomorrow, and long after that gives me the strength to get through this ordeal.

Rafe and I follow my brothers and Eric straight to the vestibule and up the spiral staircase to the first floor. The ground floor is not the first floor, which I explain to Eric along the way. Dùndubhan used to be a medieval castle, and its layout was altered through the centuries, giving it a modern sort of layout the resulted in the first floor being the second level.

Once we reach our destination, we head straight down the hall to the office door. It stands closed, and I know Rory keeps it locked. But he gave Gavin and Jamie Douglas the key, since they run the museum that Dùndubhan has now become. It also houses a bed-and-breakfast on the upper levels. But we are headed for the office, and Thane produces the key when we reach the closed door. Then we all file into the room.

Thane shuts the door and leans against it.

Ramsay sits down in the executive chair behind the desk.

Eric takes one of the two chairs on the opposite side of the desk, seeming rather unsure of himself. He shifts around in the chair, then winces, just before he scratches the back of his neck.

"Dinnae fash, Eric," Ramsay says. "We won't batter you until your brain turns to sludge. Thane and I have forgiven you for harassing our sister."

"Uh, thanks?"

Thane saunters over to the other chair, sitting down beside Eric. "If we wanted you dead, you'd have been a human puddle months ago."

Rafe and I have sat down in the two high-back chairs positioned near the tall windows, but we can hear what Eric and my brothers are talking about since the office isn't overly large.

And I speak up. "Thane, you and Ramsay had no idea Eric was pestering me for months. You only found out recently."

"Our knowledge is retroactive."

Whatever that means, I don't have time to figure it out. Thane enjoys being cryptic sometimes. But I can't worry about that right now. I need to tell my brothers, as well as Eric and Rafe, about the man who has instigated this madness.

First, I look at Rafe and give him a tight smile.

He squeezes my hand and offers me a sweetly encouraging smile.

No more procrastinating. It's time to do this. I take a deep breath and dive in. "Until recently, I didn't realize how my life had become inextricably linked with two men—Rory MacTaggart and Graham Oliver." Since Eric and Rafe know nothing about either man, I need to explain. "Rory is a solicitor—a lawyer, for the American in the room. He's been everyone's favorite solicitor in Loch Fairbairn and surrounding areas for more than twenty years, though he's semi-retired these days."

When I pause, all four men swerve their attention to me. That might disconcert some people, but I've been a journalist for long enough that I don't get flustered easily.

"It all began with Rory, when he took on a new client." I let my gaze turn inward as I recall the singular event that started a chain reaction. "Eight years ago, Rory handled a divorce case that should have been routine. Of course, any divorce can turn heated if the parties have become angry. Yet when Graham Oliver's wife left him, he blamed everyone but himself. Rory negotiated a generous settlement for Graham's wife, one she had earned after years of living with the *bod ceann*."

Eric raises his hand. "May I ask a question? Sorry, that's a dumb thing to say."

"You can ask me anything, Eric. And you are not stupid."

He wriggles in his chair. "Was Graham always a complete asshole?"

I cannae help laughing. "Yes, Graham always was. He got worse over the years, though, and I'm about to tell you why."

"Cool." He relaxes in his chair. "Can't wait to hear about that."

Rafe and my brothers also seem anxious to hear the rest.

"Graham did a terrible thing," I say, "something that almost rivals what he's doing now. You see, Rory's new wife, Emery, had a nasty ex-boyfriend who posted nude pictures of her online. Graham got hold of those pictures and plastered them all over the front page of *The Loch Fairbairn World News*, his filthy scandal sheet. He also invented outrageous lies about what a deviant Rory was. Fortunately, no one believed him, and the so-called scandal faded away quickly. But that enraged Graham. And this is where I come into the story."

Seven Years Ago

*O*n a beautiful, sunny day in Loch Fairbairn, I walk into the offices of the former *Loch Fairbairn World News*. I'd practically needed a crowbar to unlock the door, which must not have been oiled in at least ten years. Graham Oliver was never known for being neat and tidy or careful. Cannae believe I'm doing this. I've bought the scandal sheet Graham had given up on after Rory annihilated him. Business can be war at times.

Somehow, I will resuscitate this newspaper. The village needs real news, not rubbish peddled by Graham Oliver.

I had spent years working at various jobs, none of which ever felt right for me. But I had no choice. Any work is better than none. So, when Rory suggested I should take over the newspaper and offered to give me startup capital, I jumped at the chance.

Do I know anything about running a newspaper? No, but I can learn. And I dinnae see anyone else volunteering for the job.

I amble through the outer office, where Graham's desk still sits. Then I wander into the inner office that the *bod ceann* had used as a storage area. But I want this place to seem like a real newspaper. Graham had been an alcoholic and a compulsive gambler, so it's no wonder the place is in shambles. Several old editions of Graham's tabloid lie on the floor, crumpled and faded. One paper catches my attention, and I pick it up to study the headline—"Famous Venture Capitalist, Gilbert Beckham, Caught In Lurid Sex Scandal."

The story came from a London tabloid that had picked up Graham's article about the Beckham situation. Gilbert had become senile in his old age and took up with an exotic dancer. He even tried to change his will to favor her instead of his loyal son who had cared for him during his last years.

Naturally, Graham exploited the situation for his own benefit. He made a fortune off his version of the story being syndicated to all the tabloids.

I drop the newspaper and shuffle into the inner office.

Nothing but more rubbish in here. This place will need a lot of cleaning up. Fortunately, I have two burly brothers and quite a lot of mates who would be happy to help.

The front door opens, activating a bell.

I hurry back to the front area—and freeze. "What are you doing here, Graham? I thought you ran away to England."

Though I hadn't met Graham personally, I'd heard all about him from other people in the village. He looks older than he actually is, thanks to his habit of smoking constantly. His gray hair is messy, and deep lines fan out around his eyes. His khakis are rumpled, just like his shirt.

"What am I doing here?" he says. "You are trespassing."

"I own this office now. You are the one trespassing, Graham."

He stalks up to me, glaring down at me with a curled lip. "Ye cannae take my newspaper away from me. It's mine, you hear, mine."

I thrust my arm out, pointing toward the door. "Leave now, before I ring the police station."

"This isn't over yet, Iona Buchanan." He spat those words, and spittle landed on my cheek. "I'll get back what's mine even if it takes years."

Graham stomps out of the building.

I hurry to the window to make sure the *bod ceann* has actually left the vicinity. He has, thank goodness. I blow out a breath, and my shoulders drop. I hadn't realized how tense I was until that encounter with Graham was over, but now I feel almost lightheaded. The sensation only lasts a matter of seconds. Then I get back to work.

For the next month, I strive to restore the newspaper to what it should have been rather than what Graham turned it into over the years. My brothers and friends assist whenever they can. But my first order of business is to provide a visual announcement to ensure everyone understands this is a new and improved newspaper.

I create a new sign, and my brothers hammer it into place above the door. Everyone in the village who drives past this office will now see the words "*Loch Fairbairn Daily News*" emblazoned on the building. I've erased the tarnished image of this office and returned it to what it should have been all along.

A few days later, I receive an unexpected visitor.

Graham Oliver waltzes into my newsroom as if he owns the paper, halting a few feet from my desk.

My head pops up, and I stare at him, unable to comprehend why Graham has come here. I'm speechless, though, and can't speak even one syllable.

The *bod ceann* stretches his lips into a smirk. "Good afternoon, Ms. Buchanan. I couldn't resist paying a visit to the newspaper you stole from me."

"I haven't stolen anything. You lost the newspaper because of your abhorrent behavior. What did you expect? No one trusts a man who smears other people with lies."

His lips work as if he's trying to form words but can't do it. He clenches his teeth, pushing words out between them.

I rise from my chair. "Go home, Graham. You have no place here."

He slams his hand down on my desk, causing it to thump and wobble. "I'll get back what you took from me one way or another. Not even Rory MacTaggart can save you from my retribution."

The anger in his voice makes my pulse accelerate, but it's the look on his face that sends cold fear rushing through me. I believe he wants to do far more than insult me and take back the newspaper he claims belongs to him. I begin to feel a wee bit shaky, but I will not let Graham Oliver see that.

"Leave now," I tell him, doing my best to keep my voice level. "Go home and forget about the newspaper. Leave right now, or I will call the police station. You have five seconds. Four, three—"

Graham whirls around and stalks out the door, slamming it shut.

Mhac na galla. That man is off his head.

Rory had told everyone that Graham moved to Liverpool, where his mother has lived for several years. I believe what Rory said, but clearly, Graham won't give up his vendetta.

Soon, my newspaper has grown into the respectable source of information that I hoped it would become. New subscriptions come in daily. Maybe my stories mostly involve sporting events and exposés of the bad food in the school cafeteria. But everyone has to start somewhere.

Aye, my life has become everything I wanted it to be.

Until Graham Oliver reappears. This time he harasses me at my office and also at my home. The last straw breaks when he pounds his fist on my front door while my daughters are home alone. The poor lasses are so frightened that they call me instead of the police.

"Calm down, Maeve," I say. "I'm sure that man will never come back. What did he look like?"

When Maeve describes the man to me, I know who it was. Graham has come back to get his retribution. Maybe I should call my brothers or at least Rory MacTaggart, but I would rather handle the problem on my own. Well, in private, at least. I do need a wee bit of help, which explains why I march into the Loch Fairbairn Police Station and ask the constables how I can get a non-harassment order. I can't ask for one for each of my daughters. The harassment must have happened at least twice before they will qualify.

Once the order is in place, Graham stays away from me and my daughters.

But for how long?

Today

Ramsay and Thane seem to be gnashing their teeth simultaneously. I suspect they want to throttle sense into me. Maybe I did behave rashly seven years ago, but I've always been that way. Never have I endangered anyone else's life but my own. If I'd believed Graham meant to harm my girls, I would have let my brothers run him out of town.

But it hadn't seemed necessary at the time.

Thane's anger mutates into disbelief. "Iona, *gràidh*, why didn't you ever tell us about that?"

I hunch my shoulders. "You know I've always been self-sufficient. Admitting that I might need my big brothers to save me…Well, it was too much for my ego to stand. And besides, I was right about Graham. He never bothered me or my children ever again."

Ramsay shakes his head, seeming even more baffled than Thane. "What if he had hurt you? Graham is bigger and stronger than you."

"I know. I'm sorry."

Rafe sits forward, resting his elbows on his knees, and turns his head toward me. "I will hunt down that wanker and make sure he can't ever harass you again. That's why we need to interrogate Hubie. No holds barred. He will confess everything, or I will pound him into the mud until he suffocates on it."

My brothers and Rafe begin arguing about who should get to pummel Hubert Frye, though I know they won't literally do that. The argument goes on for a while, and I lose track of the time. My gaze remains downcast as I consider the bizarre things that have happened to me lately.

A flash of movement catches my attention, peripherally, and I turn my gaze in that direction.

Eric seems to be sneaking out of the room.

My brothers haven't noticed. Neither has Rafe.

What on earth is Eric up to now?

Chapter Thirty-One

Eric

As I blaze down the hall, heading for the vestibule stairs, one thought keeps repeating in my mind. *What the hell are you doing?* I can't answer that question. An impulse shot through me, and I had no choice but to follow it. Okay, I did have a choice. It's just that my brain kind of switched off a minute ago. All I can think about is protecting Iona.

Not because I'm in love with her. I never was, but I realized that fact a little too late to save face. Why, then, am I taking the stairs two at a time and almost tumbling over the railing because of that? It's simple.

I pestered Iona for months. Now I need to make amends.

How? By hunting down Graham Oliver.

As I burst out of the ground-floor door, I trip over one of the paving stones that serve as a walkway. My knee smacks into a stone. Fuck, that hurt. Will it stop me? No. Iona and Rafe deserve answers. If Hubert Frye won't give them, then I'll make sure Graham does.

I stop in the middle of the gravel driveway. I don't have my own car, which means I can't go anywhere. What are the odds one of the drivers left his keys in his limo? Maybe I'll catch a break like that. Might as well try.

The shorter limo, which looks like a regular car that's a little bit longer than usual, seems like my best shot. I jog over there. When I try the door handle, it opens. Maybe my luck is changing. I climb into the driver's seat, expecting to need to hunt around for keys, but I suddenly notice they're in the ignition slot. All I need to do is turn the key.

The second I do that, the engine grumbles to life.

Hallelujah. I push my foot down on the accelerator and race backward, swerving around the other limo until I can swing this car back around to face the open wooden gates of the castle. Then I slam my foot down on the gas pedal and roar off down the gravel driveway. Lucky for me, the metal gates that bar the road at the halfway point swing open for me, then close again behind me. Guess nobody really thought Graham Oliver would invade the stronghold.

Gravel sprays up in my wake, clattering on the undercarriage.

Soon, I'm on the paved road that leads to the village of Loch Fairbairn. I don't slow down at all until I've crossed through the village limits. Even then, I break the speed limit—but ease my foot off the gas pedal just enough that I won't wrap this limo around a light pole. As I navigate the streets, people stare at me and some shout, though I can't hear what they're saying. Probably "stop that right now, you moron." Or possibly "somebody arrest this lunatic."

I've driven around in this village enough times that I know where I'm going. Besides, I've visited this destination more than once. Never under these circumstances, though. Maybe I should've brought a baseball bat with me. No, I won't go inside. This is reconnaissance only.

Right, now I'm a cop or something.

The closer I get to my destination, the more I ease off the gas. I'm going slightly slower than the thirty-five miles per hour speed limit now. When I find an area that doesn't have many cars parked along the curb, I pull over and shut off the engine. I'm almost there. Just a short walk to go.

I climb out of the limo. Nobody notices me because nobody's around. I purposely chose a parking spot that was kind of hidden behind a tree, enough that the limo isn't too conspicuous. As I start walking up the street, I can see my destination. Though I can't read the sign, I know what it says.

The Loch Fairbairn Daily News.

About halfway to the newspaper office, I pass by a vending machine filled up with copies of today's issue. Even when she's in danger, Iona keeps pumping out stories. I'm about to skip right past the vending machine, but then the words emblazoned on the front page catch my eye peripherally. I've never known Iona to use giant bold letters on the front page, not even for the top story. Her headlines are big and bold, but not like this.

I walk backwards until I reach the machine, then turn toward it. The words on the front page...Iona didn't write them. How do I know that? Because of what the headline says.

LOCAL JOURNALIST CAUGHT UP IN SEX SCANDAL.

Whuh? No, that can't be right. Iona wouldn't smear another journalist.

Then I notice the subheading: IONA BUCHANAN IN THREESOME
WITH RAFE KNIGHT AND ERIC TAYLOR. The story itself begins below that in smaller letters: "Depraved journalist Iona Buchanan hunts for men
around every corner, seeking sexual thrills wherever she can get them. The
maneater has already sunk her hooks into an innocent American laddie and a
lunatic Brit who enjoys electrical torture."

What the flying fuck? Somebody must have hacked Iona's computer.

Then I notice the next line. It says, "See the photographic proof for
yourself."

Whatever that "proof" is, it's below the fold. I dig a few coins out of my
pocket and shove them into the slot. Then I yank the door open and snatch
up a copy. As I unfold the paper, I freeze. Where the hell did somebody get
pictures like this? One shows Iona kissing my cheek while we're standing on
her porch. The next one shows her hugging me. All of that was friendly, not
romantic. Another image reveals…Holy shit. Naked Rafe carrying naked
Iona into a sauna. I think it's the one behind Iona's house.

More pictures show me and the rest of the gang filing into Rafe's
house in England. Hubie could've taken those pictures, but the other
photos…

I sprint down the sidewalk, veering around an old guy and his little dog
on my way to the newspaper office. Sweat starts rolling down my temples,
though it isn't a hot day. When I burst through the main doors, halting just
inside, I need a minute to catch my breath. I hunch over, slapping my palms
on my thighs.

"Who the bloody hell are you?"

I jerk upright and glare at the bastard who spoke. "You must be Graham
Oliver."

The gray-haired guy with sallow skin stands behind Iona's desk as if he
owns it. A copy of the slanderous issue of *The Loch Fairbairn Daily News* lies
on the desktop.

"Aye," the creep says. "I'm Graham Oliver, the real owner of this newspaper. It was about time the residents of this town learned what a depraved
woman Iona Buchanan is. You should know all about that, laddie. You took
part in the orgies."

I jerk my head back. "Orgies? You're crazy. What you put on the front
page is total sleaze, but nothing like a wild sex party."

Graham sneers at me. "You didn't look at page two, did you?"

I know I shouldn't do it, but I can't stop myself. I need to know what
other slanderous lies this piece of human scum made up about me, Rafe,
and Iona. So, I pick up the paper he offers me, which has been folded over
to show the offending pictures.

What the…Oh, Graham is one lying, scheming, sneaky charlatan. Yeah, I'm being kind in my assessment of him.

I slap the paper down on the desk. "You boned up on Photoshop, huh? These days, anybody can manufacture shit like this with AI. And what makes you think anybody will believe your lies? You went so overboard that it's laughable."

Yeah, the "photos" depict me, Rafe, and Iona, and the others who stayed at Rafe's house, all engaged in a naked orgy on a huge bed. I guess this bastard had to create an AI version of the inside of Rafe's house, because the bedroom shown in these pictures looks nothing like that. Hubie must not have been able to sneak inside to snap images of the real thing.

Graham smacks his palms down on the desk too. Now we're eye to eye.

"You'll regret this, you slimy, conniving bastard."

"Dinnae think so, laddie."

As much as I want to punch this guy's lights out, I know that would only give him justification for having me arrested. I need to speed back to the castle and alert everyone about Graham's disgusting "story."

I snatch up the newspaper and hightail it back to Dùndubhan.

Chapter Thirty-Two

Rafe

Shortly after Eric slipped out of the room, we began discussing in earnest how to interrogate Hubie. He'd been listening to our discussion. That was on purpose. We wanted him to wonder what we might actually do to him, and so we mentioned a variety of torture techniques that we have no intention of utilizing. But the tactic worked. Forty-five minutes into the discussion, Hubie started shaking and crying. After another half hour of glowering at him in silence, the prat finally decides to speak.

"I'll tell you anything," Hubie whines. "Anything, I swear it."

Ramsay chuckles darkly. "Glad to hear it, laddie."

Where is Eric? I assumed he'd gone to the loo. But relieving himself couldn't possibly take this long.

I glance at Iona. "Do you know what's become of young Eric?"

"No. I thought he went to get a wee piece or…something."

"Getting a sandwich doesn't take an hour and fifteen minutes."

Toby brings out his mobile and flicks his fingers over the screen, then taps as if he's typing something. "Oh, bollocks. You are daft as a bush sometimes, Eric."

"What has your best mate done now?" I ask.

Toby shoves his mobile back into his pocket and shakes his bowed head. "Eric stole one of the limos and drove back to Loch Fairbairn to find Graham Oliver."

Iona leaps out of her chair. "He shouldn't have done that. Graham is dangerous. Only a lunatic would do the things he's done, and who knows what he might try next."

Toby lifts his head and winces. "Graham, ah, fabricated filthy pictures with AI. Apparently, they show all of us having an orgy at my dad's house. He used just enough real images to make it seem believable. We'll all get to see what Graham's done once Eric comes back."

How bloody long will that take? My hair-trigger temper is beginning to get tired of waiting.

Iona approaches my chair and crouches there, placing her hands on my knees. "Dinnae get upset, Rafe. We need to find out everything Hubie knows, now that he's ready to talk. Stay calm—for now."

Just hearing her voice makes me feel more relaxed.

But I still want to pummel Hubie—and Graham Oliver.

Toby's mobile chimes. He reads the text, then flattens his lips.

"What is it?" I ask.

"Eric thinks we should meet him near the newspaper office. He'll wait for us there."

"Yes, that would be quicker than Eric driving back to this castle only so we can race into the village again."

Thane taps one finger on his chin. "What will we do with Mr. Frye? We haven't interrogated him yet."

"Let's do that in the car. The girls can stay here at Dùndubhan." I cup Iona's cheek. "I wasn't including you in that statement."

"Good. I won't need to stow away in the boot of the limo after all."

Thane and Ramsay take possession of Hubie as we exit the office. The rest of us trail behind as we make our way down the spiral staircase. We stop to duck into the guest wing and let the girls and Phillip know what's going on. He vows to protect the women. I hadn't expected that, but I believe he means to do just that if anyone should breach the castle.

Then, we're away. Eric left us with the larger limo, which means we'll have plenty of space for making Hubert Frye talk.

As the car starts rolling down the drive, Toby sends another text to Eric. He's asking his best mate to send photos of the newspaper issue Graham Oliver wrote and printed. That way, we'll know what to expect when we get to the village. In a matter of minutes, we have those images.

That bastard. He plastered these lewd AI images all over the village.

Both Iona and her brothers insist upon seeing the fake photos. I watch as their expressions shift from shock to disgust and finally anger.

I'm currently sitting beside Iona on the bench across from Hubie and Iona's brothers, who flank the prat. "If you two don't mind, I'd like to talk to this bastard face to face. Would you be comfortable with moving onto this bench with Iona? Then I can have Hubie all to myself."

"Of course," Thane says.

"Aye, that'll work," Ramsay declares.

Hunched over, we all shift about until we've reached our assigned positions.

I drape an arm over Hubie's shoulders. The second he cringes, I lean in and speak in a soft yet menacing tone. "Did you help Graham craft those fake images?"

"Um…yes?"

"No uncertainties, Hubie. Yes or no are the only valid responses."

The prat cringes again. "Yes, all right, yes. Graham didn't know how to use AI, but I'd been playing around with it for a while. AI is even better and easier than normal identity theft."

"So you could destroy innocent people's lives more easily. How entrepreneurial of you, Hubie."

The git begins to shiver. "P-please, don't kill me."

"Kill you? Oh, no, you slimy little maggot. You will not get out of your predicament that easily." I curl my fingers around his wrist like a handcuff. "It's prison for you. Maybe your mate Graham Oliver can share a cell with you."

"Prison sounds perfect. I'll plead guilty, I promise."

"Glad to hear it." I place my mouth within millimeters of Hubie's ear so I can whisper to him. "Tell me all about Graham's master plan. You can skip the bits we already know and start from right now."

"Graham said the fake photos and the newspaper story were one half of the final phase." Hubie chews on his lip with the speed of a beaver gnawing on a tree. "The second half involves getting Iona arrested for money laundering."

"Why? What does he hope to gain from that? Aside from the obvious prison time."

"He really just wants to humiliate Iona and take control of the newspaper."

Thane leans forward to stare directly at Hubie. "His plan is unhinged, but I reckon that's the point. Graham was always a scheming liar who felt the world owed him whatever he wanted. But I thought he became a pig farmer in Liverpool."

Hubie nods. "Yeah, he did that for a while. But Graham always had, ah, higher aspirations."

I fist my hand in Hubie's hair to yank his head back. "So, you aren't as much of a moron as you want us to think. Higher aspirations? I'd wager you studied at university before deciding a life of crime was easier than working."

He glances at me sideways. "Well, it is easier. Unless you get caught."

The limo has just slowed down, and a moment later, it stops altogether. We are here, wherever that might be. I assume our destination is the newspaper office. I peer out the shaded window and see the other limo with Eric standing alongside it.

And I waste no time. I thrust the door open and leap out, rushing across the street to where Eric is waiting. "Where is the newspaper office?"

He points toward a building across the street, about two blocks further ahead of where we stand.

"Thank you, Eric. Stay here."

I barrel down the middle of the street, angling toward the shops and other establishments on the far side, and I don't stop until I reach the newspaper office. One car beeped at me, but I did not step aside for the vehicle. At last, I burst through the doors of the newspaper office.

Graham is sitting in Iona's chair.

Oh, no, the bastard will not get away with that—or his vile plans for revenge. I am his reckoning.

Graham rises from the chair. "Rafe Knight. How kind of you to pay me a visit and congratulate me on taking back my newspaper."

"Your newspaper?" I hurl my entire body at the desk, flying across it, dragging Graham down onto the floor with me on top of him. "Care to rethink everything you've ever said or done in your entire life?"

Spittle sprayed from my lips when I snarled those words. And I notice a large brown bag of some sort lying on the floor near my cheek. So, that's his infamous satchel.

Graham sneers at me. "If you kill me, that will only make me a martyr."

"Oh, I have no intention of murdering you. That would be too simple. You deserve a long prison sentence with a cell mate who enjoys orgies."

I stand up while gripping his shirt with both hands, hoisting him off the floor. His shoes dangle in midair. "You have one minute to retract every fucking lie you ever told about Iona Buchanan. I will permit you to fall down at her feet and literally kiss the ground she walks on."

As I hear the bell above the door chime, I turn round while still holding Graham off the floor.

Eric, Toby, Iona, and her brothers walk into the office. Ramsay has taken command of Hubie, who seems completely deflated. My mates and my son stare at me.

"Someone ring the police," I say. "Fergus and Sorley will have the privilege of dealing with this piece of rotting rubbish."

Toby dials his mobile. "Hello, this is Toby Knight. My father has just, ah, detained the two men who harassed Iona. We're in the newspaper office. Graham Oliver has unlawfully taken control of the building, which is owned by Iona Buchanan. Yes, good. Of course we'll wait, and we'll be happy to provide statements."

My son ends the call.

Thane turns his attention to me. "Why don't we take the *bod ceann* off your hands?"

"No. I will maintain control of the prisoner until the constables arrive."

And that's precisely what I do, though I set Graham on his feet. He has no chance of escaping, not with three of my mates and my son on hand."

Iona steps closer to me and my prisoner. "You don't own this newspaper anymore, Graham. You lost control of it seven years ago."

"You are not the legitimate owner." He lifts his chin high, gazing down his nose at Iona. "I sold the paper to a fellow journalist a few years ago, and now I've bought it back. *The Loch Fairbairn World News* belongs to me."

Thane scoffs. "Your business was liquidated during the bankruptcy proceedings. Iona bought it after that—legally."

Sorley and Fergus enter the building. For a moment, they simply sweep their gazes over everyone as if they're assessing the situation.

Then Fergus shakes his head. "Graham Oliver, what are ye doing here in someone else's office? Ye dinnae own this place anymore."

Graham thrashes and bellows. "I have always owned the paper! It's mine forever!"

"Is that so?" Fergus brings out his handcuffs. "The government disagrees. Sorley, why don't you take that little man who's wilting in Ramsay's arms."

"That would be Hubert Frye," I tell Fergus. "You know who my prisoner is."

"Aye. Everyone in the village knows and despises Graham Oliver."

"You lot might want to grab the satchel on the floor behind the desk. I suspect that's where Graham kept all his secrets."

"We'll do that. Thank you for the tip, Rafe."

Once the constables have secured their prisoners, they drag the pair out of the building and straight into a patrol car.

As soon as the coppers drive away, Iona flings herself into my arms. "I was so afraid of what Graham might do to you—until I remembered you are the lightning sorcerer. Nothing can harm you."

"That's a wonderfully strange compliment. Thank you."

As our group files out of the newspaper office, a pickup truck screeches to a halt directly in front of us. Rebecca Taylor scrambles out of the vehicle, rushing toward Thane and Eric. She hugs her son fiercely and kisses his cheek. Then she throws her arms around Thane, kissing him passionately.

When the couple finally disentangles, Rebecca looks at the rest of us. "Is everybody okay?"

Some of us nod, others voice our agreement, and Toby gives the thumbs-up sign.

Ramsay sighs. "Well, the excitement is over, but the adrenaline is still pumping. What should we do now?"

I glance at Iona and grin. "Shag, eat, and sleep."

Ramsay groans. "That's all well and good for you couples. I dinnae have a girlfriend."

Thane pats his brother's shoulder. "Bonnie from the café likes you, and I've seen the way you look at her. Go order some *cranachan* for two and charm the lass."

His brother grins. "I think I'll do that."

Eric shakes his head at the sky. "Man, it sucks to be the only guy who doesn't have a girl waiting for him."

Rebecca winks at her son. "I happen to know there's a place full of beautiful young women only half an hour away."

"What are you talking about?" Eric's expression freezes, then he laughs. "Dùndubhan, here I come. Taxi!"

Oh, yes, everyone will have a good time today.

Epilogue

Rafe
Two Months Later

Who could have guessed my life would turn upside down and I would love every minute of it? Not me. Iona flipped my boat right side up, though I refused to admit to that for a bloody long time. Iona Buchanan changed my life, reinvigorated me in body and soul, and showed me that relationships don't need to be filled with angst and pain.

The biggest news, to me, is the fact that I finally found out what the American Wives Club is. They're a group of nosy but goodhearted women, and a few blokes, who step in to meddle whenever one of their mates needs a hand in finding his or her true love. A few months ago, I would have scoffed at that idea. Now, I might volunteer to assist the club.

I also learned that Magnus and Piper hadn't been able to track down Hubie for us because their car broke down. Bad luck for a private investigator. But then, everyone experiences bad luck once in a while. Iona and I thanked them for their efforts, of course.

Toby and I are closer than ever. I have to thank Eric Taylor for that. His mild obsession with Iona became the impetus for me meeting her and realizing I'd found the woman of my dreams. Many new things have happened since the day I pounded on Iona's door.

Eric Taylor is dating Rowan Buchanan, and he has relocated to Inverness. Eric found a much better job in geology, one that will ensure he can visit his mum and his girlfriend as often as he likes.

Thane and Rebecca have been married for nearly a month now, and the whisky business is booming.

Courtney has remained in England with Phillip, but now has the option of flying to Scotland whenever she pleases, thanks to her stepfather's wealthy friends.

Ramsay did not date Bonnie for long. After two weeks, he realized he couldn't handle a relationship with a much younger woman. She understood.

Fergus MacRae, the copper, is trying to work up the courage to ask Maeve Buchanan to go picnicking with him. Yes, he has a crush on her.

Those are only the highlights of recent events. Right now, Iona and I are heading back to Dùndubhan for a ceilidh—a Scottish dance. I haven't tried to dance in at least six years, and it was a disaster back then. I had been a rather good dancer up until the lightning strike. Iona claims I use that as an excuse to avoid "hoofing it" since my coordination is not an issue. Maybe that's true. But I'd much rather watch everyone else as they spin around the floor.

Naturally, Ramsay and Thane insisted I must wear a kilt featuring the Buchanan clan tartan. If they thought that would embarrass me, they still have a lot to learn about the lightning sorcerer. I amble around the floor, waiting for the woman I adore to make her appearance. When she finally enters the great hall, the sight of her takes my breath away. Iona wears a kilt fashioned from the Buchanan tartan too, but it's short and shows off her shapely legs.

As Iona approaches me, she rakes her gaze up and down my body. Then she licks her lips. "My, my, Rafe, don't you look handsome—and deliciously lickable."

I wrap my arm around her waist, tugging her close. "And you are a vision of Scottish beauty, darling. If any other blokes try to steal you away, I'll toss them into my lightning simulator. They'll be quite crispy after that."

I dance with Iona for a while, then her brothers take turns.

According to Thane and Ramsay, I am required to at least pretend to dance or else they will toss me into the garderobe. That's a medieval toilet, essentially. No one even knows if the garderobe still exists. It might have been filled in.

But I know they're simply harassing me.

A few minutes later, Iona grows excited as an older couple enters the great hall. She grabs my hand, tugging to make me move. "Come on, Rafe. They're finally here!"

"Who?"

She only grins and drags me over to the older couple. Then she... introduces me to them. "Ma, Da, please meet Rafe Knight, the man I love. Rafe, these two wonderful people are my parents, Elsa and Keith Buchanan."

I shake their hands. "It's a pleasure to finally meet you. Iona has told me all about you two."

Keith slaps my arm. "We weren't sure if we could accept a Brit in the family, but Iona told us you are the sweetest, kindest, grumpiest, cleverest, most electrifying lightning-struck man she's ever met."

"That's quite a mouthful."

Elsa clasps my hand, holding it between her palms. "We have never seen our daughter so happy. Thank you for that, Rafe."

"You don't sound Scottish."

"I was born in Sweden. But I became an exchange student in Scotland, and that's how I met Keith. We've been together ever since."

Will my relationship with Iona last that long? No one could divine the answer to that question, but I mean to find out—by staying with her until she can't stand me any longer. But for now, we live in sin while shuttling back and forth between Norwich and Loch Fairbairn, always flying on our mates' private jets. Marriage might be an option, but we're too busy right now to think about that. Aren't we too old? Perhaps not. After years of feeling like an outsider in my own life, I now have everything I need and want. It's a bloody good life.

After the festivities have ended, Iona and I go home to discuss our next adventure. "Would you like to visit my favorite spot for storm chasing?"

"Ooh, aye, where is that?"

"Tornado Alley, in the American Midwest."

She slides her hand down to my groin. "I have a feeling storm chasing with you will lead to plenty of shagging."

"Oh, yes, pet. You can count on that."

Love the

Hot Scots

series?

Visit
AnnaDurand.com

to subscribe to her newsletter
for updates on forthcoming books in the series
&
to receive exclusive content!

*A*nna Durand is a bestselling, multi-award-winning author of contemporary and paranormal romance. Her books have earned bestseller status on every major retailer and wonderful reviews from readers around the world. But that's the boring spiel. Here are the really cool things you want to know about Anna!

Born on Lackland Air Force Base in Texas, Anna grew up moving here, there, and everywhere thanks to her dad's job as an instructor pilot. She's lived in Texas (twice), Mississippi, California (twice), Michigan (twice), and Alaska—and now Ohio.

As for her writing, Anna has always invented stories in her head, but she didn't write them down until her teen years. Those first awful books went into the trash can a few years later, though she learned a lot from those stories. Eventually, she would pen her first romance novel, the paranormal romance *Willpower*, and she's never looked back since.

To get exclusive content, join Anna's Facebook group, Anna's Romance Addicts, or sign up for her newsletter.

VISIT ANNADURAND.COM TO SIGN UP.